THE MAN IN RED SQUARE

ALSO BY BILL MOODY

The Evan Horne Series

Solo Hand
Death of a Tenor Man
Sound of the Trumpet
Bird Lives!
Looking for Chet Baker
Shades of Blue
Fade to Blue

Other Titles

Czechmate: The Spy Who Played Jazz

BILL MOODY

THE MAN IN RED SQUARE

Down and Out Books, LLC
3959 Van Dyke Rd, Ste. 265
Lutz, FL 33558
www.DownAndOutBooks.com

The characters and events in this book are fictitious. Any similarity to real persons, living or dead, is coincidental and not intended by the author.

Cover design by JT Lindroos

ISBN: 1937495450

ISBN-13: 978-1-937495-45-9

For Karin Haggar, the first real reader in FDH 230

Prelude

At first glance there was nothing to distinguish the slightly built man, body thickened by a heavy parka, standing opposite the Lenin Mausoleum. A look, a nervous gesture, a tell-tale tic behind the wire-framed aviator sunglasses, none of these would have been evident to the casual observer. It's difficult to recognize a man poised, however reluctantly, on the brink of his own destiny.

He'd been standing there for nearly an hour, squinting into the glare of an unseasonal sun that had briefly thawed Moscow and brought its bewildered and confused citizens out in droves to bask in the unexpected mid-winter warmth.

A lot of the snow had melted, still scattered about Red Square, thick jagged patches remained, like a chain of white islands stretched from the dark, red stone walls of the Kremlin to the incongruous onion-like domes of St. Basil's Cathedral.

The icy wind blowing off the Moskva River swirled briefly about the Kremlin towers and whipped across the square towards the GUM Department Store, stinging the faces of lunch time shoppers scurrying in and out of its ornate facade.

Was it an omen perhaps, this freakish weather? Nature bestowing her approval? He couldn't decide. He only knew the earlier confidence and assurance had deserted him now, vanished like the puffs of his own breath in the wind, leaving him with only a cold knot of indecision clawing at the pit of his stomach.

It wasn't going to work. He was sure of it.

But even now, as his mind flirted with abandoning the whole idea, playing with the notion like a child with a favorite toy, he could feel several pairs of eyes, watching, recording his every move, tracking each step. There was no turning back now. One step and he would set in motion a chain of events from which there was no retreat.

He was committed, as surely as a diver who springs off the

high board and waits only for the water to rush up and meet him.

Only his reason for being there defined him, set him apart from the swarm of foreign tourists and Muscovites waiting patiently in the long line snaking towards him across the square. Weary pilgrims to a godless shrine, shuffling ever closer for a fleeting glimpse of Lenin's waxen figure encased in glass.

Still motionless, his eyes restlessly wandered over the slow moving file. The Russians were easily distinguishable. Uniformly dressed in drab olives and dark browns, their enduring somber faces wore resignation like a mask. They were in sharp contrast to the animated group of Japanese, nervously chattering, eyes darting everywhere, clutching cameras and thumbing guidebooks.

Just ahead of the Japanese group, his eyes stopped and riveted on a man and woman. The man—tall, angular, seemingly oblivious to the cold in a light coat, tie flapping in the wind—stood ramrod stiff next to the much shorter woman. A mane of blond hair spilled over the folds of her thick fur coat.

They were exactly as he remembered.

The woman's breath expelled in tiny puffs as she gushed in obvious delight and pointed around the square. The man nodded absently, occasionally following her gestures. Once, they turned in his direction; he thought for a moment the man's eyes locked with his own. He turned away quickly, pulling the hood of his parka up around his face. Then, almost angrily, realizing he couldn't possibly be recognized at this distance, jammed his hands in the pockets of the parka, and felt his hand close over the small slip of paper.

Relax. How long had it been? Years. He forced himself to take several deep breaths and tried once again to shake off the anxiety. Was this all it would take? A hastily scribbled note?

The file was moving faster now. He would have to make his move soon. But there was something wrong with his legs. They wouldn't move. Again, almost angrily, he took off his sunglasses, as if they were the cause of his immobility. He turned into the wind and strolled casually towards the line.

He pushed through a large crowd coming out of the tomb, unmindful now of the grunts of protest as he jostled for a position nearer the Japanese group. A few turned to eye him curiously as he suddenly veered away and broke into a kind of slow jog. His boots crunched over a patch of snow; the blood began to pound in his ears.

Abruptly, he changed direction. He turned quickly, pushed through the orderly file, directly in front of the man and woman. Startled, the woman cried out, clutching her handbag close as he brushed against her. The fur of her coat lightly grazed his face. Angry voices filled his ears. Someone was shouting for the guards. The man, equally surprised said something but it was lost in the shouting.

He palmed the folded slip of paper and slid it easily into the tall man's coat pocket.

For a fleeting moment, so vital that everything depended on it, he turned his face squarely to the man. He saw the flashing spark of recognition dissolve into shock, the mouth drop open to speak a name, silently formed on bloodless lips. Then he was gone, melting into the crowd, past curious stares, indignant voices.

It was done.

He walked hurriedly, zigzagging across the square, glancing back over his shoulder, knowing there would be no pursuit. He paused at the steps of the Metro, free at last of the crowds.

Perhaps, free of Russia.

Tommy Farrell was waiting for Santa Claus.

He'd had other plans for Christmas Eve–plans that didn't include freezing his ass off in the back of a broken down van on the New York Thruway. He sat hunched on the floor near the rear doors, shifting his position for the third time in as many minutes but finally gave it up as a useless exercise. There was simply no way to get warm or comfortable. He could only take solace in the knowledge that the red, disabled vehicle tag flying from the van's aerial was as false as his hopes that the Jets would make the Super Bowl.

He looked out the van's rear window. The late evening traffic rushing by was lighter now than when he'd taken up his position nearly an hour before and moving steadily. The road had been cleared, but new snow flurries were already starting to fall and a heavy storm was predicted by midnight. Perfect weather for Santa Claus, Farrell thought, lighting a cigarette and pulling the collar of his coat up around his ears.

He checked the luminous dial of his watch. Eight o'clock. He dragged deeply on the cigarette and tried to dredge up thoughts about duty to country, but they were easily obscured by the vision of his wife, at home in front of a glowing fire, putting finishing touches on the tree and explaining to their two young children why daddy had to work on Christmas Eve even if he is in the FBI.

He shivered again and poured the last of the coffee from a thermos. It was still hot but flat, tasteless. He felt the van shudder and turned sharply as the interior was suddenly bathed in blinding light, revealing for a moment the tripod-mounted Nikon with a long-range telephoto lens. A klaxon horn shattered the night as a heavy diesel thundered by dangerously close.

Farrell's hand shook; the coffee spilled. He cursed the huge truck as the hot liquid splashed on his hand. Tossing the cup aside, he wiped his hand on his jacket and squinted through the lens of the Nikon.

The camera was trained on a phone booth across the expressway.

He carefully adjusted the focus and checked the meter reading. With high speed, infrared film to compensate for the poor expressway lighting, the pictures would be sharp and clear if conditions held. He rotated the lens slightly until he could read the number on the dial of the telephone.

"Bingo One, Bingo One, this is Caller." The metallic voice crackled out of the small hand-held radio beside Farrell.

"Go, Caller," he answered.

"The Navy's on the way. Just passed the toll booths. ETA, four minutes."

"Gotcha." Farrell laid the radio aside, checked his watch and the camera once again and nervously watched the minutes tick off. In just under four minutes, a dark blue sedan pulled off the expressway and parked in front of the phone booth.

The driver emerged cautiously from the car, briefly scanned the oncoming traffic and gave Farrell's van a cursory glance. For an instant, the driver's face was framed in the lens. "Gotcha," Farrell murmured aloud. The Nikon's motor drive whirred as he clicked off several frames.

Through the lens, Farrell continued to track the man as he strode towards the phone booth. Inside, a dim light came on over his head as he closed the folding door. Farrell watched tensely as the man took a large envelope from under his coat and stuck it under the shelf below the phone. He hung up the receiver and quickly returned to his car. Farrell shot the last of the roll at the retreating car as it merged with the traffic heading toward New York City.

With practiced hands, Farrell rewound the film, loaded the camera with a fresh roll and re-adjusted the focus. He paused for a moment, lighting another cigarette, then picked up the radio.

"Caller, this is Bingo One."

"Go Bingo," the voice replied.

"Santa's helper has come and gone."

"Roger, Bingo. Santa should be along in a minute. How you doin' out there?" The business-like voice suddenly became friendly.

Farrell smiled. "Okay if I ever thaw out."

"Hang on. I'll buy you a drink when we wrap this up, okay?"

"No thanks. It's Christmas Eve remember?"

"Aw, you married guys are all alike. Why don't you...wait a minute. Santa just went through the gate. Black Buick, four-door."

"Right," Farrell said. He snapped off the radio and rubbed his hands together. He counted off three minutes and forty-two seconds before the second car pulled off and parked near the phone booth. For more than a minute, the flashing tail lights winked at Farrell, but no one got out of the car.

"C'mon, c'mon." The snow flurries were beginning to

thicken. As if responding to Farrell's anxiety, the door opened and a man got out. Short, thick-set, and as with the first man, his face was briefly framed in the lens.

Farrell's breath quickened at the sight of the familiar face. He pressed the shutter button. Swiveling the camera, he tracked his prey to the booth and locked in for a waist-high shot.

This time there was no pretense of dialing. The man simply held the receiver in one hand and felt under the shelf for the envelope. He seemed to stare directly into the lens, as if he knew it was there, Farrell would remember later.

While the man grappled with the folding door, Farrell shot the remaining film and grabbed the radio, almost shouting now. "All units, go!"

Red lights flashing, tires screeching in protest, a police cruiser arrived seconds later. It skidded to a halt blocking the outside lane and was quickly joined by three unmarked cars. Together they boxed in the black Buick.

Farrell continued to watch through the lens. The expression of bewilderment and shock on the man's face quickly gave way to resignation as he was led away to one of the waiting cars. Then, police cruiser in the lead, one of the policemen driving the Buick, the convoy roared off, leaving the phone booth deserted once again.

Farrell quickly packed up the camera and lens in an aluminum case. He jumped out of the van's rear doors, tore off the red tag from the aerial and climbed into the driver's seat. Turning the ignition key, he smiled in relief as the engine came to life easily.

He paused for a moment wondering as always where his photos might end up. On the desk of the Bureau Chief? In the Kremlin? Well, it didn't matter really. He'd done his job.

He shoved the van in gear and pulled onto the expressway. With any luck he'd be home in time to help with the turkey.

One

It was nearly nightfall as the jumbo jet burst through the heavy dark sky over Washington and touched down at Dulles International Airport. The chirp of tires and sudden reverse thrust of engines jolted John Trask, brought him to the surface of an uneasy slumber. He rubbed a bony hand over his sharply chiseled face, blinked out the window at the airport lights flashing by and unbuckled his seat belt.

Once inside the terminal, Trask eased through customs and immigration. Diplomatic status has its rewards, he thought, smiling at the novelty of traveling under his own name. He moved quickly to beat the crowd to the ground transportation exit and scanned the rank of taxis for the car that would take him to Langley.

There was snow on the ground and the night sky promised more of the same. In a moment he was joined at the curb by a much younger man and directed to the waiting car. Trask eased in the back seat, and closed his eyes as the driver negotiated the airport traffic and angled towards the Virginia Expressway.

Gratefully, he sank back against the seat, feeling the fatigue spread through him. But even his weariness could not stop the jumble of thoughts racing through his mind. It was happening again. Just when he thought he had the answer, it slipped away, triggering the familiar signs he'd grown to trust that meant something didn't quite fit.

The arrest of a Soviet official—especially one without diplomatic immunity—was always welcome news, but this one didn't make any sense at all. Why would a senior trade delegate, with an unblemished record, jeopardize his career and usefulness to Moscow with a stupid blunder?

Yes, the stakes were high and the target, seemingly ready-made: a dissatisfied young naval officer, up to his neck in debt with access to a guidance system project. Normally an ideal situation, but not for Dimitri Zakharov. He was an old hand and knew better than anyone how Moscow viewed mistakes. The evidence was undeniable. The photos wrapped it up very neatly and were no doubt giving the Kremlin fits. Too neat? It all stacked up on paper, but Trask couldn't shake the feeling something was wrong.

Zakharov had seemed oblivious to the FBI surveillance. There were several meetings on film and the financial arrangements were astonishingly amateurish. Cash wrapped in brown paper and deposited the morning after a drop. Still, the material he was buying was top grade so maybe he could be excused the indiscretion and the speed of the operation.

Moscow normally took months to set up a recruitment. Zakharov had moved in on the naval officer in weeks. Maybe he was coming over. It was an unusual approach, but it had been done before. To avoid suspicion in Moscow, a would-be defector forces an arrest, then quietly disappears into a new life, new identity and leaves the Kremlin to wonder what went wrong.

For the moment, Trask discarded these thoughts. He had his own defector to worry about. An American defector.

"How much further driver?" Trask asked. He sat up straight and lit a cigarette. He'd lost track of where they were.

"Not long, sir," the driver replied. "Turnoff is just coming up."

Trask looked out at the rolling hills blanketed with snow as the car swung off the George Washington Parkway and sped up to the Langley complex. Identification cards were checked quickly and they were waved through towards the seven-story main building. The car submerged into the basement garage. Trask nodded his thanks to the driver, grabbed his briefcase and took the elevator to the Director's conference room. Only the quiet hum of the heating system and the faint throb of the computer center broke the stillness.

Trask saw he was the last to arrive. They all looked up as he entered. Eugene McKinley, sitting in for Director Richard Abrams, a young aide from the State Department, a gruff looking Admiral from Naval Intelligence, and of course, Charles Fox, old friend, former mentor, looking a bit tired, a bit older, but Trask was happy to note, the sparkling blue eyes were bright as ever.

"Ah, John, at last," Charles said rising. "Good to see you again. How are things in Moscow?"

"Fine, Charles. Good to see you. It's been too long." They clasped hands warmly, memories reflected in both their eyes. Field work in Budapest, debriefings in Berlin and Prague. They had crisscrossed Europe together. Looking at Charles Fox, one would be surprised to learn that this urbane, distinguished gentlemen had once run one of the most effective networks in Eastern Europe. It was just too bad about Prague, Trask reflected.

He nodded greetings to McKinley and was quickly introduced to the others. A Filipino mess steward brought in coffee and sandwiches while Trask dropped into one of the easy chairs arranged around the fireplace. The blazing logs gave off a pleasant aroma of cedar and pine. A fireside chat, Trask thought. This should be interesting. Abrams from State, looking far too cool and young for such a job, shuffled through a pile of papers and munched on a ham sandwich. The admiral puffed sullenly on his cigar and stared into the fire. The amenities were quickly over as Eugene McKinley led off.

"Well, gentlemen, shall we get started," he began. He was a beefy man and bulged under his dark suit. His face was pink and freshly shaved. "The Director asked for this meeting to iron out the initial details, give us a starting point so to speak, and hopefully, after tonight we'll have our bearings. As I'm sure you're all aware, the Director is devoting his time, as is the president, to the current situation in Iran." He looked around the group for confirmation and found it in the expressions and silence of everyone present.

It was unthinkable, but fifty-two Americans were at the mercy of a fanatic Islamic leader and the U.S. Government, with all its power and resources, was seemingly helpless. Everyone there silently contemplated the consequences of an unfound solution.

Trask wondered if it were true that at the time of the hostages were taken, there was not a single operative in Iran with the exception of those in the embassy.

McKinley broke the silence and turned to Abrams from State. Trask eyed him coolly. Sharp, perhaps too sharp. He had Ivy League written all over him and reminded Trask of those young, ambitious men of the long but not forgotten days of Watergate who had hovered about the Nixon White House.

"Richard, suppose you bring us up to date on the Zakharov arrest," McKinley said.

Abrams barely referred to his notes as he began. "Dimitri Zakharov, a senior official of Amtorg, the Russian trade organization based in New York City, arrested December twenty-four by an FBI surveillance team. At the time of his arrest, he was in possession of highly sensitive classified material secured from," he paused to check the name," Lieutenant Mark Hopkins, U.S. Navy." Abrams flicked a glance at the Admiral and got a stony stare in return.

"What about this Hopkins?" Charles interrupted.

"I was coming to that," Abrams said. He seemed slightly annoyed at Charles's question. "Hopkins, age thirty-seven, was working on a guidance control project. I don't really know all the details, but he had apparently gotten above his means. New house, new car, charge accounts, and of late, some gambling debts." Abrams paused again. "As we all know, this is exactly the tailor-made situation the Soviets ferret out these days."

No one disagreed with Abrams. Blackmail, subversion, compromise, even the odd assassination were still very much a part of the Soviet arsenal but in recent years, they had gone right to the core of things—money.

"Hopkins was put under routine surveillance as part of a periodic security check when he was accidentally seen in the company of Zakharov," Abrams added.

"Accidentally?" Charles broke in again and exchanged the briefest of looks with Trask, who was thinking the same thing.

"Well, not exactly by accident." Abrams appeared slightly flustered. "He and Zakharov were spotted together in the same restaurant on two separate occasions. Coincidence was ruled out enough to step up surveillance on Hopkins and take a closer look at Zakharov, although at the time of his arrest, his record was clean."

"Maybe somebody should have been a little more careful with Zakharov," the admiral put in from behind a cloud of smoke. His edginess was understandable. Hopkins was the navy's responsibility and the admiral would be held accountable.

"I'm afraid I'll have to agree with the admiral," Charles said.

"Oh, certainly Zakharov had been routinely checked out a number of times, as I'm sure you're well aware, Mr. Fox, the FBI's most conservative estimates set the number of Soviet operatives at about three thousand. Or, in effect, one in three Soviets in the U.S. are engaged in some type of clandestine activity. That requires a lot of manpower to keep track of them all." It wasn't the State Department's fault Abrams was saying.

"Yes, quite right," Charles said, shrugging at the admiral.

McKinley looked like he'd heard it all before and Trask noted that Abrams was now regarding Charles with a good deal more interest. He shuffled his papers and continued.

"Over the next several weeks, Hopkins and Zakharov met several times in which no exchange was detected. Naval Intelligence was alerted. Hopkins' record was spotless, but he was engaged in highly sensitive work. The meetings became more frequent and less covert. Parks, hotels, bars, convincing the FBI something was in the offing."

Everyone digested the information Abrams read out in his precise, clipped tones. Even if both were out of character, a high-ranking Soviet official and a naval officer in a sensitive job spelled just one thing.

"At first," Abrams continued, "the FBI thought there might be some sort of sting operation through naval intelligence. Unhappily that turned out to be negative. Finally, Hopkins was discovered lifting photo-copied material and later dropped. But the actual exchange was not detected."

"And the material?" Charles asked.

"Low grade stuff," Abrams said, smiling reassuringly. "It

was obviously a first step so a decision was made to allow Hopkins to go all the way in hopes of a bigger drop."

What was Charles after? Trask wondered. He knew the mechanics of an operation better than anyone. Was he just trying to keep Sonny Boy on his toes or was something bothering him as well? He looked forward to a private talk with Charles.

Abrams rearranged his notes and continued. "There was a hurried meeting before Christmas Eve, quite in the open this time. The FBI pulled all the stops, and on Christmas Eve, Hopkins made a drop in a phone booth on the New York Thruway. A few minutes later, it was recovered by Zakharov. Both were arrested immediately. Hopkins of course, will be court martialed."

"What's the man's state?" Charles asked, turning to the admiral.

"He's made a complete confession, claims the money was too good to pass up. His family is taking it pretty hard. His wife apparently knew nothing, but his father is also Navy, which makes it difficult. Looking at Hopkins record, well, financial problems or not, it was a shock to everyone."

Charles sat back in his chair and stared pensively into the fire. He only half heard McKinley's question. "What about Zakharov?"

"He's being held pending further investigation, and although he doesn't have diplomatic immunity, the Soviets have lodged the standard protest over his incarceration and accused us of withholding information. I assume, however, Zakharov will stand trial and be sentenced by Federal Court following lengthy debriefings. Returning him to Moscow is naturally out of the question and for once we can do more than simply declare him *persona non grata.*" Abrams paused dramatically, to ensure he had everyone's attention. "Gentlemen, I don't have to tell you what an opportunity this is." His attitude was almost as if he'd single handedly brought about Zakharov's capture.

"Yes, well, I think John has something to add that might complicate matters," McKinley said. All eyes turned to Trask who had been quietly absorbing Abrams' monologue and

Charles' probing.

"Yes, John, what's all this about a defector coming home?" Charles sat up and faced Trask.

"Defector? I..." Abrams was clearly perplexed.

"Sorry, Richard," McKinley said. "This is all pretty recent. That's why we recalled John from Moscow. He's senior man and talked to Mason himself."

"Mason? Is that the defector's name?" Abrams was frantically searching through his papers.

"No, Owens is the defector," McKinley said. "Well, go ahead, John. It's your show from here."

Trask got up and stood in front of the fireplace. "I guess I should start from the beginning. Five years ago, in late 1974, Robert Calvin Owens, an employee of Triton Industries in Sunnyvale, California, turned up on the doorstep of the Soviet embassy in San Francisco. He was five years back from Vietnam and seemingly on the verge of a brilliant career in microchip technology, Triton's specialty. Owens' mother—he has no other family—was shocked and his friends, what there were of them, were dumbfounded. The Soviets, of course, could hardly contain their excitement. Silicon Valley is one of their prime targets, and with Owens background, they didn't stop to ask questions. He was on the first plane to Moscow before anything could be done. Since then, we've had only sketchy reports about his whereabouts, but we do know he was assigned to Bureau T in Zelenograd, the Russian version of Silicon Valley." Trask paused, aware of the attention of the others.

"Three weeks ago, an American couple, Arthur and Joan Mason, were in Moscow, sightseeing in Red Square. Owens apparently appeared out of the crowd, brushed against them and stuffed a note in Mason's pocket."

"What did it say?" Charles asked.

Trask paused again, looking around the group. McKinley stared into the fire; Abrams clutched his briefcase and listened open-mouthed. The admiral reached for another cigar.

"It was a simple message: My name is Robert Owens. Can I come home?"

"Extraordinary," Charles said. He searched Trask's face

for some sign.

"And you interviewed Mason?" McKinley asked, looking away from the fire.

"Right. I have a transcript of the interview. Mason came directly to the embassy with the note. He was quite sure it was Owens. They had worked together briefly at Triton, but he said Owens seemed to be almost making sure he was recognized. I have the note also." Trask opened his case and took out a sheet of paper. "This is a photo copy," he said, handing it around. "We've done a preliminary hand writing check but it will get a full analysis."

"Any report yet?" Charles asked, looking at the note.

Trask lit a cigarette and nodded. "This is either Owens' hand or an excellent forgery."

"Forgery?" Abrams was sitting on the edge of his chair. "But why would you suspect forgery? I mean..."

"I didn't say we suspect anything," Trask shot back. He looked at Charles and saw the realization already spreading over his face. Only Abrams and the admiral didn't know, he guessed.

"But I don't see the connection between this and the Zakharov arrest," Abrams said. "This..." His voice trailed off as if he suddenly realized his own execution was known to everyone and he was just finding out for himself.

"Tell him, John," McKinley said.

Trask stared for a moment at Abrams. Time to drop the bomb and send this whiz kid back to State with his tail between his legs.

"Moscow wants a trade," he said evenly. "Owens for Zakharov." He threw his cigarette into the fire and listened to the silence. Charles, he noted, was smiling.

Abrams began to stuff papers into his briefcase. "Oh really, I mean how can we even discuss this. A defector, a traitor for a top Soviet caught in the act. I've no doubt the Russians would like Zakharov back. Of course they want a trade." Abrams ignored the admiral, but looked imploringly from McKinley to Trask to Charles.

"Well, I'm afraid that's the way it has to be worked out, Richard, and we'll expect full cooperation from State on this.

Thank you for your part. We'll take it from here," McKinley said, clearly dismissing Abrams.

Abrams nodded and was joined by the admiral as McKinley accompanied them out. Trask and Charles were left alone.

"Well, John, you've managed to pull out another surprise," Charles said.

"I don't know what I've pulled out, Charles. I'm only a messenger on this one. But anyway, you're ahead of me on surprises. Are you back in the fold or is this a special guest appearance?" Neither man would mention Prague.

Charles shrugged. "Your guess is as good as mine. They keep threatening to retire me and I keep resisting. I do some consulting now and then for the Eastern desk. Still, perhaps this means something substantial is in the works."

Trask nodded. "I guess it will be a routine exchange, but we'll have to see what Eugene says."

"Yes, I'm inclined to agree, but it does seem a bit strange, Zakharov's arrest, I mean. Still, as you say..." Charles seemed preoccupied, drifting off before Trask could pursue him. McKinley returned and broke out a bottle of brandy.

"Now then," he said, sitting down and filling three glasses. "Let's get down to business. I'm afraid our young man from State is a bit miffed. The Zakharov case was his baby and he's been liaison with the FBI. I couldn't resist letting you break the news, John. The president has already been advised, of course, so I think Abrams can stand a little feather ruffling."

"So," Charles began, "I can understand Moscow wanting Zakharov back, but why are we so keen to welcome Owens home?"

"Owens could be invaluable," Trask answered. "Technology is the Soviets highest priority these days, and according to our sources, Owens has been at Zelenograd all this time. Someone who's been on the inside, even a defector, will have a wealth of information. Then, there's also the possibility Owens was recruited much earlier, maybe while he was in the army, for example. A kind of reverse sleeper. Don't forget, we're well ahead of the Soviets in development. Owens could confirm that."

"Yes," McKinley said, "or refute it. If only we could stop the insane student exchange program. We send our students to Moscow University to study Russian fairy tales and they send us older graduate students to study physics and laser development." McKinley sighed. "The main thing is to ensure Owens' attitude is going to be cooperative."

"And," Charles said, "that he is indeed Robert Owens. Which makes it difficult for us if I'm correct in assuming that, with the exception of this fellow Mason, nobody's seen Owens for what, five years?"

"Exactly," McKinley said. "I believe John has the only viable plan if we're to go ahead with this. To positively confirm Owens, we've got to come up with someone from his past—college roommate, co-worker, army buddy—someone who could ask questions only the real Owens could answer. Even with intensive background briefings, there are certain details of a man's life that can't be anticipated, especially if you go back far enough." McKinley paused a moment. "I don't like to think about it, but there's certainly a consideration Owens could be a ringer. Find someone who looks enough like him, plastic surgery, well you both know how it works."

Charles nodded and then said. "What about this fellow Mason he contacted in Moscow? If Mason worked with Owens, surely he could make a positive identification."

"No, Charles. It was seven years ago, and besides, he didn't know Owens very well. In any case, I don't think he'd be a willing candidate."

"Well, suppose we find such a person. What then?" Charles asked. "Even assuming Moscow will agree, won't it mean sending an inexperienced man into a potentially dangerous situation?"

"How do you mean?" Trask asked.

"Moscow will certainly stipulate any such confirmation be made on their home ground won't they? They're certainly not going to let Owens just walk away while we still have Zakharov."

McKinley allowed himself a smile. "As usual, Charles, you're absolutely correct. We want you to find this man for us and convince him a trip to Europe would be a grand experience. With the help of our computer records of course. We'll iron out the details after we see what we have to choose from. I can think of no one more qualified, right, John?"

Trask nodded. It was true of course. Charles Fox had recruited and run agents all over Eastern Europe under the worst conditions. His natural, persuasive charm would be perfect. People talked to Charles. Trask had seen it time after time.

"Well, it's settled then," McKinley said. "John will go back to Moscow and work out things there. Charles, I'll authorize all the computer time you need starting tomorrow, but we have to work fast. We've pulled Owens' file already, there isn't much to go on, I'm afraid." McKinley drained his glass. "In fact, what I've seen makes me wonder if Robert Calvin Owens even existed."

Charles caught McKinley and Trask exchange an almost imperceptible glance.

A shared secret? I wonder, he thought.

Two

Speeding along an endless, two-lane asphalt strip towards Cable Falls, Montana, Charles Fox smiled, remembering a sports commentator's description of a boxing champion on the eve of his retirement. An aging pro in the twilight of a fading career, the sportscaster had said.

An aging pro perhaps, but his career, if somewhat dimmed, had not faded completely. Not yet. At fifty-seven, Charles Fox had been an American citizen for more than twenty-five years. But the traces of his native English accent, the Etonian mannerisms could be called upon and unleashed in full if the situation required it.

The hair was silver and thinning, complimented by a narrow white mustache. The compact body, except for a few extra pounds, was the same as when he'd roamed the back streets and alleys of Eastern Europe.

First with the OSS and later with the CIA, he eventually ran a network of operatives which had become as legendary as Fox himself. The Soviet invasion of Czechoslovakia in 1968 had changed all that, though he rarely allowed himself to think about it anymore.

In recent years with his wife dead and a daughter in college, Fox had been a consultant for Eastern European operations, lecturing, teaching, drawing on his knowledge of the area. Since Prague field work had become a thing of the past.

It was rumored there was a woman somewhere although no one thought to ask. Fox was often seen in the more fashionable restaurants around Georgetown. Always impeccably dressed, usually in the company of an old friend or former colleague, Fox was seemingly content to enjoy the delights of good food and wine.

But beneath the veneer of complacency, he harbored a longing for a return to action. The blue eyes still sparkled and the mind was as wily and cunning as ever. Charles Fox was glad to be back in the fold, even temporarily. Even in Montana.

The snow, so he had been told by the Hertz clerk in Billings, had stopped several days ago. The road was clear and the hard packed snow gleamed like polished stone in the bright sunlight. Frozen lakes and streams flew by in a blue blur, and despite the heavy sheepskin jacket, the car heater was going full blast. Montana was cold and lonely. He hadn't seen another car for nearly an hour.

He flipped around the radio dial but continued to find only weather and farm news, laced with the heavy staple of country and western music. Grimacing, he gave up finally, snapped off the radio longing for a Beethoven Quartet. He let his mind focus on why he was in Montana.

After further meetings with Eugene McKinley and John Trask, the list of possible candidates for Owens's confirmation had been shortened to five. It had been agreed to concentrate on the period which encompassed Owens' stay at college, military service and finally, the point of his defection. But even with the aid of the Langley computers, Owens' life was virtually a blank slate. Preliminary inquiries had confirmed the initial impression that Owens was indeed a loner. With the exception of his mother—and she had refused point blank to discuss her son's defection to the Soviet Union—Owens had no other family. Anyone who did remember him could make only vague references. In the end, they were left with Owens' army service and his employment at Triton Industries.

It now fell to Charles Fox to narrow down this short list to one. Final approval of the project was dependent upon finding a suitable, reliable man to verify Owens as genuine. One man. To go where? Western Europe? Hungary? Czechoslovakia? Russia? It still wasn't agreed where the meeting would take place. Trask had returned to Moscow to make those arrangements and once there, this man, singled out purely by chance, would be called upon to erase any doubts about Robert Owens identity. At least that was the idea.

Charles warmed to the task before him, flushed with

anticipation at the thought of playing an active role again. Choosing the right man would be important and Charles was convinced the answer would be among the survivors of Owens' unit in Vietnam. Two of the five candidates had already been eliminated. One had been killed in a car crash three years ago. The second, a bleeding mind that had never recovered from the horrors of Vietnam, was institutionalized in a Veteran's hospital in California. For the remaining three, Charles was left with a high school teacher in Las Vegas, the security chief of Triton Industries, and if the file could be believed, a Montana farmer with long hair, an even longer record of drug arrests and decidedly leftist politics. To Charles, none were promising.

Nearing Cable Falls, Charles braked, skirted a slow-moving tractor and watched the sun, now an orange disk, sink into a sea of snow. He drove slowly past the city limits sign toward a cluster of wood frame buildings. The town looked nearly deserted as he reached the end of the main street and pulled up in front of what appeared to be the town's only motel.

Charles gazed through the windshield at its run down look, guessed he would find lumpy beds and moaning water pipes. Sighing, he parked and got out of the car, feeling the chilled air on his ears. His feet crunched over the hard-packed snow as he tramped up the steps to the entrance. A hand-written placard in the window read: Vacancy. "I should think so," he muttered to himself as he surveyed the empty parking lot.

A tiny bell jangled as he opened the door. Behind a scarred desk, a rail-thin man lounged sullenly, head bobbing to the blaring radio, moaning a mournful song of a trucker's lost love. Charles shuddered inwardly and walked up to the desk.

The clerk regarded Charles curiously, shifted a toothpick to one corner of his mouth and grunted. "Hep ya?" A gnarled hand clawed at the radio and turned it down slightly.

"Possibly," Charles said. "I'm looking for the Savage farm."

"That so," the clerk replied. "You a friend of Mike's then are ya?" His voice was almost a whine and thick with contempt. His already narrowed eyes grew more suspicious.

"Not exactly. This is kind of an official visit." Charles produced a wallet crammed with credit cards and casually let the clerk take in the government identification. "No problem however. Mr. Savage might even thank you for pointing me in the right direction."

"Mr. Savage, eh?" The clerk snorted at the address and spat out the toothpick. He paused for a moment in indecision. "Well, I reckon you'd find him anyway. Usually down at Maggie's Bar come supper time. Drives a pickup. Anybody down there can tell you how to git to his place," the clerk added, making it obvious it wasn't going to be him.

"Fine," Charles said, deciding the clerk wasn't going to volunteer any more information even if he pressed him. "In the meantime, have you got a room? I'd like to clean up a bit."

"Spoze so." The clerk dragged a dusty ledger off a shelf and opened it to a page of indecipherable scrawls to which Charles added his own. The clerk glanced at the name and handed him a key attached to a wooden block. "Ah, we pay in advance here—cash," he drawled as Charles turned to go.

"Of course," Charles said, trying to keep the amusement out of his voice. He laid two twenty-dollar bills down. "Will this be sufficient?"

"Yeah, I reckon so. Have to git your change to you later."

Charles nodded and left the clerk to gnaw another toothpick as the radio resumed full volume. He took his bag out of the trunk, found room five—only a slight improvement over the office—and dropped on the bed. The drive had been tiring, but he was surprised to find he'd slept for nearly an hour when the knock came at the door. It was the clerk with his change.

"Don't see Mike's truck at the bar," the clerk said, peering over Charles shoulder into the room. "Course on the other hand, he might have gone up to the mountains." The hint of a smile crossed his face.

Especially if you've warned him off, Charles thought. "Well, thank you for your trouble. Where can I get something to eat?"

"Bar's the best place. Maggie does a good chicken fried steak."

"Right," Charles said. "Thanks again."

It took ten minutes for the water to get hot. Under the shower, Charles decided it was going to be difficult to even find Mike Savage, much less talk to him. He began to regret his decision to arrive in Cable Falls unannounced.

He dressed quickly, put a well-placed paper clip in the door and headed for Maggie's Bar. It was dark now. The shapes of the buildings were silhouetted against the white landscape. A dog barked somewhere as he passed several small pickup trucks and pushed through the door.

Three men in heavy overalls huddled at the bar. At one of the tables, two grizzled old men slapped checkers on a board. In one corner, under a stark hanging light, two younger men were shooting pool and drinking beer out of bottles. A third leaned against the wall in boredom. Everyone looked up as Charles came in. He could feel their eyes follow him as he walked to a table in the rear.

"What'll it be, mister?" A woman Charles guessed must be Maggie appeared out of the kitchen. She had a hard lean face, rough, red hands and strands of hair hung down over surprisingly soft brown eyes.

Charles smiled at her. "The man at the hotel says you do a good chicken fried steak. That would be fine. Oh, and a beer please."

Maggie nodded and shuffled away, returning a few minutes later with an ice cold beer and the steak, batter fried, alongside a heaping mound of mashed potatoes swimming in brown gravy. There was also a small dish of sweet corn.

Charles ate hungrily, listening to the snatches of conversation over the drone of the radio, the crack of pool balls and checkers. He was acutely aware of the searching glances of the few customers. A few newcomers came in, but none of them was Mike Savage. Maggie seemed to read his mind though; he was sure the hotel clerk had already spread the word.

"Mike won't be in tonight," Maggie said, ringing up the bill on an old cash register. "If he comes in, it's always earlier than this." She slammed the register drawer shut with a bang.

"I don't suppose you could direct me then?" Charles ventured. "It's rather urgent that I see him." The pool game had stopped. Charles was aware of the heavy silence that swept over the bar.

Maggie studied Charles for a long moment, glanced toward the pool table and pushed back a wisp of hair from her eyes. "Follow the road out of town north about twelve miles. There's a turnoff on your right. Can't miss it in this moonlight. Little ways up, there's a fork. Take the one on the left. Mike's place is about half a mile further up." She turned abruptly and headed for the kitchen.

"Thanks," Charles called after her. The crack of pool balls resumed as he stepped out onto the street.

He walked back to the motel for his car and drove out of town, checking the odometer and the rear-view mirror as he drove. No company and the turnoff was exactly twelve miles. He turned and soon reached the fork Maggie had described. He stopped the car for a moment. The one on your left she had said. Charles went right. Another couple of minutes and his headlights caught a sign: BEWARE OF OWNER. Smiling, Charles parked the car off the road and got out.

He tramped up the hill along a worn trail recently cleared of snow. Every few paces he stopped, listened intently for any sounds, but there was only the wind through the trees until he'd gone a few more steps.

"Hold it right there, mister." Charles froze. A shadowy figure emerged from behind a tree and moved toward him cautiously. "Hands on top of your head."

Charles complied and looked at the man as he came closer. Just over six-feet tall, he guessed. Bushy eyebrows, heavy mustache and dressed in faded jeans and a scuffed sheepskin jacket. Despite the cold the man wore no hat, but his long hair was tied back in a ponytail. Charles knew he'd found Mike Savage and he was now looking down the double barrels of a shotgun pointed at his middle.

"They tell me at Maggie's a government man's lookin' for me. That must be you, eh?" Savage moved closer. In the moonlight, Charles could make out his features, but he was not close enough to make a grab for the gun even if he wanted to.

"I confess," Charles said. "May I be permitted to identify myself?"

"That's the idea. Real careful now, with one hand, take out your wallet and lay it down in front of you."

Charles knew the drill. He complied again and stepped back. "You're a very careful man. I guess news travels fast around here. Do you always greet visitors this way?"

Savage grinned as he glanced at the ID card. "Mister, you're trespassing on private property and this is a small town." He studied the card for a moment, keeping one eye on Charles. "Okay, this looks good. Now what can I do for you? My taxes are up to date, I don't owe anybody anything and I send my ex-old lady two hundred a month." Savage shifted the shotgun to the crook of his arm.

"Nothing like that I assure you," Charles said, putting his hands down. "I came to talk to you about Vietnam." Even in the shadowy light, he could see Savage's grin vanish.

"What about it? Nam was a shithole and I don't recommend it," he said flatly.

"Your time there is actually what I mean. More specifically, an officer you served with. Lieutenant Robert Owens."

"Owens?" Savage spat out the name like a curse and laughed without humor, a hollow, chilling sound. "Served with, huh? Yeah, I guess you could say that. He left us to join some intelligence unit after. What about him?"

"He defected to Russia about five years ago and now he wants to come home."

Savage lowered the shotgun further and flipped Charles his wallet. "You're CIA, right?" Savage studied Charles intently.

Slowly, Charles returned his wallet to his pocket. "Let's just say government attached. Can we talk about it?"

Savage gazed at Charles for a full minute before answering. "Why not? You're the first guy that's asked. C'mon, we'll be more comfortable inside."

Savage turned abruptly and started up the trail. A few minutes later they arrived at an expanse of cleared land. A small, rough-hewn cabin squatted near the edge of a bluff. A wisp of smoke curled up from the stone chimney. From the edge of the bluff, Charles could see a wooded meadow stretching below. He could only imagine what the view was like in daylight.

A honey Labrador bounded around from the back of the cabin with a tail-wagging greeting for Savage and a curious sniff for Charles. "That's Pappy," Savage said, roughly stroking the dog. "Come on in."

Inside the cabin, Savage lit an oil lamp, threw a couple of logs on the fire and motioned Charles to a battered leather chair. "Coffee or whiskey?"

"Whiskey's fine."

Savage returned with a tumbler of Scotch and a beer for himself." I didn't figure you for a beer drinker," he said, dropping into another stuffed chair next to Charles. The moonlight spilled in the window and snow flurries began to cling to the glass, forming tiny patterns of crystal before sliding wetly down. The fire made the room glow and Charles suddenly wished he were there for some other reason.

"Built it myself," Savage said, sensing Charles' silent approval. "Good place to get away from things." He took a gulp of his beer. "Look, I'm sorry about the greeting, but there are a couple of people I don't really want to see again. The town is alright once you're accepted, but they can be a bit tight-lipped."

"I noticed." Charles smiled. Savage seemed suddenly more relaxed, as if he were happy to have a visitor, unannounced or not. Charles guessed few people had seen the inside of the cabin.

"You eaten? I got some chili on if you don't have a squeamish stomach."

"No, thanks. I had one of Maggie's steaks before I came up. She told me the way. Well, almost the way. She made a slight mistake about the turn at the fork."

Savage laughed. "No mistake, but Maggie figured if you could find the way, you must be okay. She's alright, kind of adopted me when I moved here. Her son bought it in Nam."

Savage stood and went to the kitchen. He brought Charles

another drink and a steaming bowl of chili in a stone bowl for himself. He ate in silence, occasionally glancing at Charles who sat contentedly, warmed by the fire and Scotch, letting his gaze roam over the cabin. On one wall, some rough shelves held an impressive collection of paperback books.

Savage followed his gaze. "Passes the time," he said. He finished eating and lit a cigarette. "What do you want to know about Owens?" he asked as he popped open another beer.

Charles shifted in his chair. "I'd like to hear about you first." He regarded Savage with real interest. Remembering the file, he wondered how a boy from the streets of Chicago survives Vietnam and ends up on the side of a mountain. "How did this all come about?" He waved a hand around the room.

Savage smiled understandingly. "That's what my dad wants to know. He doesn't like this either," he said, fingering the pony tail. "I haven't cut it since Nam." Shrugging he went on. "After I was discharged, I went back to Chicago. Got married, got a nothing job—probably exactly what I would have done if I hadn't gone to Nam, but it didn't work. Nam changed a lot of guys. Me for one. I got into some heavy dope dealing. I guess you know about that. Anyway, I made some money, got lucky on some investments and split for the open skies. Just got in my truck and drove till I saw this place. It's about as different from Nam as you can imagine. Parked the truck, built this place and well, here I am." He flipped his cigarette into the fire.

Charles sat back. How many were there like Mike Savage? Scarred invisibly by a war they didn't believe in but fought nevertheless. Returned to scorn, confusion, hopelessness and broken lives. Scattered about the country, their fears locked away, dreams unfulfilled.

Charles took out a briar pipe and a pouch of tobacco. "Owens was only with your unit a few months, right?"

"I got something better to pack that with if you feel like it."

"No, thanks. I tried it once with my daughter. Didn't do anything for me," Charles said.

Savage shrugged and took a stubby pipe from over the fireplace. He filled it from a stone jar. Lit, the pipe produced the pungent aroma of marijuana. On the floor, Pappy raised his head, sniffed the air and moved to the corner.

"Pappy doesn't approve?"

"Naw, doesn't like the smell, I guess. Found him when he was a puppy. Just a stray, like me." Savage settled back in his chair and stared into the flames. "Yeah, Owens wasn't with us long, a few months was enough. Guess you've done your homework," he said, looking at Charles.

"How is it you remember him so easily?" Charles sat forward and sipped his drink.

Savage's laugh was hollow again, like a rattle. "Remember him? Hell, I almost killed the bastard. Had him right in the sights of my M16, then just as I pulled the trigger, one of the guys jerked it away and I missed." He laughed again. "Just think, I might have saved you a trip up here and you'd have one less defector to worry about."

"How did it happen?"

Savage took a pull on his pipe, sucked in some air and coughed slightly. "Owens was a replacement. Nam wasn't like your war. We didn't train together, ship over together, fight together or come home together. Everybody shipped in one at a time. Our second in command got wasted when he stepped on a mine and what was left of him was sent home in a bag." Savage paused, shaking his head.

"No real experience. Owens, I mean. Green as they come. A twink with bars on his shoulders. There were some nineteen year olds that were scary, man."

Charles nodded. Child men, transformed overnight into hardened combat veterans with blank gazes, storing up memories they'd never be able to shake.

"Anyway, on this one patrol, Owens panicked under fire. He called for support mortar shelling, but he fucked up the coordinates. Our own guys were shelling us. Everyone begged him to hold off, but he wouldn't listen. He hadn't paid any attention in the briefings. Always had his face in some computer book. He'd been to college, he was always telling us.

"We were caught in some pretty heavy action about then, which if we got out of it was okay because that meant we could up the body count. That was the big thing in Nam, man. Body count. If it was really good we'd get a shipment of ice cream and cold cokes dropped by chopper." His shoulders slumped and he looked at Charles with a pleading expression. "I mean what was that war about anyway?"

Charles wished there was something he could say that would penetrate what Mike Savage was feeling, even after all these years.

"Like I said," Savage continued, "Owens thought he knew better than anyone else. A few of our guys bought it. One took a direct hit. He'd been in Nam three days. He was seventeen. Hello and goodbye war."

Savage seemed to sink even deeper in the chair. His pipe had gone out. "We survived, the rest of us, though, I don't know how. The mortar fire was finally straightened out and I guess Owens got his ass reamed good when we got back. Big fucking deal. We got into a light skirmish on the way. Owens was just up ahead and when I saw him there in my sights, I thought, fuck it, I just..." His voice trailed off and he stared into the fire.

Charles remained silent. The wind rustled the snow against the windows. The dying fire crackled and hissed. After a bit he said, "And Owens left after that?"

Savage sighed, returned from wherever his memories had taken him. "Yeah, not long after. They disappeared him somewhere behind the lines where he couldn't do any harm. Lucky for him, too. Someone would have wasted him sooner or later if the VC didn't." He shook his head again. "And while that was going on, those assholes in Paris were arguing over the shape of the goddamn table."

Charles had no answers. He could feel for Mike Savage, but this was not his man. The ten years of pent up emotions seething inside him threatened to spill over at any moment. Savage would not fail to kill Owens a second time if he were given the opportunity.

"What are your plans now if you don't mind my asking?"

"Oh, I don't know. I just kind of cruise along up here."

His smile returned and Charles could almost see the tension visibly drain from his face. "I've been trying to get my brother out here, help me clear some more land, maybe build some kind of lodge. You know, catch the Canadian tourists who want to get away from it all."

Charles smiled. Savage would be an expert at that. He put down his glass and stood to go. "Well, it's getting late. I'd better be getting back to town. Thanks for the drinks and talk."

"No problem, man. I hope you got what you came for. I'll walk you back down."

Pappy led the way as they retraced their steps down the trail to Charles' car. He gripped the young man's hand firmly. "I hope everything works out for you," Charles said.

Savage nodded. "Watch it going back. Might be some ice on the road." He started to go then turned back. "You know Owens isn't worth the effort."

Who knows? Charles thought as he drove away. Maybe Savage was right. He headed back to town somehow relieved that he could leave Mike Savage on his mountaintop.

Three

In the study of his comfortable *dacha* twenty miles outside of Moscow, Colonel Vasili Aleksevich Delnov, Second Chief Directorate KGB, was pleased; quite pleased.

He sat at a huge oak desk and let his eyes roam over the dozen color enlargements spread out before him. Pulling the heavy woolen robe closer around his massive body, naked under the robe, he pursed his lips and whistled softly as he studied the photos one at a time. His eyes, cold and hard, flicked around the desk, now here, now there, as if playing a game with himself, willing his eyes to find some tiny discrepancy somewhere.

Without taking his eyes from the photos, he reached to his right into a carved wooden box, took out a long Cuban cigar and lit it with a small, heavy, gold Dunhill lighter. He pulled the swivel lamp down over the desk closer to the photos, at an angle that all but made the harsh glare on their glossy surface vanish.

Continuing to study the photos, he weighed the heavy lighter in his right hand, clasping and unclasping his stubby fingers over its smooth finish, bouncing it lightly in his hand. Over the years, this action with the lighter had become his own peculiar version of worry beads. Occasionally, as now, the mannerism signaled intense pleasure. The gesture was well known to his subordinates in the Seventh Department, although none of them, even Delnov's most trusted assistant, was ever sure if the gesture meant pleasure, simple annoyance or intense anger.

He shifted the position of the photos, studying them carefully, much in the way a casting director might do, agonizing over a choice for a major role in a film with a multi-million dollar budget. But in this case, there was no decision to be made, no array of stars to choose from. The photographs were all of the same man.

The twelve photos—six profiles, six full facial shots—revealed the smooth even features of an almost handsome man. The eyes that stared back at Delnov were soft and deep brown. The lower lip protruded slightly under a narrow nose and the chin was also narrow and tapering. The dark, straight brown hair was neatly parted on one side, and although the man could be no more than thirty-five, the hair was already thinning. On the full-face shots, the expression was blank, vacant, full of resignation.

Choosing one at random, Delnov picked it up and held it closer to the light, turning his head slightly to tap ash in an onyx ashtray. As his gaze returned to the photo, he felt the familiar feeling of power that he held over this man. Impulsively, he turned the photo over and glanced at the letter neatly printed in felt tip pen.

Nodding in self-approval, he raised his eyes to the window in front of him and peered out at the white landscape. The hint of a smile curled around his mouth. The lighter bounced happily in his hand.

"Yes," he murmured softly to himself and leaned back in his chair. His eyes returned to the photographs. They were like a magnet, giving him an inner warmth as delicious as the furry slippers holding his wriggling toes. He continued to inspect the photos for another few moments, then put out the cigar, rose and crossed the room to a small drinks cabinet. For a large man, Delnov's movements were quick and graceful. He broke the seal on a bottle of spiced Vodka, poured out a hefty tumbler full and walked back in front of the desk to stand at the window.

He stood gazing out at the woods to the left of the *dacha*. The moon shone through the trees bouncing light in soft slivers through the slim birches onto the snow. He toasted his reflection in the glass and downed the vodka in one gulp, feeling the burning warmth spread through his body immediately.

"Who is he, Vasili?"

Delnov turned sharply from the window. He was so absorbed in his thoughts he hadn't heard Natalya come into the room. She was standing over the desk looking at the photographs.

A light silken robe was draped casually about her body, her bare feet wriggled in the soft carpet. She's like a polar bear, Delnov thought. She never felt the cold. The light from the desk lamp silhouetted her body beneath the robe. Delnov took in the easy rise and fall of her breasts, the taut nipples jutting ahead stiffly, eager to be released from the confines of the fabric.

"No one important, my pet," he said, joining her at the desk. "Do you think he's handsome?" His gaze followed her own to the photos.

Her lower lip pouted. She shook her head and wrinkled her nose. After a moment's hesitation, she shook her head again. The light blonde hair fell about her face haphazardly. It was damp and fresh from the bath and he could smell the faint aroma of perfumed soap on her skin.

"No," she said finally. "Not ugly, but not handsome either." She turned toward Delnov. "Not at all like you, Vasili. You are handsome," she murmured throatily.

Delnov smiled, accepting the lie as she rose on her toes, grazed his cheek with her lips and blew softly in his ear. She slipped her hands inside the robe, around his body and pressed herself against him.

"But, Vasili," she persisted. "He must be important for you to have so many pictures of him. He's not Russian is he?" She pulled back slightly, looking into his face with that innocent expression of curiosity he had come to know so well.

Delnov's eyes narrowed. At first he had believed her to be one of Shevchenko's stooges, sent to ferret out information. That would have been typical of him. Shevchenko had opposed him from the outset, cautioning at first, then raising objection after objection, and finally, even threatening. But Shevchenko's threats were empty, like those of a small boy and not to be taken seriously. And, despite Shevchenko, he had triumphed in the end, overcoming all objections and receiving approval from Andropov himself. *That* had silenced Shevchenko.

Still, one could never be too careful. He'd had Natalya checked out to his complete satisfaction, and even though he was reluctant to admit it, relief. She was evidently nothing more than what she appeared to be: a beautiful but largely untalented actress with a Moscow theatre company, and apparently, she was in love with Delnov.

"Nothing to worry your pretty head about, my pet," he said soothingly.

She was quick to recognize the tone of finality in his voice. The issue was not to be taken further.

"Now, go and warm up the bed for us. I'll join you shortly. I have a little surprise for you."

Natalya's eyes sparkled like a child's. "Oh, tell me, tell me," she squealed in delight.

"Later," he said. "If I tell you now it won't be a surprise." He pushed her away gently, but let his hands linger for a moment over her supple hips. He felt a tremor of excitement rush through him as he watched her pad to the door in almost liquid motion. The robe fell open as she walked, affording him a teasing view of her smooth thighs.

She stopped at the door and looked coyly over her shoulder. "If you don't hurry, I shall be asleep," she said mockingly, with practiced skill.

"Then I shall just have to wake you, won't I?" She smiled and shut the door noiselessly behind her. Delnov sighed. She was beautiful and she was his.

He turned back to the desk, and after one last glance, gathered up the photographs. Stacking them neatly, he put them in a large brown envelope, closed its clasp and returned it to a drawer in the desk. He frowned as his hand brushed against a similar envelope. It too contained photographs, three in all, also enlargements, but printed in black and white. He spread them on the desk. Unconsciously he felt for the lighter as he studied the new photos.

The light was not good, but the images were clear and unmistakable. They showed a man standing in a phone booth, staring into the lens. "Zakharov." He spat the name and gripped the lighter tightly.

In the second photo, Zakharov was between two other men, obviously the FBI agents. Zakharov's expression was one of resignation tinged with fear. It was a waist high shot and even there, Delnov could detect the slump of the shoulders, the sagging face, the blank stare. The third photo showed Zakharov getting into a car. The lighter felt cold in his hand as he gripped it tighter.

What was considered Zakharov's apparent blunder had nearly ruined everything. His ingenious plan, the greatest stroke of his career, a plan that promised the highest praise from his superiors, perhaps even the Order of Lenin. Yes, that was certainly possible. All nearly, but not quite ruined. Instead, he had turned Zakharov's arrest, exactly as planned, to his advantage, arguing it was not a disaster as Shevchenko had, but merely extra leverage, perhaps even a blessing in disguise. Delnov had not counted on such violent opposition from Shevchenko. In the end, Andropov had agreed and from that point, Delnov was once more in command.

Of course they wanted Zakharov returned and Delnov himself would be there to greet him. He relished the thought of being a witness to Zakharov's debriefing, his disgrace, his sentencing. A pity but sacrifices must be made. It's too bad, he mused, that Zakharov would never know how he had advanced his own career.

He gave the Zakharov photos one final glance, returned them to their envelope which he placed in the desk drawer. He locked the drawer, poured himself another vodka and again toasted his own reflection.

The photos of Zakharov had been delivered to him only yesterday by his assistant following a meeting with the American John Trask. Obviously, Trask thought they would influence their decision to allow the verification of Owens to be made outside the Soviet Union. Perhaps they would concede, Delnov thought. Not completely, of course. Prague, or perhaps Budapest, would be equally safe. Just enough to keep the Americans convinced. No more, no less. Yes, it was all falling into place, exactly as he had engineered the plan from its inception.

He could well imagine the surprise of the Americans that Owens wanted to return and also their elation that he would be allowed to. Fools, he thought. Were he in their place, Owens would be left to rot in Siberia. But then, that's what makes the game so interesting. The varying viewpoints, the diverse allegiances, the differing approaches. Delnov enjoyed it all. He downed the vodka. Well, enough of this for tonight.

His mind turned easily to Natalya, lingering over the vision of her waiting submissively on the huge bed, her golden hair spread out over the pillow, her breasts rising and falling, his erection pressing between their warmth ever closer to her inviting lips.

Still, he would have to oversee everything carefully. Trask was no fool and there was Fox to contend with, the old devil. Delnov chuckled. If Charles Fox was involved, however indirectly, he would have to tread with caution. He had dueled with Fox before and not always triumphantly. But of course there had been Prague. Even now Delnov savored the memory.

Extreme care must be taken during the verification period the Americans were insisting on and the actual exchange when it took place. If only they could get Zakharov first, the rest would be easy. Perhaps too easy and then all the fun would be out of it.

Well, there was still time to decide and now Natalya waited. He snapped off the light, grabbed another cigar and headed for the bedroom, whistling softly to himself, the lighter bouncing happily in his hand.

If Mike Savage had a complete opposite, it was Mel Highlands, the security chief of Triton Industries. Fox spotted him immediately from the personnel file in the arrivals lounge at San Francisco International Airport. Medium height, short brown hair, well cut three-piece suit and carrying a light attaché case. Fox caught his eye and stepped out of the crush of passengers.

Highlands was all business as he greeted Charles. "Mr. Fox?" He extended his hand in a firm grasp. "I have a car waiting. Do you have any other luggage?"

"No, just this bag," Charles said. "I left some things in Los Angeles."

"Right then, shall we?" Highlands guided them through

the labyrinth of the tunnels and passageways to a car. They were whisked across the airport to the executive terminal and the Triton plane. It was a small Lear jet, fitted as a company plane might be expected: comfortable lounge chairs, a bar, and a television. A quick nod to the pilot from Highlands and they were off. Once airborne, Highlands filled Charles in on their day.

"The telex said you're cleared for anything which makes it easy for me. You have anything specific in mind or is this just a general look around?" Highlands' manner was easy, efficient, and reassuring. Charles suspected he was good at his job.

"No, just a quick look around and of course anything you can tell me about Owens. I'd like to see his personnel file." Highlands knew about Owens, but had not been informed about his planned return.

The security man nodded and stared out the porthole of the small jet, reflecting for a moment over the city of hills. "You know, even now," he said, "after all these years, it's hard for me to believe anyone would leave all this."

Charles wasn't sure whether Highlands was referring to the company jet or the city of San Francisco. "People are motivated by different things," he said. "Perhaps Owens was fighting some inner battle."

Highlands' answer was a disapproving shrug, but Charles could sympathize. His job was an unenviable one at best. Despite the stepped up security measures in recent years, the Soviets continued to concentrate their efforts in securing technology and Silicon Valley was a prime target. The Soviet consulate and communications facility sat atop one of the highest hills in the Bay area and targeted the valley as well as Mare Island Naval Base where the U.S. nuclear submarines were serviced. Here and in other principal areas of Soviet activity, such as New York and Washington, D.C., the centers were staffed with the cream of the KGB crop. And despite the massive campaign by the FBI to stem the tide of information flowing to Moscow, Robert Owens had simply walked into the Soviet embassy and offered himself, his head crammed with data the Russians must have salivated over. And all right under the noses of men like Mel Highlands who tried to prevent such occurrences. It was no wonder Highlands felt little sympathy for Owens.

"We'll be landing in a moment," Highlands said, breaking the silence. The plane glided in smoothly and taxied to a small terminal. Another short drive brought them to Triton, a complex of manicured lawns, low white buildings and impressive landscaping. Triton was but one of hundreds of companies in Silicon Valley that had become the very heart of the computer industry and microchip technology. Triton, Charles reminded himself, was the only company with the dubious distinction of having one of its former employees defect to the Soviet Union.

They checked in at the front gate where Charles was given a visitors pass and Highlands led them to his office. "Thought it would be better to talk here," he said, motioning Charles to a comfortable chair. "I'll order us some lunch in if that's all right with you. Then we'll do the big tour."

"Fine," Charles said. "I suppose we can get started by telling me about Owens' work here at Triton. What kind of projects was he working on when he left?"

Highlands leaned back and clasped his hands together. "Developmental stuff mostly." He consulted a dark green file folder on his desk. "We do all kinds of things here. Research into laser physics, non-linear optics, spectroscopy, as well as tunable lasers."

"I'm afraid you've lost me already," Charles said laughing. "Science was not one of my strong subjects."

"Nor mine," Highlands said, slapping the file. "But the list goes on and on. I know about enough to know how valuable it would be to any foreign power, never mind the Russians." His eyebrows knitted into a frown. "We might just as well open the gates and let them walk in and take notes. We've almost done that already, though not at Triton," he added quickly.

"How do you mean?" Charles asked.

Highlands leaned back in his chair again and lit a cigarette after offering one to Charles. "A few years ago, the State Department, in its infinite wisdom, arranged for a group of

Soviet aircraft specialists to visit some of our factories—Boeing, Lockheed, McDonnell Douglas—to improve relations," Highlands said sardonically. "Give them a look at our production lines, have a little shop talk, that kind of thing. Well, it turns out that this supposedly benevolent group of visitors the tour were wearing special shoes to picked up metal scraps and shavings from the factory floors. Those particles were later analyzed back in Moscow and eventually led to the Soviets being able to acquire the metal alloys necessary to produce their Illyushin Il-76T transport plane." He paused to give Charles a rueful smile.

"Want more? Okay. I was told that story, by the way, to impress on me the importance of security at Triton." He shrugged again. "The Soviet embassy in Washington spends several million dollars a year for copies of thousands of technical reports on file at the Department of Commerce's Information service. They get this stuff *legally*. The magazine *Aviation Week & Space Technology*, each issue mind you, is flown directly to Moscow and translated en route. A friend of mine at the FBI tells me they get up to ninety percent of their intelligence from open sources—unclassified material, seminars and trade shows." Highlands angrily stubbed out his cigarette. "You figure it out. Then along comes a guy like Owens and well..."

"What exactly was Owens working on?"

Highlands consulted the file again. "Oh, nothing important," he said. "Just a device called an accelerometer. Apparently, it measures changes in the pull of gravity on an airborne vehicle. It's crucial to guided missile systems. I'd say that would be fairly high on the Soviet shopping list, along with high-speed micro pressers and integrated circuits. All stuff we do here at Triton."

Charles got up and walked to the window. Over the complex he could see a number of white-coated employees hurrying in and out of buildings, reading printouts on the run, talking, laughing. He tried to imagine Robert Owens in this setting. What had made him do it? And more important, why were the Soviets willing to let him go now? According to the latest word from Washington, the Kremlin was getting impatient over Zakharov. Why again? It wasn't as if Zakharov was a prize catch and they must have him back at all costs. Zakharov was not a known operative, so why the panic?

Charles fought to grasp the thread of an idea running in his mind, but it continued to elude him. What was the key? He turned back to Highlands.

"Anything you can tell me about Owens' personal life?" There was always the chance there was a name that hadn't already turned up.

Highlands shook his head. "No, not really. He didn't have one. Clean record but a real loner. Obsessed with work, seldom if ever spent any time outside with anyone. Lived with his mother, definitely not a bar hound. We were pleased with that because the Soviets trawl the singles bars for any likely tidbits. Owens had been doing a lot more than that. Art Mason might help you there. You still want to talk to him?"

"Yes," Charles remembered. "If you can arrange it." Arthur Mason had at least seen Owens in Red Square, but Charles felt there was little he could provide considering the shock the sighting must have caused him.

A buzzer sounded on Highlands' desk. He picked up the phone. "Right," he said. "I'll be right down." He hung up and turned to Charles. "Something has come up but I shouldn't be long. Make yourself at home. I'll have lunch sent in."

"Fine," said Charles. He sat down wearily. There was nothing here and Highlands certainly didn't fit the bill. In a different way he was just as unsuitable as Mike Savage, who would have been ideal had Charles been recruiting for an anti-terrorist group. Highlands' attitude in regard to Owens was equally negative and Charles realized he was no closer to finding someone to identify Owens. Only one name remained on his list.

With Highlands gone, he took the opportunity to look at the file the security chief had left on his desk. Almost absently, he flipped through its pages, but halfway through, something caught his eye.

***

When Highlands returned, he found Charles already at work on lunch. "Sorry about that," he said. "Minor problem."

"I'll take the tour now if you don't mind," Charles said.

"Sure," Highlands said, grabbing a sandwich. He brightened slightly. "Might as well make your trip worth something. This is a pretty interesting place you know."

Charles followed Highlands out of the office, struck suddenly by the thought that Robert Owens must have felt the very same thing.

The interview with Arthur Mason had proved to be as fruitless as Charles expected. The tall computer scientist had worked with Owens briefly, but could add nothing more to what Charles already knew. He was sure it was Owens he'd seen in Red Square, and he'd been obviously shaken by the experience.

The news from Washington was equally disappointing. Moscow had reluctantly agreed to a confirmation of Owens identity, but reserved the right to choose the site and demanded the operation be a joint effort between the CIA and KGB. That will be the day, Charles thought.

John Trask was holding out for neutral ground but wasn't optimistic. As expected, the Soviets were outraged over Zakharov's arrest and were screaming frame. Until the time of his arrest, the Russian was a seemingly innocuous trade official, not a known operative and yet Moscow was apparently willing to trade for Owens, who had spent five years in one of their most sensitive installations. Charles was still puzzling over it all when he found Harry Peck leaning on the fence of his chicken ranch just north of San Francisco.

"I think the sun agrees with you, Harry," Charles said getting out of the car.

Peck smiled and glanced at the sky, the sun beating down its late afternoon heat. "Good thing I guess, eh?" He was a tall gaunt man with a weathered face and narrow set dark eyes. "What brings you out here, Charles?"

"Can we talk inside?"

"Sure. Betty's gone into town for some shopping." They walked across the yard to a low frame house, past rows of chicken coups. Hundreds of chickens squalled in protest over the intrusion.

"Retirement seems profitable," Charles said.

"Yeah, I guess so, if you like chickens. I can't eat eggs anymore though," Peck said.

They sat at the kitchen table while Peck poured coffee from a pot on the stove into two chipped mugs. Charles took it all in for a moment and flashed on his own retirement reflected back at him in Harry Peck's lifeless face. Peck had been out of the bureau five years now.

"So, what's up, Charles?" Peck drawled. "You didn't come all the way out here to see my chickens. You still globetrotting for the competition?" The FBI and CIA had always been rival organizations, but often their areas of concern overlapped. Charles and Harry Peck went back a lot of years.

"Names, Harry, names. I need some help. A defection in 1974. Robert Owens worked at Triton Industries. Remember it?" Charles studied Peck's lined face almost hoping he was wrong.

Peck rubbed a hand over the stubble on his chin and looked out the window. "Yeah, always thought there was something strange about that one. I wasn't working the case, but I know we were getting a file together on the guy. I was working the Russian end, keeping tabs on one of their boys who had just come over from Moscow. New kid on the block." Peck sneered and lit a hand rolled cigarette.

"What was funny about it, Harry?"

Peck shrugged, "We just about had the Russian nailed down. He got pretty careless."

Charles took out a photo and pushed it across the table. "Was this the man?" he asked.

Peck took the photo and studied it a moment. "Yeah, that's him all right. Is he in trouble again?"

Charles returned the photo to his pocket. "What happened, Harry? Why didn't the operation continue?"

Peck shrugged and sipped his coffee. "We got word from Washington to drop it, forget the whole thing. They even sent someone out here to make sure we understood."

Charles felt a shudder go through his body. "Who was that? Do you remember?"

"C'mon, Charles," Peck said, smiling. "It was one of your people. Said it was going out of our jurisdiction." Charles held himself still. Moscow was certainly out of the FBI's jurisdiction.

"Trask I think his name was," Peck said. "Yeah, that was it. John Trask."

Four

"Today is failure day," said the metallic voice from the wall-mounted speaker. "All teachers are reminded grade sheets and failure notices must be in the office by three o'clock today." There was a slight pause then, "Have a nice day." A click and the speaker was once again silent.

Christopher Storm scowled at the speaker, as always amazed at the assortment of announcements it spewed forth daily. He hated it, but like his desk, the blackboard and the rows of student desks, it was part of the standard equipment in room 323.

He ignored the stack of computer printouts on his desk—one for each of his five classes—and let his gaze travel around the empty classroom, allowing himself a brief indulgence in his dream. He could draw on it at will and it was always the same.

In the dream, he stood in front of a small university class, discussing and probing the merits of the great works of modern literature—Henry James perhaps, or Hemingway, F. Scott Fitzgerald. His students were eager, attentive, inquisitive, taking notes, making comments, perhaps lingering after class to ask about some subtle point in a Faulkner story. He would nod wisely at the student's observation, smile at the inquiring face, then gather up his book and notes in a worn leather briefcase—given to him when he had published his doctoral dissertation—and retire to his book-lined office to prepare for a graduate seminar or perhaps polish an article for a literary journal.

Reluctantly, he let the dream slip away, dissolving into the reality of grade sheets, failure notices and the one hundred, seventy-five bored teenagers he shared his classroom with. The dream, he realized with an almost final acceptance, was becoming more out of reach with every passing day at Meadows High School.

He picked up one of the sheets, scanned the list of familiar names. Beside each name on the pink and white printout was a series of small circles to be bubbled in under the student's grade, days absent and behavior, with the standard IBM No. 2 pencil.

His eyes stopped beside the name of a boy who carried a skate board around like a security blanket. Where is the circle to indicate this student tries hard but is just not into modern literature? Or this girl? How can I show that her work has dropped considerably since her parents split up?

He threw down the pencil, leaned back in his chair and tried not to think about the individual notices for failing students and the obligatory teacher comments. One original and two copies. One for the teacher's files, one for the counselor and one sent home with the student. That one usually ended up in the trashcan before lunch. When grades came out, there would be angry calls from the parents of Todd or Chip or Darcy—whatever happened to regular names—demanding to know why their kid was failing. It wouldn't do any good to explain a warning notice had been sent home six weeks earlier. A meeting would be arranged with the counselor, the student would demonstrate sufficient remorse, solemn vows would be made promising a better effort and the whole cycle would begin anew.

Although there were few exceptions, Storm had come to realize most of his students were uninterested, apathetic, their principal concerns being designer jeans, hair styles and who was going to be at the big game on Friday night. Modern literature rated a poor last.

If it was done at all, homework was haphazardly pursued in front of a blaring television. Most could barely write a coherent sentence much less a critical essay. Books were chosen by thickness rather than content and the favorites were those written after the movie had been made. The few exceptions—students genuinely interested and planning college careers—*did not*, as Storm's university advisor had promised, make up for the dismal, depressing experience of teaching high school English.

He was reminded of something one of the guys had said

after coming back from Vietnam. "We are the unwilling, working for the unqualified, doing the unnecessary for the ungrateful." Vietnam and Meadows High School had a lot in common, Storm thought, suddenly flashing on another dream. It came only rarely now, in the black of night or the bleak hours just before dawn. A horrific vision of a steamy jungle, torn and broken bodies, death and...

"Hey, Chris, how about some coffee?" Storm looked up to see two arms pushing through the door. The hands held paper cups and were followed by the misshapen body of George Dunne.

"Yeah, George, c'mon in." Storm cleared a space on his desk as Dunne dragged a student desk over with his foot and wedged himself into it with considerable difficulty.

Halfway through his first year at Meadows, Storm had bumped into George Dunne at a coffee shop. The accidental meeting had blossomed into a quick friendship. They found they shared the common experience of combat—Dunne in Korea—and a dislike for Meadows principal, Lester Dawson. Dunne had shown Storm the ropes, pointed out shortcuts through the maze of paperwork, listened to his doubts about himself and generally eased the confusion and frustration of a new teacher finding his way.

Storm was grateful and enjoyed their talks, which had become something of a ritual each morning before classes. Dunne was nearing fifty, Storm guessed. He had a thick crop of unruly hair, a lined face which seemed perpetually weary. He peered out from behind black, horn rimmed glasses. The breast pocket of his wash n' wear sport shirts always bulged with an array of ball point pens. Dunne taught science and his lab classes were something of an institution at Meadows.

"How are you doing with those?" Dunne pointed to the printout grade sheets.

Storm grinned back sheepishly. "Same as always, George. I hate them. You know that."

"The computer age, my boy," Dunne said, "applied to education to facilitate a more accurate recording of the students' progress, or lack of it. Without those, we'd all need a secretary." He pushed the glasses up the bridge of his nose.

"I've been teaching long enough to remember when everything was done by hand, including the discipline. Got mine..."

"I know," Storm said, laughing. "Already finished." He thumbed over his sheets. "I just can't take it seriously, George. What has any of this got to do with teaching?"

At first Storm had been impressed with Dunne's attitude. He seemed totally nonplussed by all the meaningless tasks filling a teacher's day, robbing him of precious time for real preparation. But more and more, he came to suspect that buried beneath the jovial exterior was a core approaching, if not surpassing, Storm's own disillusionment.

"Why do you stay with it, George?"

Dunne shrugged and looked away. "I've got sixteen years in now. Four more and I can call it quits. I'm in too deep." He said it like a gambler who had spent his stake. He turned back to Storm. "What about you, Chris? It's not too late for you. What was it you told me during one of our first talks? Vietnam was so ugly and deceitful you turned to something full of truth and beauty—literature. How much literature are you teaching now? Where's the truth and beauty here? Get out, Chris, now while you still can. While you still have the incentive." There was a bitterness in Dunne's voice Storm had not heard before.

"How?"

"I don't know," Dunne said, shaking his head angrily. "You were halfway through a master's degree. Go back finish it. Get a Ph.D. for Christ's sake. Get a job at a small college where the pay is low but they still care. They don't care here, Chris. You know what that idiot Dawson told Connie Goodwin, the best Spanish teacher this school ever had? 'Why don't you have a Mexican food day instead of all this homework?'" He slapped his hand on the desk and crumpled his coffee cup in the wastebasket.

Storm nodded silently, remembering his own interview with Dawson. Noting his military service, Dawson had asked, "You kill any gooks out there in Vietnam?" Storm had never told Dunne about his dreams. He wondered if Korea haunted him.

"It's not that easy George. It all comes down to money and I haven't got it. I'd have to quit teaching for two or three years to finish a doctorate. I still have to pay Jennifer child support for Danny and..."

Both their eyes flicked to the framed photo of the small boy on Storm's desk. "Find a way, Chris. Find a way. You've got what it takes to be a good teacher, but they'll beat it out of you here." As if embarrassed by his outburst, Dunne took off his glasses and began to polish them furiously.

They sat in silence for a few moments then a bell sounded, startling them both, breaking the mood. Storm glanced at the wall clock.

"Well," Dunne said, getting up, "the teeming horde will be arriving shortly. At least they'll be quieter today since it's failure day. Especially the ones who think they're failing. See you at lunch."

Storm shoved the grade sheets aside and grabbed a literature anthology. He decided to assign a reading for today. SSR the school district called it: silent sustained reading.

He might even finish the grade sheets by three o'clock, if he was lucky.

"Mr. Dawson will see you now." A small neat woman with glasses attached to a silver chain around her neck smiled at Charles Fox and led him down a short corridor. They passed a scrubbed blonde girl in a green, pleated mini-skirt and floppy white sweater with a huge *M* emblazoned on its front. She also carried two green and white pom-poms.

"Morning, Melinda," the secretary smiled, barely looking at the girl.

"Hi, Mrs. Cranston." The girl smiled at Charles, exposing a mouthful of wire and metal.

"Here we are," Mrs. Cranston said, stopping before a door. "Go right in."

"Thank you," Charles said, opening the door. The office was crowded with photos, trophies and various other bits of memorabilia collected during Lester Dawson's six years as principal at Meadows High. Charles still couldn't get over the name, but the taxi driver assured him that in Spanish, Las Vegas means the meadows.

Lester Dawson popped out of his chair as Charles came in and hurried around a large glass-topped desk. Charles caught a glimpse of a photo of a frail woman flanked by two small boys.

"Mr. Fox, nice to meet you," Dawson drawled and stuck out a bony hand. He was partially bald and had protruding eyes. Charles placed the accent as somewhere in west Texas. Dawson motioned him to a chair and disappeared once again behind the desk. His bulging jaw muscles worked placidly on a wad of chewing gum. "So, how can we be of service to the Department of Health, Education & Welfare? You letter mentioned a fact finding tour and some kind of pilot program."

"Well, as I said on the phone, we're conducting some preliminary studies on teacher training practices in the Southwest. Meadows High, I believe, has some rather remarkable methods for teacher review and observation."

Charles had decided to forego direct contact with Christopher Storm as he had done with Mike Savage and Mel Highlands. With both of them eliminated on paper at least, Storm looked like his last resort, and unless he was deceiving himself, a good prospect. He had quickly devised the HEW cover story, but Dawson was clearly uncomfortable. What was he hiding?

"Well, that certainly is true," Dawson said. "Of course we're honored HEW is aware of our practices. We believe here at Meadows High," he continued, quoting from a recently delivered speech at a Parent Association meeting, "in keeping up with modern technology. We have our own television station, you know. Fully student operated."

"Indeed." Charles let the word hang in the air for Dawson to retrieve as he saw fit. From his uncomfortable appearance, he seemed to take it as an accusation.

He stared glumly for a moment then brightened suddenly. "Perhaps it would be best to show you one of our advanced concepts. TOS."

"TOS?"

"Yes. Teacher Observation Screening." Dawson popped up out of his chair again and beckoned for Charles to follow. They went out of the office, down a long corridor lined with gray metal lockers. Two girls passed them, each with an arm full of books.

"Morning, Sue, Mary Ann," Dawson called. "Y'all hurry to class now." The girls scurried off stifling giggles as Dawson and Charles turned down another corridor taking them past the library. Dawson stopped in front of a door marked COMM. He pressed a buzzer and the door sprang open.

The room was like the director's control room in a television studio. One wall was taken up by a bank of monitor screens. Charles counted fourteen. In front of the monitors was a huge console with an array of dials and glowing amber lights. A heavy-set man with dark hair sat at the console sipping coffee from a stoneware mug. His eyes flicked around the soundless screens.

"Morning, Walter. All quiet on the western front?" Dawson quipped.

"Yeah, Mr. Dawson. No problems," Walter answered. He eyed Charles curiously.

Directly behind the console was an arrangement of comfortable looking chairs with small writing tops attached. Dawson motioned Charles to one. He sank into three inches of leatherette and stared in fascination at the color monitors, each depicting a classroom scene.

Dawson registered Charles' surprise with obvious pleasure. "How about that?"

"You have cameras in all the classrooms?"

"Well, there are some dummy ones, of course. We only have facilities for these fourteen, but we can always switch a live camera over a weekend so no one really knows whether they're on candid camera or not." Dawson chuckled at his own joke.

Charles eyes roamed over the screens as he sought a face from a file. He found it in the second row. "No sound I suppose."

Dawson smirked. "Name your choice."

"Well, in keeping with the spirit of Las Vegas, number

seven seems appropriate."

"Walter," Dawson said, "you heard the man."

Walter flicked some dials and the room was suddenly filled with the voice of Christopher Storm. "...and so if you finish the Steinbeck story before the end of class, you can do the questions I've put on the board. Okay? Let's get to work." Storm's instructions were met with a chorus of groans.

On the console a phone rang. Walter picked it up, grunted into it and handed it to Dawson. "Yes, yes, tell them I'll be right down." He hung up and turned to Charles. "'Fraid you'll have to excuse me for a minute. I got some angry parents waiting. You just stay here and enjoy yourself. Walter can answer any questions you might have."

Dawson slipped out and Charles joined Walter at the console, studying Storm, who was now seated at his desk. Thirty was about right, Charles decided. Dark curly hair, slim build and according to the file, just under six-feet tall.

"How do the teachers feel about this?" Charles asked, indicating the screens. He wondered how cameras in class had gotten past the teachers union.

"Well, a lot of 'em don't like it, that's for sure. 'Course they're used to it now, seeing the camera and not knowing whether theirs is on or not." Walter's accent was similar to Dawson's.

"And have they proved useful?"

"Oh, yeah, no doubt about it. You'd be on your toes if you thought you was on camera every day. Helps with security, too."

"Security?" Charles kept his eyes on Storm. The class softly droned in the background.

"Well, we can sort of keep an eye on things. There's a panic button in all the classrooms. Teacher just has to press it. Screen goes black and we know there's trouble."

"You mean like there, at number six?" Charles asked.

Walter jerked his eyes to the screen and slammed his coffee cup down. He began to adjust the dials. "Could be just a malfunction. Happens sometimes. Nope, something's up."

A red light began to wink beneath screen six. Walter grabbed a telephone with a crank handle on the console.

"Security? Three twenty-two. I'm gettin' a red light. Better check it out." He put down the phone and looked at Charles, who was already on his feet.

"I'd like to have a look. Where's three twenty-two?"

"As you go out the door, first corridor on your left then halfway down."

Charles found the corridor and was passed by two uniformed security guards jogging ahead of him. He reached the classroom just after them and looked inside.

The students were back against the wall on either side. A woman, the teacher he guessed, stood near her desk. Several desks were overturned and in the back of the room, Christopher Storm faced a gangly, freckle-faced redhead.

He had his arm around the neck of a smaller, black student and held a thin knife to the boy's throat. The security guards stood frozen behind Storm.

"Okay, Harvey," Storm said quietly, "I don't know what the beef is, but this isn't the way to handle it. Now, why don't you just give me the knife and we'll talk about it, okay?" Storm inched a step or two closer.

The boy called Harvey moved back a couple of steps, dragging his captive with him. The black boy's eyes bulged in fear.

"Stay away, Mr. Storm. This ain't your business." His eyes darted about the room. Some of the girls were crying; the boys looked on in fascination, but no one moved.

Sensing the security guards behind him, Storm waved them back silently, never taking his eyes off the two boys. "Okay, Harvey. Just you and me. Let's talk about it. Let Rudy go and give me the knife." In a crouch now, Storm edged a step closer.

"Do something, Mr. Storm," Rudy pleaded.

"Shut up, nigger," Harvey spat. His eyes flicked around the room again. He seemed to falter, as if trapped, unsure what to do next. "Get them outta here, too," he ordered. His eyes were on the guards, who were also moving closer.

"You heard him," Storm said. They started to protest, but Storm's glare won out and they complied. One took the teacher, who was now crying; the other motioned the class to file outside

A bell sounded and the corridor was immediately crowded with onlookers. There was more confusion as Lester Dawson, panting and red faced pushed into the room.

"What's going on here?" he asked Charles. Dawson crowded closer to see for himself.

"Okay, Harvey, they're all gone. Now, give me the knife." Storm's voice was even, calm.

Harvey nervously glanced about again. He relaxed his grip somewhat on Rudy; the knife eased down a bit. Sensing his chance, Rudy twisted and broke free. He ran behind Storm for a moment to glare at his attacker, who was now suddenly without a hostage.

"Go, Rudy. Get out of here," Storm said. Rudy backed up a few steps then turned and scrambled for the door.

Storm took his eyes off Harvey for a second to see Rudy clear the room. At that moment, totally frustrated and enraged by Rudy's escape, Harvey lunged at Storm with the knife. Storm turned just in time to sidestep the boy's clumsy attack, but felt the blade slice into his arm. He turned to the side, using Harvey's momentum, chopped him across the back of the neck. Harvey went sprawling into a desk, the knife clattered to the floor. Storm was on top of him, pinning his arms behind his back. Harvey yelled and squirmed uselessly beneath Storm.

"Well, c'mon," Storm shouted toward the door, "I can't hold him all day."

Charles and Lester Dawson moved aside as the two security guards took charge and dragged the now sobbing Harvey to his feet and out through the crowd. There were cat calls from the mob of students as they reluctantly moved aside to allow the guards to escort Harvey.

"Y'all get back to class now," Dawson shouted. "Move!" He began shoving students back. Some other teachers arrived and began to herd students into the classroom as order was restored.

Dawson turned back to Storm. His arm was bleeding slightly. He had torn the sleeve of his shirt to wrap around the wound. "Let's have a look at that, boy," Dawson said. He glanced uncomfortably at Charles Fox.

"It's alright," Storm said. "It looks worse than it is."

Dawson looked closer. "Well, better get down to the nurse and have her look at it." Storm nodded, holding his arm. He glanced at Charles curiously.

"I'll want a full report on this, Mr. Storm," Dawson said, as he walked away.

Storm shrugged and looked again at Charles. "I hope you're not a parent."

"No, no," Charles said. "I would like to have a word with you if I may."

"Sure, soon as I get this taken care of. I've got a free period coming up. Why don't you wait in my room? It's just next door."

Charles wandered around Storm's empty classroom. It was identical in every way to the room where the confrontation had taken place except for the ten-speed bicycle leaning against the blackboard. A faded army knapsack hung over the back of Storm's chair. One wall held a small cork bulletin board full of school notices, fire drill instructions, and in one corner, three student essays. One, Charles noted, was by Rudy. The papers were an exercise on *The Short Happy Life of Francis Macomber* by Ernest Hemingway.

An English classroom in Las Vegas was a long way from a Montana mountaintop, but like Mike Savage, Christopher Storm seemed to have found his own way of dealing with things. After seeing Storm in action, Charles was eager to talk with him. He wondered where the other survivors of Company C were.

The door burst open suddenly. Storm kicked it shut angrily and strode to his desk. He began opening and closing drawers. "Dawson and his fucking reports," he muttered. He stopped, suddenly aware of Charles' presence. "Sorry, I forgot you were here."

"More trouble?"

Storm sighed and dropped in his chair. "Dawson. He wants a complete report, in triplicate of course, typed and on his desk this afternoon. George is right. I've got to get out of this place."

"George?"

"George Dunne, science teacher. He keeps telling me I should get out of teaching."

"Maybe you should." Storm was puzzled by Charles' amused expression. It was as if the older man knew something Storm didn't. "Do you ride that to school every day?" Charles asked, pointing to the bicycle.

"Most days. Good way to stay in shape, but the real reason is I can't afford a car. What did you want to see me about? Are you with the school district?"

Charles smiled. "No, not at all. I'm with the government actually. Health, Education and Welfare so your Mr. Dawson thinks. I'd like to keep it that way."

"Why the secrecy?"

"It's an old Vietnam matter," Charles said. "One of the officers you served with. Lieutenant Robert Owens." Charles saw it immediately, as he had with Mike Savage. The eyes clouding over, the curtain being drawn. Storm continued to stare for a moment then his expression of disbelief dissolved into understanding.

"Oh, I get it. Owens must be in line for some government job and you're doing a security check, right? I thought the FBI did that kind of thing?"

"Normally they do," Charles said, "but I'm not with the FBI. Do you have some time to spare?"

"Sure, why not. No one's asked me about Nam since I got back, but I'm tied up with this until late."

"How about dinner on me, well, actually the government. You name the place."

Storm thought for a moment. "Mexican food okay? I know a good place and it's not on the Strip. Mr...."

"Fox. Charles Fox. Mexican food will be fine. What's the name? I'll find it."

"El Fuego. About seven."

Five

"Well, who is he?"

"I don't know. Wants to talk about Nam."

Storm was stretched out on the couch of the small apartment he shared with Valerie Hunter. She was a blackjack dealer on the Strip and over Storm's protests, paid most of the bills. Valerie easily made double his teaching salary.

Except for the desk in one corner of the tiny living room, most of the furniture was hers, as was the Volkswagen parked outside. On the television, Walter Cronkite had just reminded America that the hostages in Iran were in their 145th day of captivity.

"You want to meet me after my shift?" Valerie was standing over him.

Storm looked up sleepily. She was dressed in her dealer's uniform: tight fitting black slacks, long sleeve white shirt, black plastic name tag and a ludicrous gold medallion that hung on a gold chain between her small breasts. The slacks molded over her body like a glove and her dark hair, blown dry and neatly brushed back, framed her face. Valerie was twenty-six but she could easily have passed for one of Storm's students.

"Yeah, maybe. Depends on how long it takes with this guy Fox."

"Okay, I hope you can make it." She kneeled down and kissed him lightly. She touched the bandage on his arm. "How's the wounded teacher?" She said it jokingly, but her eyes were troubled. "Chris, isn't it about time to quit? You know I could..." His eyes stopped her. It was an old debate.

"Okay, okay, you win." She held up her hands in surrender. "I gotta go. Bring your friend with you. We'll have a drink. You want the car?"

"No, I'll get a ride with someone." She gave him a last smile and was gone.

Storm sat up, lit a cigarette and glanced at his watch. He sat for a few moments, head down, arms dangling between his knees, smoking pensively. He got up, took a beer out of the refrigerator and walked out onto the tiny balcony. There was just enough room for one chair and a small hibachi grill. He leaned on the railing and stared out across an expanse of desert that was soon to become a parking lot.

The lights of the Strip winked at him mockingly. He rarely visited the casinos unless it was to meet Valerie. They only served to remind him of the money he didn't have. The divorce settlement called for $250 a month. One day late and a letter from Jennifer's attorney would slide through the mail slot like a brick.

Their marriage had collapsed like a building on a faulty foundation. Neither of them really knew why, but Jennifer had retreated to the safety net of her mother in Ohio; Storm had grabbed for a teaching job like a drowning swimmer at a lifeline. There had been no home to sell and little to divide. A few pieces of furniture, books, records, a photo collection, all neatly packed in cartons and shipped to Ohio.

But Danny couldn't be divided. He was with Jennifer now, and although Storm knew he was really better off with his mother, the boy's absence hurt. Danny was the only thing of value their volatile union had produced.

He was surviving but there were scars. The residue of Vietnam, the alienation when he returned, the sense of being alone, which was perhaps the hallmark of the Vietnam experience. Storm wasn't unique in that respect and even now, with an almost involuntary burial of the past, he seemed lost in a fog of depression, heavy, thick, wet, that hung on him, stifling interest in anything but getting through the endless days one at a time.

He'd been with Valerie for just under two years. They shared their lives in the tiny apartment—a carbon copy of a hundred and twenty-six others in the complex that changed managers as often as tenants. Air conditioned boxes, housing dealers, cocktail waitresses and occasionally, someone like himself who was not connected with the gaming industry, as they liked to refer to gambling in Las Vegas.

He went back to the living room. A rerun of *M*A*S*H* flickered on television. He eyes went to the stack of literature notebooks squatting ominously on his desk, daring him to grade them. Spring vacation was roaring toward him and he hadn't even begun to prepare exams. He dropped the beer bottle in the waste basket, breaking it against another.

He would have to do something soon, he realized. He'd been treading water with Valerie for a long time. It was she who'd helped him pick up the pieces of his life when all he'd wanted to do was crawl away like an animal and lick his wounds. But where was it going? He was comfortable with her, but he wasn't sure if it was love he felt or just relief that she was the first woman he didn't want to get away from as soon as they'd made love. Hell, maybe that's all love was.

He dressed quickly and tried to remember Robert Owens.

El Fuego, Charles discovered was on Main Street, halfway between the Strip hotels and the garish glitter of downtown Las Vegas. Nestled among an assortment of second hand furniture stores, cheap motels and garages, it didn't look like much more than a greasy diner. He got out of a taxi in front of the low, white building next to dirt parking lot. Storm was inside already, nursing a beer. There were no other customers.

Charles slid into a booth opposite Storm. A young dark girl brought a hand written menu in a plastic cover, a plate of corn chips and a small bowl of salsa. Uncertainty was written all over Charles' face.

"Everything is good," Storm said reassuringly. "It's family-owned and the price is right. Try the number six combination plate."

Charles nodded to the girl hovering nearby and ordered a beer for himself and another for Storm. "How did things turn out today?"

Storm took a long pull on his beer. "Usual story. Harvey is suspended for five days. Rudy's parents pulled him out of school. Next week it'll be all forgotten."

Charles studied Storm thoughtfully. "How long have you been teaching?"

"Too long. Almost two years." He shook his head. "I never thought it would be like this. The first year one of our counselors was caught showing a porno film to the senior girl cheerleaders. Right in his office. Two months ago, the Boy's Dean was arrested for shoplifting and the teacher you saw today, Connie Goodwin, had a nervous breakdown right in front of her class. Just totally lost it. She's only been back to work for a month. Today will probably finish her off. They're calling it teacher burnout. What it amounts to is the same symptoms as combat stress and I've already had that." He paused. "What did you want to know about Owens?"

"You've been thinking about that, I gather, since this morning."

"Yeah, I've been thinking about it. I've been wondering why Owens is up for a government job and I'm babysitting a hundred and seventy-five teenagers."

"Actually it's not a job at all. At least not for Owens," Charles said. "Did you see him at all after Vietnam?"

"No, I spent some time with him in Japan on leave, but Owens shipped out and I went back to the lines. What is it? The job is classified? Is that why you can't tell me about it?"

"No, not at all," Charles said, measuring his words carefully. "As I said, it's not a job for Owens. The job is for you, if you're interested."

Charles turned his attention to the plate of corn chips. "These are quite tasty."

Storm's beer bottle had paused in mid-air. The girl brought their order. Two steaming platters of tacos, enchiladas and refried beans, all smothered in melted cheese. Storm was still staring as Charles began to eat.

"You're right, this is excellent," Charles said. The steam curled around his face as he pierced the cheese crust and speared a chunk of beef.

"Me?"

Charles nodded and continued eating. After a moment, Storm began to pick at his food. Charles devoured the two enchiladas and started on the taco. He paused long enough to take of drink of his beer and wipe his mouth with a checkered napkin. "Five years ago, Owens defected to the Soviet Union.

He's been there ever since, but now he wants to come back. We need someone who can positively identify him." Storm's eye met his before he resumed eating.

"That's the job? Identify Owens? Don't you know it's him already?"

"Of course," Charles said, careful not to betray his own doubts. "But we have to be sure. No one has seen Owens for several years and there's always the possibility, I grant you it's remote, that our friends in Moscow might try to pull a substitute on us. It's been done." He watched Storm eat while listening intently. Charles felt it was sewn up. It was all there.

"What makes you think I can identify him? It's been even longer since I've seen him." It was the question Charles was hoping for. Storm was careful. He didn't rush in without thinking. That was good.

"Good point but you were in a combat unit together, under extreme stress. Alliances are forged very quickly in those circumstances. Experiences are not often forgotten. It's not so much identifying Owens as to see if his memory jibes with yours."

Storm's gaze went blank for a moment. He had tried to push it out of his mind, bury it until it was possible to find. It was always there, appearing without warning.

The Christmas Eve ambush out of Cantigny. Mortars, their own, lobbed with textbook precision, exploding in the branches, spraying shrapnel down on the platoon like deadly rain. And Walker, a black kid from Detroit, whom Storm barely knew, looking at the stumps of three missing fingers and saying, "What's happening? What's happening?"

They'd huddled together in a shell hole until dawn, listening to the moans and screams, and only then realizing the VC had been moving behind a human shield of women and children.

Storm's voice was almost a whisper. "You seem to know a lot about it."

"Yes, I suppose I do," Charles said quietly.

"There's one other thing."

"What's that?" It was now Charles who paused, the napkin halfway to his lips.

"I saved Owens' life once," Storm said, a grim sort of smile on his face. "You didn't know that did you?"

Charles already knew, but he wanted to hear it from Storm. "How did that happen and when?"

Storm looked down and studied the tablecloth, moving the salt and pepper shakers around in a pattern before him. "One of our guys wanted to waste Owens." Storm shrugged. "It wasn't that uncommon a feeling over there, and Owens was a prime candidate. He got us into a real mess. We got out, just barely. On the way back to base camp we were ambushed by some VC stragglers. This guy decided then was a good time to take out Owens. I saw what he was going to do, jerked the gun away. Owens never knew."

"Why?"

"I don't know really. Owens wasn't worth a court martial even if he did deserve it. I guess the VC would do it for us sooner or later."

"That would be Mike Savage wouldn't it?"

Storm look relieved. "So you did know."

"Not about you. About Savage? Yes. I met him recently." Charles laid his napkin aside. "What are your feelings about Owens now?"

"Nothing I guess. I haven't thought about him until you mentioned his name. Look, that was a crazy war. It'll never be all told."

"They're all crazy, Christopher. Vietnam wasn't unique in that respect." Storm nodded his head slowly. "What about Japan? The time you spent with Owens there?"

"That was different. We whored around the bars, got drunk, talked about a lot of things." Storm paused. "What makes somebody defect anyway?"

Charles smiled and took out his pipe. "Why don't you ask him yourself? Oh, by the way," Charles added. "I don't think I mentioned. The identification will probably take place in Europe. Most likely, Moscow."

Storm felt almost giddy, like a dazed gambler who has just thrown his third seven on the craps table and suddenly realizes he's a winner. The lights of the Strip blazed as the taxi negotiated the heavy traffic.

"Damn tourist," the driver said, slapping his hand on the wheel with every lane change.

Storm was barely conscious of even Charles next to him, impassively taking in the sights, noting the names of the showroom stars on the giant marquees. He could still not believe it. Not really. Plucked from the drudgery and obscurity of a high school classroom. Singled out like a lottery winner who had forgotten he'd even bought a ticket, but has only to complete a minor formality to collect his prize.

And all because of something that had happened ten years earlier. The pure chance that had placed him in the same patch of jungle in Southeast Asia as one Robert Owens.

He had simply to confirm the identity of an army officer he'd served under. How could he fail? His part in the affair was a simple "yes" or "no" answer. No more, no less, according to Charles. Then the reward was his.

The pick of any graduate school in the country, a loan that needn't be repaid, to cover tuition and all expenses and in the end, he would become Dr. Christopher Storm. The fantasy class flew to the surface of his mind with ease and in complete clarity.

The taxi stopped briefly at Caesars Palace, long enough for Storm to run in and leave word for Valerie to join him and Fox later. They retraced their route, back out the long drive, past the mock Roman statues and fountains, to merge with the Strip traffic once again. They turned left in front of the MGM Grand and went east to Paradise Road and Charles' motel.

Over drinks in the small bar, Charles briefly outlined the mechanics of the process by which Storm would confirm Owens. The questioning, of course, would center on Vietnam, Charles said, but he was careful to keep it in the most general terms.

Sufficiently disillusioned with teaching, stymied from any further advancement without external help, a trip to Europe and graduate school had to be an attractive prospect. If Charles had a momentary pang of alarm at Storm's quick acceptance, he reminded himself he was not in Eastern Europe; he was not asking Storm to risk his life, become an enemy agent. He brushed aside those doubts with little trouble especially in light of the phone call he had received from John Trask.

Trask's contact had reported that Moscow was pressing and anxious for the arrangements for the exchange of Zakharov and Owens to be completed. They remained adamant the site would be at an as yet undisclosed location. They would continue to stall, but Charles knew in the end it would be Moscow.

No, it would be Storm. There wasn't time to look further. They couldn't chance the Soviets changing their minds now. Still, the nagging doubts persisted, nibbling at the corners of his mind. An idea almost so remote as to be valid was struggling to surface, it had yet to come into any sort of tangible form. This too he brushed aside, at least for the moment.

"What about school?" Storm asked, smiling, unable to hide his anticipation.

"Leave that to me. Our friend Mr. Dawson will be informed you are taking a leave of absence. He'll be reminded about HEW grants and told that we appreciate his cooperation."

Storm laughed. "I'd love to see old Lester's face when he hears that. How long will I be gone?"

"Not more than a couple of weeks I shouldn't think. There'll be some briefing in Washington and then you'll meet with Owens for a few days. Long enough for you to be satisfied beyond doubt he is indeed Robert Owens."

"I still can't believe it," Storm said shaking his head. He rattled the ice cubes in his glass.

Charles seemed amused. "We have a job to do and you happen to fit the requirements. It's really quite simple."

"C'mon, Charles," Storm persisted. "Nothing is simple with the CIA. I have to admit you're smooth, but I saw enough of those so called 'visitors' jumping out of choppers in Nam. Saigon was thick with them, driving around town in Ford Pintos. They might as well have worn name tags."

"Have it your way," Charles said flatly. "Our involvement doesn't pose a problem does it?"

"No, I guess not," Storm said. He looked toward the door and spotted Valerie. She stood at the entrance, scanning the bar. He half rose out of his seat to wave to her.

"Christopher, for the moment..."

Storm nodded his understanding and Valerie joined them.

"Hi," she said, smiling at Charles. "Is this some kind of celebration?" She slid in next to Storm as Charles got to his feet.

"Yeah, you might say that," Storm said. "Say hello to Charles Fox."

Charles took her extended hand. "A pleasure. How do you do, Miss Hunter?" He signaled a passing waitress and ordered a round of drinks.

Valerie's eyes flicked between the two men as the drinks arrived. "Well, are you going to let me in on it?" Her gaze was questioning, somewhat apprehensive, Charles noted.

"No big thing," Storm said, glancing Charles for reassurance. "One of my old Nam buddies is in a bit of a jam. Charles just wanted to talk to me about it." He paused, catching the slight nod of approval from Charles. "I may have to be away for a little while." He touched Valerie's shoulder.

Charles watched her weak smile fade into a searching look. She held her glass with both hands and stared into it. "I see," she said, not looking up. "For how long?"

Charles answered quickly, sensing potential trouble brewing. "Don't worry, Miss Hunter. You'll have him back in no time at all."

But Charles could see her eyes were disbelieving, unconvinced as she returned his steady gaze.

"Get down! Get down!" Storm screamed. The trail erupted in a hail of mortar fire. He saw flashes of light to his left. Clumps of dirt kicked up in front of his face.

"Chris, wake up, wake up!"

"I told you to get down." He pressed her down on the bed, pinning her arms in a vise-like grip. His breathing was heavy and labored.

"Chris, Chris, please." She fought and tried to twist away.

"What?" His grip suddenly relaxed. Slowly, he released her and sat up. His face was bathed in sweat.

Valerie stared at him, her eyes wide in fright. He turned slowly toward her in the shadowy glow of the street lamp that seeped into the room. He looked at her as if she were a stranger. His whole body trembled. He flinched as she touched his shoulder.

"What happened?" he asked finally. He took several deep breaths.

Valerie rose up slightly. "You were dreaming," she said. "Like before." She threw back the covers and got out of bed. "I thought that was all over."

She left the room and returned moments later with cigarettes, a glass of water and a wet wash cloth. She turned on the bedside lamp, watching Storm closely. He gulped down the water while she lit cigarettes for both of them. Then she began to bathe his face with the cloth.

"I'm sorry, Val." He took deeps drags of the cigarette. "It was all there again, so clear."

"I know, I know," she said softly. Inside she was churning with fear.

"Scared you, huh?" His smile was weak.

She just nodded and continued to bathe his face.

"Used to happen all the time when I first got back." She could see the disbelief in his eyes that it was happening again.

They had talked about it a lot when they were first together. Jennifer, he'd told her, had never been able to handle it. But Valerie, wanted to be better than Jennifer, so she hid her revulsion and listened as he spun out tale after tale of horror and death. She had thought it was all behind them.

"I used to go out drinking until two or three in the morning when I first came back. It was crazy. One day I had a license to kill; the next a cop stops you for driving too fast. My dad would be waiting up for me with a pot of coffee. We'd sit in the dark and just talk, sometimes until dawn." His voice had become a monotone. "I don't think I could have made it without him. He kept telling me to go back to school, get a degree, become a teacher in a nice college somewhere."

He shook his head. "I thought it was all over, Val, I really did." But even as he spoke, he remembered. Ninety hours back and still coiled like a spring, he'd sent his kid brother crashing into the bedroom wall when he'd tried to shake him awake on a dark morning.

Valerie angrily crushed out her cigarette. "It's all this talk with this guy Fox. This job, whatever it is you can't or won't tell me about. That's what brought it back. Goddamn him!" Her eyes were blazing.

"Val, it's not his fault. He doesn't know." His face suddenly hardened. "And he's not going to know either. I can handle it."

She couldn't look at him without betraying her doubts. She turned off the light and crawled in next to him, kneading his shoulders till she felt the tension begin to leave his body. "Relax, Chris. It's all right now," she whispered.

He lay back turning toward her as her hands roamed soothingly over his body. She blinked away tears in the darkness and nestled her head against his chest. His tenseness washed away as her stroking became more insistent, her hands encircling his hardness. She straddled his body then, mounting him, letting him feel her warmth as he entered her. She threw back her head as their bodies merged and convulsed then collapsed on top of him, crushing her breasts against him. She lay still, motionless over him like a protective covering.

She lay awake long afterwards, staring into the darkness while he slept beside her. She decided at last she would have to gamble.

At a table near the imitation marble railing encircling the casino bar at Caesars Palace, Charles Fox sipped a gin and tonic and watched, fascinated by a fortyish woman in baggy slacks and bouffant hairdo.

She was perched on a high stool and clutched a paper cup full of coins, which she fed into the machine with hypnotic precision. Every drop of a coin was followed by a pull on the slot machine's handle that had now blackened her hand.

Nearby lights flashed, bells rang as other luckier players pocketed their winnings. The woman glared in annoyance whenever another machine paid off and frowned at her own as if she had been betrayed. But she made no move to switch machines. Her concentration was total as she relentlessly pulled the handle again and again.

At last her face broke into a grim smile as three bars centered themselves on the machine. A bell rang and one hundred coins spilled out and clattered into the metal tray below. Charles raised his glass in a silent toast as the woman excitedly scooped up the coins and filled yet another paper cup.

The already large casino crowd was swollen by the Friday afternoon exodus from Los Angeles, just five hours away by car, and weekend revelers were already lining up for show reservations. With rare exceptions, such as the two minutes of silent homage for President John Kennedy, the action was continuous.

On his left, Charles caught sight of a relief crew of dealers emerging from somewhere off the casino floor. Filing out, almost in formation, dressed in uniform black and white, they broke off in small groups to man their respective roulette wheels, crap tables or blackjack positions, to begin another forty minute shift sticking dice, turning a wheel, dealing cards.

Minutes later, a similar group, cigarettes already lit, weaved its way through the casino, oblivious to the shouts of the winners, the groans of the losers. Charles watched one group pass the bar and Valerie Hunter peel off when she spotted him.

He was uneasy about her call. It spelled one thing: complications and there were enough already. She'd contacted him, obviously without Storm's knowledge, and Charles had done his best to dissuade her. But she'd been insistent, so he'd reluctantly agreed to the meeting. He didn't know how much Storm had told her, but felt certain he wouldn't have divulged the details of their discussion. He had known of their relationship, but not its depth. Storm had been vague on that point, but it was clear Valerie Hunter's influence was more than passing.

"Sorry to drag you out," she said, joining Charles at the table. Her manner seemed forced. Charles looked at her and thought she had the eyes of a stricken widow.

He held up two fingers to a toga-clad waitress and looked inquiringly at Valerie. She shook her head. "Just coffee. Dealers are like cops. We don't drink on duty."

She fumbled in her purse for cigarettes, got one going and smiled nervously at Charles. "Look," she began, "Chris doesn't know I'm seeing you, but there's something I think you should know about." She averted her eyes as the waitress brought their drinks. She looked to Charles like someone about to violate a trust.

"Chris had the dream again last night."

"The dream? I don't understand?"

She nodded and explained. "I don't know what you want him to do. I don't want to know. But all this this talk about Vietnam has brought it all back again. All the hell he lived through and has managed to survive. You're bringing it all back again." She flung the words at him like an accusation and her voice had taken on a hard edge.

Charles parried her assault with silence, sensing her discomfort. Only his eyes sparked with interest.

"You must know what the Nam guys went through," she continued. "A lot of the ones who made it back are in hospitals still trying to figure it all out. The lucky ones, like Chris, have buried it, like it should be." She paused, blinking back tears. "He'd kill me if he knew I was here telling you this." She took a tissue out of her purse and blew her nose.

"I met his brother once. He told me the first year Chris was back they went to a Fourth of July picnic. There was a fireworks display. Chris hadn't given it a thought, but when the bombs went off, the rockets, he dived on the ground, covered his head "

Charles nodded, thinking of the loneliness of Mike Savage on his mountain. It was a daily battle none of them escaped.

"I just, I just don't want Chris to go through any of that again. If you could see him when he has these dreams." She broke off again, stabbing at the ashtray with the half-smoked cigarette. She hadn't touched her coffee.

"Miss Hunter, Valerie," Charles began. "I understand your concern. No one wants to see Christopher suffer. Certainly not me. I'm not forcing him to do anything. I'm merely offering him a chance to help himself by helping me."

"I know, I know," she said. "I couldn't stop him if I wanted to. But he's making it now. Oh, teaching is not what he thought it would be and he's so goddamn stubborn he won't let me help him with grad school. Now you come along and..."

"You love him very much, don't you," Charles said quietly. She nodded, head down, as if in prayer. "You're quite a girl, Valerie. He's a lucky man."

She looked up at him and smiled cynically. "Look around you, Mr. Fox. There are girls like me all over the Strip. Dealing cards, hustling drinks, hooking." She looked down again. "Chris is the one good thing to happen to me." She brushed away another tear. "Well, I just thought you ought to know." She glanced at her watch. "I hope I won't regret this. I have to go back to work now."

"You won't, I promise you," Charles said. "You're wrong about one thing though."

"What's that?"

"There aren't many girls like you anywhere." He smiled and took her hand.

She managed a weak smile. "You're an old charmer, Mr. Fox. You know that?" She hurried away then, swallowed up in the casino crowd.

Charles remained at the table for another few minutes. Nothing Valerie had told him had changed his mind about Storm. There would have to be some adjustments—Washington would demand them—but they could be easily managed.

Yes, Christopher Storm would do just fine.

Storm found two messages scrawled on the pad by the phone when he got home. Valerie was gone, off to visit her sister in Los Angeles. He grabbed the phone and hurriedly dialed Ohio.

"Jennifer? It's Chris."

"Hello, Chris." Her voice was restrained, hesitant.

"What is it? Has something happened to Danny?" Jennifer never called unless it was for money and he'd already mailed the check.

"No, Danny is fine. Well, it is about Danny."

He knew before she said it. The promised Easter vacation visit was off. It had been all arranged and agreed on. "What about Danny?" His voice was tense.

"I've decided it wouldn't be a good idea for you to see Danny now."

"What do you mean it wouldn't be a good idea?" He gripped the phone tighter. "What about Danny? Won't he be disappointed? Let me talk to him."

"No, Chris, you can't talk to him. I haven't told him yet."

"Why not, for Christ's sake?"

"Don't shout at me," she retorted.

"I'm not shouting." He forced himself to lower his voice, curb the rage that coursed through him.

"Danny's settled in school now. I don't want him upset. He's only five you know." He could hear the tremble in her voice, but he wanted to scream back at her.

"Of course I know he's five. I'm his father."

"I don't want to have to explain about that woman."

"That woman? Oh for God's sake, Jennifer, we've been divorced for three years. Stop acting like it only happened yesterday. Val wasn't coming with me anyway. We've already discussed that." He felt totally frustrated by the phone, unable to see her face. He could picture Jennifer's mother sitting nearby, listening, frowning in disapproval.

"I'm sorry, Chris. I don't want to argue about it. That's the way it's going to be, at least for now."

"Jennifer!" The dial tone purred in his ear. He stared at the phone then slammed it down. He paced the room like a caged animal. It took him several minutes to calm down long enough to make the second call. Charles answered on the first ring.

"I'm ready, Charles."

"You're quite sure, Christopher?"

"I've never been more sure of anything."

"Fine," Charles said. "We'll leave tomorrow then." Storm put down the phone quietly. There was nothing to hold him now.

Nothing.

Six

"Ah, Stefan, come in, come in," Delnov said, opening the door for his assistant Stefan Dolya. He had close cropped, straw-colored hair and finely-chiseled features, dominated by wide-set blue eyes giving him an expression of perpetual concentration.

Removing his heavy coat and gloves, he quickly tried to account for his chief's good humor. The recent victory over Shevchenko? The smooth, continuous process of the operation? Or was it simply the residual afterglow of a weekend with Natalya?

Dolya hung his coat in the hall and followed Delnov's casually dressed hulk—thick baggy sweater and corduroy slacks—into the main room of the *dacha*. Logs blazed in the corner fireplace; a bottle of vodka rested invitingly on a slab-like table wedged between two overstuffed chairs. He caught a glimpse of Natalya, lounging like a cat on the sofa, thumbing a magazine. It was French he noted immediately and without effort, not daring to let his gaze linger on her for more than a moment.

"Sit down, Stefan," Delnov boomed, like a gracious host with an unexpected guest. He dropped into one of the chairs and motioned Dolya to the other. "Of course, you know Natalya."

He looks so strange, thought Dolya, dressed like this. Relaxed, content, in control. Yes, that was it, in control. Not at all the impression he gave as he strode the halls of the Seventh Department. The frightened clerks and cowering secretaries would be surprised at this scene of domestic bliss.

"Yes, of course," Dolya answered, nodding at Natalya. She peeped over the top of the magazine, giving him little more than a cursory glance. Willfully, he tore his eyes away, acutely aware the magazine did little to hide the outlines of her body under the flimsy robe, nor the fact that she was obviously naked beneath it. Bitch, he thought.

Delnov poured them both glasses of vodka and settled back in his chair. "Warm yourself, Stefan, then we will talk. Something important you said." Taking her cue like the actress she was, Natalya rose, stretched and pulled the robe tightly around her, but not before both men had a brief glimpse of her body. It was mostly for his benefit, Dolya thought. Or was this exhibition Delnov's idea? This is what you cannot have her actions said. Not now perhaps, but later? Who knows?

"I must have a bath, Vasili. You will excuse me? I will leave you men to your boring talk."

"Of course, my pet."

Dolya cringed inwardly. My pet indeed. It is you who are the pet, Comrade Delnov, only you don't know it yet.

Natalya smiled sweetly, bent over and gave Delnov a peck on the cheek. Her hand grazed his shoulder as she turned, dropped the magazine and walked out of the room. It was an impressive exit.

"She is beautiful, is she not?" Delnov asked. He downed his vodka and poured them both another.

"Very," was all Dolya could manage without betraying his own hunger for the girl. She had teased and taunted him on more than one occasion. But someday, he thought, someday. He guessed her attraction to Delnov was based purely on power and privilege. Certainly there could be no other explanation.

But suppose Shevchenko proved right? He had fought Delnov hard over Owens' return and Dolya had to admit his argument had merit. Dolya had witnessed their struggle as a detached observer. Well, almost detached for his own fortune was, at least for the moment, tied to Delnov. But Shevchenko's star was rising as well and glowed perhaps even brighter than Delnov's. It behooved any ambitious KGB officer to cast his lot with a winner.

Warmed by the fire and the spiced vodka, both men lapsed into silence. Dolya allowed his thoughts to wander. What a picture they made. D & D. Delnov and Dolya. Damnation and Deception. He knew that was the English nickname that rang about the halls of the department. He wondered if Delnov knew as well. Probably. He could almost imagine Delnov enjoying it, basking in it. And which was he, Stefan Dolya, bright young officer on the rise? Damnation or Deception? Deception, he decided at once, for he wore it like a cloak, successfully hiding the hatred he harbored for his chief.

"You have met with Trask?" Delnov asked suddenly.

"What?" Delnov's voice startled him. He cursed himself for the lapse of concentration, but of course it was so like Delnov to quickly get down to business. He was not a guest after all, but an underling, dutifully reporting to his superiors. "Yes, last night."

"And?"

"They have a man," Dolya said, replying almost too quickly, instantly regretting his haste. If anything went wrong, Delnov could convict him with his own words.

"Good," said Delnov, smiling benignly and slapping his thighs. "Tell me about this man they have found."

"He's a teacher," Dolya said, measuring his words carefully, able to recall exactly the conversation with the American.

"A teacher?" Delnov threw back his head and laughed loudly. "Forgive me, Stefan, but a teacher? That really strikes me as quite funny."

"Yes," said Dolya, attempting a smile of his own. "I suppose it is. His name is Christopher Storm. He apparently served in the same unit with Owens in Vietnam. The Americans are satisfied that he can confirm Owens as genuine." He could think of nothing else to add except Trask's impatience and insistent pressing for the meeting to take place outside of Russia. He swallowed the remains of his vodka and poured himself another.

"And what do our computers say about this teacher Christopher Storm?" Delnov lit a cigar with his familiar lighter and began to bounce it in his palm.

"Nothing. No record of any previous visits to the Soviet Union or any connection whatsoever with intelligence work. His name was run through the computer and cross-referenced in all categories." Dolya gazed steadily at his chief. Here at least he was on solid ground. He had run the computer checks himself. He couldn't be faulted later.

"Good, Stefan, excellent. Your assurance pleases me. Still..."

Dolya looked up quickly. Now what? "We must keep in mind Fox is behind this. A factor we must take into account from this point forward. This Storm, as you say he is called, could he be a new operative, unknown to us? Is that not possible?" Delnov arched his bushy eyebrows.

It was not only not possible, it was ridiculous. "Yes, I suppose, but the possibility is so remote and..."

"No, Stefan, we must be absolutely sure," Delnov continued. "Perhaps some further checking on Mr. Storm is in order before he meets with Owens. Give it some thought, Stefan. We can discuss it further tomorrow at the center."

Dolya nodded his compliance, wondering again about Delnov's maddening obsession with Charles Fox. Whatever had happened in Prague between the two men had obviously left a mark on his chief. He could not recall Delnov being wary of anyone before. He himself rejected the idea that Storm could be anything but a hastily chosen figure from Owens' past. The Americans were too anxious for him to be anything else. Still, he would have to placate Delnov's suspicions somehow.

"And Owens? He is prepared?"

"Of course. Owens knows exactly what will take place and has been carefully instructed."

"That leaves only comrade Zakharov. The Americans still agree to the trade?" Just mentioning Zakharov's name seemed to make Delnov frown.

"Yes, I made it clear to Trask we were only willing to release Owens because of Zakharov." Dolya reproached himself silently, perhaps without cause, wondering if he'd overplayed his hand. But now, reviewing his meeting with Trask, he was sure he had used just the right amount of urgency to whet the American's appetite.

"The Washington residency reports that Zakharov is undergoing almost daily interrogations," Dolya said.

"Meaningless," said Delnov defiantly. "What can they learn from one who knows nothing?"

Delnov stared into the fire for a moment then rose quickly. He towered over Dolya, who struggled out of his chair, realizing he was being dismissed. What was on the agenda for the rest of this snowy Sunday? Some cozy lovemaking with Natalya in front of the fire? Dolya turned toward the door.

"I am pleased as always with your efficiency, Stefan. Very pleased. Your efforts will not go unrewarded," Delnov said. Dolya flinched inwardly as his chief put his huge hand on his shoulder in a gesture of what? Approval? Friendliness? No, Delnov was incapable of that.

He shrugged into his coat. Outside the gusting winds whipped snow across the drive. It would be a lonely journey back to Moscow.

"Tomorrow we will also visit the clinic, eh? I want to see how our patient is doing." Delnov smiled brightly.

Driving away, he could see Delnov in the rearview mirror, standing in the doorway, watching the car. He looks like a bear at the entrance of his cave, Dolya thought.

The image shot across the darkened projection room and flashed on the screen with blinding intensity, startling Storm as he sat hunched down in the leatherette chair.

Instinctively, he closed his eyes, blocking the image from view. But even with his eyes shut tightly, the scene was a vivid, painful, vicious swipe at his mind. He could almost smell the cordite, the burning flesh as the claymores exploded, spraying hundreds of tiny steel balls in a fan-shaped arc for nearly fifty yards. The small hut bursting into flames, the woman carrying the child running and screaming into the lush green wall of jungle.

"This is a village in Quan-Tri province," a voice said, as the camera panned across the scene of carnage and eventually came to rest on the face of the reporter. He was crouching near the trail and dressed in army fatigues. He held the microphone stiffly and tried to look steadily into the camera, but his eyes darted to either side as off screen as more shells exploded.

"These men you see behind me," the reporter continued, "are members of the First Calvary Division, Company C. Their valiant efforts here this morning are yet one more step toward what analysts hope will be the final push in the Tet offensive, mounted by..."

Storm shut his eyes again and mentally tuned out the reporter's voice droning on over the actions. He felt a wave of nausea coming again. The headache had been with him since breakfast, an unrelenting throb at the base of his skull.

"You watching this, Storm?"

Garrison's voice cut across the darkened room like an instrument, probing, prodding his body and mind, demanding acknowledgement. Storm kept his eyes closed and didn't answer. He opened them only when he heard the click of the video recorder as Garrison stopped the tape. The action was frozen on the screen. He focused on the greenness of the jungle, remembering the stifling heat, the implacable insects and snakes, avoiding that part of the picture showing the hut, flames licking up its sides. Another click and the screen went mercifully black.

Garrison suddenly loomed over him, tall, muscular, a granite face and knife-like creases in his trousers. An expression of contempt and disapproval clearly shown on his sharply etched features. "What's the matter, Storm? You don't like the Saturday morning cartoons?" he mocked.

It had been like that for three days now. "We want to jog your memory," Charles had said. "You're going to be questioning Owens primarily about the war so you'll spend some time with Major Garrison viewing some Vietnam film." Charles referred to it as if he was talking about home movies of somebody's vacation.

Garrison, so Storm had been told, was on loan. Charles didn't say from where, but he recognized the type immediately, saw it written all over him like an identification badge: Special Forces, two maybe three tours in Nam. Hard, steely-gray eyes hungering for combat. He'd seen them jumping out of choppers, shouting, searching the bush before they hit the ground, sneering at the wild eyed terror of

Company C replacements, the haunted eyes pleading only for survival. Search and kill missions were designed for Garrison and the Green Berets.

If only he could tell them none of this was necessary. It was all a meaningless exercise in redundancy. He already had it all in his mind in frightening detail. He didn't need news telecasts, films, tapes, replays of the six o'clock news that had turned Vietnam into America's only television war.

"It's getting boring, Garrison," Storm said. "Anyway, I already know the ending. You know, the part where we abandon the embassy and turn over Saigon to the VC?" He tried to sound flippant, casual, but he knew he wasn't fooling Garrison.

"It's *Major*, soldier," Garrison shot back at Storm angrily.

"And it's *ex-soldier*, Major," Storm said, feeling his own anger. "I'm not one of your gung-ho recruits so you can drop the drill instructor routine." He was tense, trying to muster more defiance than he felt. He remembered his own basic training, the instructor's face inches from his own, shouting obscenities, driving, pushing. The closeness was menacing and now he felt the same thing from Garrison.

Garrison stared for a moment, obviously holding himself in check. "One difference, Storm. There's no discharge from this outfit." He glanced at his watch. "We'll quit for today. Mr. Fox will be here in a minute to pick you up." Storm nodded in relief and collapsed against the back of the chair, but Garrison's barb had struck home.

What would Charles say if he told him he'd changed his mind? Could he just walk away, catch a plane back to Las Vegas and forget the whole thing? What had seemed so appealing was now a nightmare of churned up memories and regimentation. Maybe Valerie had been right. In his eagerness to collect his prize, he had glossed over Charles' reminders that he would undergo briefings and preparation. And now, he felt he was getting more than he'd bargained for.

He didn't go anywhere alone. Since his arrival at Langley, he'd been picked up and carted everywhere; collected and dropped off like a parcel, a virtual prisoner in the massive CIA complex. No letters, no calls, no visitors. Security was the byword and it was uttered without the hint of apology.

They'd arrived at night. He'd been immediately issued a visitor's limited access badge and reminded it was to be worn at all times. Even asleep, he wondered? Did someone check for pin holes in your pajamas? Exhausted from the flight and confused by the twists and turns of Langley's maze-like streets, he eventually found himself in a Spartan but comfortable room on one corner of the several hundred acre complex.

There was a bed, a small bureau and desk, a metal wardrobe and a television. A three-quarter bath opened off the room. Except for a handful of paperback books crowded on the desk, it might have been a room at a Motel 6.

He explored briefly, trying to imagine who had occupied it before him. A spy in training for a secret mission? A captured foreign agent? He was intrigued by the books but they offered no clues. Most of them were fairly recent bestsellers, a classic or two and a book of quotations. Nothing to reveal the former occupant's identity. Or were the books simply part of the furnishings? Were the other rooms in the block similarly equipped with exactly the same titles?

Outside he could see the building was surrounded by well-tended lawns and gardens. In front was a large parking area, but no cars. He didn't have to check to know the door was locked from the outside. Where did they think he was going? He decided in the end it was nothing more than a fairly comfortable cell and dropped off to sleep.

A security aide had awakened him in the morning and escorted him on a short walk to a large cafeteria for breakfast. Charles and Garrison were already there. The dining room was busy and as Storm watched the breakfast crowd lingering over coffee and cigarettes, he was struck by the notion that this could be the staff dining room of any major company in America. But of course, he reminded himself, the CIA *was* a major American company.

Over breakfast, Charles had explained the need for the Vietnam film and introduced Garrison, who Storm would come to think of as his minder, and later, his nemesis. He was immediately aware of the soldier's close attention, watching him, weighing him, sizing him up like a new recruit, albeit one with special circumstances. And even in the first meeting, Storm sensed Garrison's tacit disapproval. Charles had made the wrong choice.

After breakfast, he'd spent three hours reviewing old Vietnam film. He'd had no stomach for lunch afterwards. Under Charles' watchful eye, he'd pushed a lamb cutlet from one side of the plate to the other as if it was some kind of game. Lunch was followed by a couple of hours reading over files and other material on Robert Owens, which included many photos, but none dated later than 1975. His strongest impression was of the changes in Owens since he'd seen him crawling in the dirt in Vietnam.

The next item on the agenda was exercise. He would have preferred a long bike ride, but—"security, you understand, Christopher," Charles had said—precluded that so instead, he had spent an hour on the deserted track under Garrison's supervision of course, jogging in circles, but content to give himself over to the release of physical exertion.

Dinner was alone—he hadn't seen Charles for the rest of the day—then back to his room to wile away the long evenings with a book or television. None of it was at all what he had expected and it was beginning to wear thin.

"Christopher?" He hadn't heard Charles come into the projection room. "Ah, there you are." He sat down next to Storm and indicated the screen. "How's it coming?" Charles seemed somehow ill at ease, disturbed about something.

Storm shrugged. In these three days, he'd come to think of Charles as some kind of mentor, a guide to see him through the preparation process, but one who had somehow let him down.

"I don't really need any more of this, you know. I remember it all well enough without a daily reminder, and I could definitely do without Garrison. What's he pushing for anyway?"

"Nothing, I assure you," Charles said. "The major may be a trifle over bearing in his attention to duty, but he means well."

Sure," said Storm, not at all convinced. Garrison made him

feel like he'd failed some kind of test before he'd even taken it. "So what's on the agenda for the rest of the day? More briefings, more photo sessions? I think I could find Owens in the dark now and I probably know him better than his mother."

"Not at all," said Charles, smiling. "We think you're looking a bit rundown so this afternoon, we've scheduled you for a complete physical examination." Before Storm could protest, Charles headed him off. "Just routine," he soothed. "It wouldn't do at all for you to get sick on us later now, would it?" Charles was casual but firm.

However, it was far from routine. The physical was as thorough as any he'd ever undergone. A complete eye exam, including tests for night vision, urine and blood samples, electro-cardiograph, even a treadmill test. It took up the entire afternoon and ended with an appointment the following morning for yet another doctor.

"Take these three times a day," the pretty nurse said, handing him a vitamin supplement. "We'll expect you tomorrow morning at ten."

"Hey, c'mon," he protested. "I've just been through the mill. Why another doctor? You want a second opinion or something?" he snapped at the nurse.

"Hardly," she replied frostily. "Dr. Groves is a psychiatrist."

That had stopped him cold. "Oh," was all he could manage. More digging, more probing, more games to play. A psychiatrist? What were they looking for?

Later back in his room, he went over everything in his mind and no matter how many times he examined it, nothing added up. Garrison, the intensive briefings, the physical, and now a shrink. All for a simple conversation with his former lieutenant? No, there had to be more to it than that unless the CIA just always played it this safe.

He fell asleep resolving to press Charles a bit, but slept badly as images of a humid jungle crowded his mind.

Doctor Maxwell Groves was much younger than he'd

expected. Lean, trim, a friendly face and Storm was relieved to note he smoked cigarettes, not a pipe. "I'll be with you in a minute," Groves said. "Take a seat."

The office was small and functional with the inevitable gray file cabinets, framed certificates on the wall, pale carpeting and Groves desk, a clutter of file folders and papers.

"Okay, Storm, ah, do you mind if I call you Chris?" Groves smile was disarming. Nothing to fear from me his expression said.

"Sure," Storm said, but he was already uncomfortable under the doctor's steady gaze. How much could he afford to reveal about himself?

"Let's see," Groves began, skimming over a file in front of him. "You did one tour of Vietnam in 1968-69, right?" Storm nodded. "Any re-entry problems?" Groves lit a cigarette, leaned back in his swivel chair and looked at Storm through a haze of smoke.

"How do you mean?" Storm hedged.

"You know, readjusting to civilian life after a combat tour. That kind of thing." His cigarette stabbed the air. "Rough out there, huh?" Groves too was measuring him just as Garrison had done.

"Yeah, it was rough, but it was rough for everybody. But coming home? No, there were no real problems I can remember."

But of course there had been problems. The alienation, the looks of disgust when you mentioned you'd been in Nam or that you jumped at every loud noise the first year back.

"Oh," said Groves, faint surprise on his face. "My records indicate some outpatient treatment at a VA hospital in California. Want to tell me about that?" Groves smiled again, still maintaining his casual, nothing to worry about attitude.

Storm looked away and lit a cigarette. Idiot. You should have known they'd know that. They've got everything and this guy is an expert.

Sensing his reluctance, Groves pressed him in a more serious tone. "Look, Chris, you've had some stress problems you've had to deal with. If I'm going to help you, we've got to talk about them, especially the dreams."

Storm turned sharply to face Groves and found a steady answering gaze. The dreams? How did they know about that? How? Was his room wired? Could they hear him screaming in the night? Or was it...Valerie? Somehow they'd gotten to Valerie. She must have seen Charles before he left.

"I wasn't aware I'd asked for any help."

"Fair enough. Okay, I've caught you by surprise, I can see that. But it still might be a good idea to talk through some of this." Groves leaned in closer. "Look, I was out there too, Chris. Third Air-Evac Group. I know what it was like."

Storm nodded, wondering if Groves was telling the truth. He continued to dodge the questions at first, parrying with Groves like a fencer. But later, as he became more comfortable, as his defenses crumbled one by one, he poured it all out in a way he'd never done with anyone. Not his father, not Valerie, certainly not with himself, realizing at last that to make it familiar and tame he must feed his fear. If he recognized and admitted it enough he might yet be able to face it. He talked almost nonstop for over an hour.

Groves listened, occasionally making a note, encouraging with his silence and gentle prodding until Storm grew to appreciate his cleverness. He suddenly realized the whole session was probably being taped and would no doubt go down in a report to Charles. It was too late to back up, but by then he didn't care. He'd left his burden with Groves to do with as he saw fit.

They shook hands briefly and Storm was ushered out, left to wonder if he'd blown the whole deal, but at the same time, strangely relieved by his confession.

His relief was short lived. Back in his room, he found Garrison dressed in a warm-up suit and running shoes, thumbing through one of the paperbacks.

"Workout time, Storm. Let's go." Garrison said.

He was too surprised to argue and changed into his own running gear, conveniently supplied right down to the correct shoe size. He laced up the Nikes tightly and followed Garrison's broad back to the athletic field. Again there was no one about and he began to wonder who used it besides he and Garrison.

"What's the plan, Major?" He stopped as they neared the track. A late afternoon sun had broken through the clouds and he could feel the warmth touch him.

"Just get the kinks out," Garrison called as he started off on a slow jog. Storm nodded and followed a few paces behind, staring at Garrison's cropped head bobbing in easy rhythm. It wasn't that he minded running, in fact he enjoyed it almost as much as riding a bike. It was being made to run that rankled him. In addition to the annoyance of being under Garrison's supervision.

Garrison maintained a steady pace as they neared the end of the fourth lap. Storm felt sweat break out on his forehead, his breath come quicker. He was gliding now. Garrison's running style, he noticed, was awkward. His legs were working harder, his arms pumping like pistons. Storm passed him easily going into the second mile. He glanced back over his shoulder and caught a brief glimpse of Garrison's red face, set in concentration. He rounded the curve, feeling good, deciding he would do one more mile when suddenly he heard Garrison pounding after him.

Garrison pulled beside him, an amused smile on his face. They ran neck and neck for another lap and despite his efforts he could do nothing to shake Garrison, who dogged his every step and appeared to be breathing easily. He can probably do this all day, Storm thought, so why the act before?

The answer came as they went into the next turn. Somehow Garrison's feet got tangled with his own and he went sprawling headlong in the dirt.

Storm was baffled. It clearly had been deliberate.

He stood up, brushing himself off, seething inside. Garrison was standing hands on hips. "What's the matter, Storm? Tired?" he sneered.

Yeah I'm tired, Storm thought. Tired of you. He charged, driving his shoulder into Garrison's midsection, hearing the whooshing sound as his breath expelled. He knew he was being foolish, making a terrible mistake. Garrison was a Special Forces instructor, he reminded himself as they both hit the ground. Garrison had been caught unawares, but he recovered quickly, gripped Storm around the waist and using the momentum of their fall, easily flipped him backwards over his head.

Storm saw a flash of sky then felt the damp grass as his back slammed into the ground. Before he could think of what to do next, he was roughly rolled over, his arm pinned behind his back Garrison's knee firmly planted on his head.

"So you want to play, eh, Storm? Well, c'mon." Garrison released him and stood up. He backed away a few steps, feet firmly planted, arms outstretched. "That was good, Storm. I liked that." His teeth were clenched and the cords of his neck stood out.

Garrison watched him warily as he stood up, shaking out his arm, numbed with pain. This was crazy. Garrison was deliberately goading him, daring him to attack, here on the deserted track of the CIA complex. Why? Where was Charles? Was anybody watching this? Was this some other test?

He searched Garrison's mocking face for some sign, but saw only anticipation. This was his element. He basked in it, like someone would in the sun or a hot bath. Well, he'd had enough. Of the briefings, the films, and most of all Garrison.

He feinted to the left and then dove under Garrison's outstretched arm, but grabbed only a handful of air for his trouble, as the big man easily side stepped his clumsy charge and chopped him on the back of the neck, driving him into the ground. He fell in a heap, tasting grass and dirt, then lay motionless. He could sense Garrison watching him from behind.

"C'mon, get up, Storm." He continued to lay still, eyes closed. "Storm?" Garrison came closer to his inert body and looked down. "Shit, hey, Storm." He bent over closer and reached down to pull his shoulder.

Storm swung his left arm out stiffly, catching Garrison full in the throat, rocking him back on his heels. His hands went to his throat even as Storm got up and charged him again, driving his shoulder into Garrison's unprotected middle. There was a grunt from Garrison again as he toppled backwards, Storm on top of him. He rolled off quickly and jumped to his feet a few paces away.

"You forgot, Garrison. Never approach a prisoner like

that unless you know he's dead." Storm was breathing hard, but he felt strangely elated. He steeled for another attack, but Garrison was on one knee now.

"Christopher!" Storm spun around to see Charles hurrying toward them across the field. Garrison got to his feet and glared at Storm.

"I won't forget next time," Garrison hissed as Charles approached. He brushed himself off, glanced briefly at Charles and stalked off.

"What was that all about?" Charles asked. He looked out of place on the dusty track in a suit and topcoat.

Storm watched Garrison's retreating figure. He hoped he wouldn't see him again. Garrison would be laying for him now. Surely Charles had seen the entire incident, but he seemed satisfied with Storm's terse reply.

"Nothing. Just a misunderstanding."

He slept well that night.

CENTRAL INTELLIGENCE AGENCY

Medical & Psychiatric Examination/ C. Storm
Your ref: Charles Fox
Date: 4/11/80

Subject is an adult male, thirty years of age. Extensive physical examination confirms health and physical condition as excellent. These findings are countered only by moderate to heavy cigarette smoking. Physical stress tests, however, suggest subject is active physically.

Psychiatric Assessment:
Subject is Vietnam combat veteran and despite the lapse of time since active service, he continues to experience the residual effects of what is commonly referred to as combat fatigue, i.e., stress. Marital problems, subject is divorced and apparently denied reasonable access to his son, and current occupation as high school teacher, contributes to the current levels of stress and the post-traumatic symptoms of irritability, recurrent fits of anger, flashbacks, which, while lessened considerably, are still in the operative stages.

Conclusion:
Subject is an articulate, intelligent individual, fully conversant with his problems and able to identify them lucidly in discussion and examination. I would, however, have some slight reservations about the individual's performance in a high stress situation, particularly in reference to the Vietnam experience without further examination and testing.

Examining Physician: J.M. Groves, M.D.
Asst. Chief, Psychiatric Division

"Well what do you think of it?"

"You were right, Charles. It certainly is worth a look," Storm said.

They were five-hundred feet above the city, inside the Washington Monument, at the peak of the column rising like a finger pointing toward the sky.

Storm's eyes traveled west, up the length of the reflection pool in front of the monument, toward Constitution Avenue and beyond to the mammoth figure of Lincoln looking back at him. Despite himself, the scene struck him with a kind of awe.

Charles nodded, taking in the view himself. "This is my favorite spot in all the city, and at this time of evening, well, it has a special magic. Don't you think?"

Directly below the bunker-like observation deck, Storm could make out a crescent of American flags. "That's where it'll go," he said, pointing.

"What? Sorry, Christopher. I wasn't listening."

"The Nam memorial, if it's ever approved and they decide to put a name on it." The plan called for two low slabs of black granite wedged in the ground with 57,692 names engraved on it. But as yet, there were no plans for naming the place where it had all happened. They turned in silence for the elevator ride back down to ground level.

Storm felt refreshed, the first time since his arrival in Washington. He wasn't sure if it was the session with Groves, the small victory against Garrison, or simply a good night's sleep. He regretted it now, the brush with the major. It had been stupid, a childish response to Garrison's bullying, but on the other hand, how would Garrison have reacted if he hadn't taken the bait. Hell, maybe he just felt good because they were having a day out, away from everything.

The doors hissed open at ground level and they strolled along the rippleless pool. "Come on," Charles said, glancing at his watch. "I promised you a good dinner. I know a nice place in Georgetown. We'll take a taxi."

They walked out near the broad avenue. It was nearly dark now and the city was aglow with lights from office buildings and monuments. Storm could just make out the Capitol dome on the hill.

He was still gazing at it as Charles flagged a taxi. It ground to a halt in front of them and Charles was already halfway inside when Storm noticed the dark shapes behind him.

There was no time to react as a powerful arm locked across his throat, choking off warning shouts. He could only watch in mute incomprehension as a second shape pushed Charles into the taxi and it roared off.

Another car arrived seconds later as Storm continued to struggle in the grip of his assailant. Doors flew open and in a blur of motion he was shoved face down on the back seat. He could hear horns honking as they pulled away. Hadn't anyone seen anything? Where was Charles? His mind raced. This wasn't a mugging or robbery. He was being kidnapped.

His arm was released as the man began tearing off his jacket and pulling up the sleeve of his shirt. He twisted slightly and saw a second man, inserting a syringe into a small bottle.

He struggled again but was unable to move at all. He tensed as the needle jabbed into his arm. It seemed he could barely breathe now, but strangely, he didn't care as the blackness overtook him, darker and darker.

"*Karasho*," the man with the needle said.

Was that...Russian?

Then there was nothing.

Seven

Dimitri Zakharov followed the guard down the carpeted corridor of the Federal Building with easy familiarity, having traversed the same route innumerable times in the past seven weeks. How many times exactly he couldn't say, but of the journey itself, his mind could reel off the statistics with precision-like accuracy.

One hundred, forty-two paces down the corridor. Turn right, up five steps, then another right turn for fifty-seven paces bringing him in front of the pale green door. The predictability of the journey was almost as comfortable as the questions of his interrogator, he decided.

He paused in front of the door and caught a glimpse of Waters through the wire-mesh glass window. The guard opened the door then moved aside for Zakharov to enter the small room and receive Special Agent Eddie Waters' now standard greeting.

"Morning, Dimitri. Sleep well?" Waters was now as familiar to Zakharov as the room's furnishings. Hard back chairs, the table with its carafe of water and two glasses, the large ashtray. The package of cigarettes and box of wooden matches were crowded only by Waters inevitable yellow legal pad and felt tip pen.

The interrogation of Dimitri Zakharov had gone on now for nearly two months. When he drew the assignment, Eddie Waters had been elated, but also suspicious since more experienced agents in the Bureau had been passed over in his favor. But Waters was not a man to quibble with what he considered good fortune.

Dimitri Zakharov could be broken, he was sure of it, despite the Russian's baffling, maddening, indifference to his obviously disastrous position.

There was enough to nail Zakharov for twenty years. Good, solid evidence that would make any federal prosecutor lick his chops waiting for a trial date. And that was another thing bothering Waters. Why was the fucking State Department dragging their ass over the indictment, deciding whether or not Zakharov was even going to be tried? He didn't have diplomatic immunity so why hadn't a trial date been set?

Zakharov himself, even when confronted with the mountain of evidence against him—transcripts, documents, wiretaps, photos—remained impassively indifferent. It was almost as if he knew something Waters didn't, or that he was holding something back. That was the key. Waters was sure of it and he was determined to dig it out. Today, he thought he had something. Today, he was going fishing.

He motioned Zakharov to one of the chairs. As usual, the Russian went right for the cigarettes, extracting one from the freshly opened pack with almost delicate care and lighting it carefully with one of the wooden matches. If the session went the usual time, he would go through the entire package. He blew out the match, flicked his eyes toward Waters and smiled thinly before dropping the match in the ashtray. The ritual complete, they could now begin.

"So, Eddie, what do we talk about today?" Zakharov settled his compact body in the chair and regarded Eddie Waters with heavy lidded eyes. The amused smile sharpened his blunt features.

Waters eased his lanky frame into the chair opposite Zakharov, his own face a mask of studied casualness to disguise the feeling of elation which was trying to crowd to the surface of his mind.

"Let's talk about San Francisco, Dimitri, shall we?"

Zakharov blinked once and studied the ash of his cigarette. "Yes, why not? It's a beautiful city."

It was only a flicker, a tiny beat of hesitation, but Waters registered it with the inner satisfaction of a poker player holding a pair of aces and suddenly knowing his opponent is bluffing.

***

Christopher Storm was nine-years-old and very unhappy. It was his birthday, but instead of celebrating he was in the hospital recovering from a badly needed tonsillectomy. He remembered clearly going under the anesthetic, the counting backwards from one hundred, feeling as though he was sinking into a pool of dark murky water.

Awakening now, the sensation was much the same. He was swimming under the water, clawing toward the surface, driven by the sounds, the light. He could see it now as his head broke through the surface.

A single bulb was attached to a cord directly over his head. He blinked at the light and lay still for moment, trying to coordinate his thoughts. Everything was fuzzy. Fragments of pictures flashed through his mind, hazy, unfocused.

Charles, the Washington monument, a taxi, Charles shoved inside, the other car...hands on his throat, face down...a needle. Instinctively, he rubbed his arm. Then some vague impressions of movement, a low rumbling sound. A plane?

He opened his eyes again, surprised to find himself stretched out on a narrow cot, still in the same rumpled clothes. A blanket had been thrown over him. He turned his head to the right and saw a small table and a chair. Further away, in the corner, a washstand, a large jug and a neatly folded towel. Nothing else.

It was some kind of cabin, roughly and hastily constructed, as if the builder had abandoned the project before it was completed. There were windows on both sides of the door and another on the opposite wall. Outside he could see branches of trees swaying gently against the glass.

He sat up, instantly aware of the dull throbbing at the base of his skull. He closed his eyes again, waiting for the dizziness to pass, then rose on unsteady legs and walked to the window. Outside, beyond the cabin was a great expanse of forest. The sun, diffused by clouds was rapidly setting behind the cabin. The ground was covered in snow and he was suddenly aware of the cold. What time was it? Late afternoon? He felt his wrist but his watch was gone.

He pressed both hands to his head and squeezed his eyes

shut tightly, desperately trying to piece together the impressions that crowded his mind. But after the car, the needle, it was all a blank. Where was he?

He turned from the window and went to the wash stand. He poured water from the heavy jug into the basin and splashed his face with cold water. He was still fuzzy, unsure on his feet. He dried his face with the towel and sat down on the bed again.

He jumped as the sound of a click in the door broke the stillness. A key turned in the lock and the door opened. A medium built man in a dark suit came in, followed by another man, huge in stature with a hard face. His nose looked like it had been broken at one time and not properly set.

The smaller man shut the door and pulled the chair up near Storm. The big man glanced at him once then went to stand by the window.

"Good morning, Mr. Storm, or rather I should say afternoon. I must apologize for the, ah, facilities, but it was the best we could do on such short notice." His voice was quiet, undemanding, almost friendly, but he spoke with an accent Storm couldn't discern.

"Who are you?"

"Yes, of course," the man said, taking off his rimless glasses. "Permit me to introduce myself. I am Fyador Malin and this is my associate Viktor. You must excuse Viktor. His training was, shall we say, less academic than my own. He doesn't speak or understand English."

"I don't understand," Storm said. The dizziness was returning again.

"No, of course not. The after effects of the drug, I'm afraid. An unfortunate but necessary precaution. You've had a long journey and you're tired and confused." He put his glasses back on and smiled.

"Long journey?"

"Yes, Mr. Storm. Allow me to be the first to welcome you to the Union of Soviet Socialists Republic."

***

Stefan Dolya sat in one of the comfortable lounge chairs in the anteroom of KGB Director Yuri Andropov's outer office. Several guards slouched nearby in front of a large-screen television, mesmerized by a dazzling display of laser beams flashing from hundreds of space ships.

"*Star Wars*," Dolya mused, realizing even before his eyes drifted below the TV screen and saw the video recorder. The guards had taken no notice of him although he'd been sitting there for over thirty minutes.

He'd gone to Delnov's office in Dzerzhinsky Square for their early meeting only to be told his chief had been summoned to Andropov's office and he was to meet him there. Dolya frowned. A meeting with the Director meant one of two things: an update on the project—unlikely as Andropov never personally participated in operations—or something had gone wrong.

Dolya suddenly tensed, briefly entertaining the thought Andropov wanted to see him as well. But no, the project was Delnov's responsibility. He was only an assistant, albeit an important one, he reminded himself.

What then? Everything was proceeding exactly on schedule. The Americans had a man to verify Owens and had agreed to the exchange. To satisfy Delnov's doubts, Christopher Storm was even now being investigated further. Owens was fully briefed and knew what to expect. And, at the clinic, well, even that situation was under control.

As his mind began a series of speculative explorations, he was shocked to see Colonel Shevchenko emerge from the outer office. He glanced at the television screen, then seeing Dolya, immediately walked over to greet him as if he was specifically there for that purpose.

"Major, Dolya," he said, smiling.

Dolya struggled unsuccessfully to get out of the confines of the soft chair with what he hoped was the proper amount of deference, but Shevchenko restrained him with a hand on his shoulder.

"Comrade Colonel," he blurted, half out of his chair. His own chief with Andropov and now Shevchenko as well and the blustery Colonel treating him like an old friend.

"Sit down, please, Stefan."

"Yes, Comrade Colonel, as you wish." Dolya sank back into the chair.

Shevchenko smiled again. "Nothing to worry about," he said, thumbing toward the door to Andropov's office. "Just some additional information Comrade Delnov was perhaps not aware of that I believe relates to your, ah, project." He paused for a moment, studying Dolya, as if trying to decide whether to say more.

"Well, I must be off," he said getting up. "You know, Stefan, I think it might be beneficial to both of us to perhaps, exchange views from time to time, eh?" He smiled again, leaving Dolya to squirm uncomfortably on the soft chair, his mind reeling from the implication of Shevchenko's remarks.

He sighed deeply as Shevchenko left. The Colonel and Delnov had opposed each other, it seemed, forever; their rivalry was common knowledge. Only because they were in different departments prevented them from clashing openly. But on the Owens exchange, their areas of responsibility apparently overlapped. There was no other explanation for them both to attend a meeting with Andropov.

Five minutes later, Dolya was still puzzling it over when Delnov emerged from the office, ashen-faced, wobbly, nodding absently at the aide who showed him out. Dolya rose and crossed the room. Delnov hadn't noticed him and almost collided with him.

"You. What are you doing here?" Delnov demanded. His eyes suddenly blazed with anger.

"Your secretary," Dolya stammered. "I was instructed to meet you here. What is it? What's happened?"

"Yes, of course, I'd forgotten. Forgive me, Stefan, it's just that..." his voice trailed off. His eyes had gone blank again. Suddenly, he grabbed Dolya.

"Come, Stefan. We must talk. There is an urgent matter requiring our immediate attention."

"Come now, Mr. Storm. Surely you're not going to persist in this tiresome denial of your reasons for being here. You had intensive briefings, did you not? At CIA Headquarters?" The friendliness in Malin's voice had faded and was replaced now with an irritable sarcastic tone.

"I'm here because you brought me—kidnapped me. Of course I saw material on Owens, but only to refresh my memory. I was supposed to come here and confirm his identity. That's all. That's all I know."

Malin got up and walked to the window. He whispered something to Viktor, who then remained gazing out the window, hands clasped behind his back. It was nearly dark now.

Malin, it seemed to Storm, was amused by his denials that he was a spy. A spy? Jesus Christ. What else was there to tell him? He didn't know anything, but the Russian continued to press for details Storm was sure he already knew and only wanted confirmed. Malin, he was certain, knew everything.

"Ah, Mr. Storm, you make it so unpleasant," he said, shaking his head. "Did you think we would simply allow you to walk into Moscow, a known spy, and walk out again with another spy? Surely you don't expect me to believe that." Malin turned again from the window to face Storm.

"Known spy? Look, I don't care what you believe. I want to talk to someone at the American Embassy."

"Impossible," said Malin. He paused to light a cigarette and offered one to Storm, then dropped the package on the table. Storm glanced at the Cyrillic letters on the package. "Very well, you leave me no choice but to report to my superiors you are being uncooperative. However, I'm a reasonable man, Mr. Storm. Perhaps a good night's sleep will clear your mind, enable you to see the futility of your denials. I shall return in the morning, and believe me, Mr. Storm, you will care a great deal about what I believe then."

He nodded to Viktor and opened the door. "Please take my advice and give this some careful thought. I would also remind you the door will remain locked and Viktor will be nearby at all times. Any attempt to escape would be very foolish." Malin left, closing and locking the door behind him.

Storm fell back across the cot, one arm over his eyes to shield them from the bright overhead light. He could still not believe it. Kidnapped in the middle of Washington, D.C., and flown to Russia. Just like that. And where was Charles? Was anybody looking for him? Did anybody know where he was?

He got up and went to the window, looking out at the darkened forest. The only light came from the half-moon peeping through the trees. How far away was Moscow? he wondered.

He paced the cabin for another hour. He couldn't just wait for Malin to return in the morning. More questions, more denials until...what? He had nothing to tell them.

Only one word kept intruding into his thoughts, insistent, demanding, until like a litany it rang in his mind.

Escape.

"It's true, Stefan. Andropov himself told me."

Dolya was stunned. The shock on his face he knew must have been evident to Delnov, who himself seemed to have aged years in the last hour. His face was puffy, cramped with anxiety, but Dolya could see he derived some relief from his own discomfort.

The stupid compartmentalization of the KGB would bring them all down. It was a point of the department's organization constantly debated by the younger officers. The obsession with secrecy, the entirely vertical chain of command, even the very size of the organization made it vulnerable. Well planned, often brilliantly executed, operations were stopped cold as they inadvertently stumbled into another section's area. Dammit, intelligence overlapped. Couldn't anyone see that?

"There's no mistake?"

"None."

They were sitting now in Delnov's office, having returned with such urgency Dolya could only wonder at the meeting's importance. But this? What would this do to Delnov's great plan? Nothing, if Delnov could be believed. Some of Delnov's assurance was restored now that he was back in the familiar surroundings of his own office.

"You're not surprised we are to continue as planned?" He

had not mentioned Shevchenko's attendance at the meeting with Andropov. Apparently the major change was a speeding up process, a new air of urgency Dolya instantly regretted.

"No, I suppose this just makes it all the more imperative, the stakes higher. A shift in emphasis?"

"Exactly. Zakharov's return is now our primary concern. Owens's performance must be flawless." Delnov's eyes bored into his young assistant. There was no mistaking the meaning of his steely gaze. Owens' preparation was Dolya's responsibility and he would be held accountable if anything went wrong.

Even as he registered Delnov's glare, a different, yet obviously related thought, burst into his consciousness, suddenly frightening him even more than the prospect of failure at Delnov's hand.

Suppose the entire Zakharov arrest was a setup? What if the Americans knew all along that Zakharov was...?

"I want you to go over everything again with Owens. Every detail must be perfect," said Delnov.

"What? Of course." He wanted to get away to think. "And if there are any problems?"

"There will be no problems, Stefan. Do you understand? No problems." Delnov glanced at his watch. "You will inform Trask we are ready for the exchange. The sooner the better. You'd better see Owens today."

Dolya nodded and left quickly, grateful for the quick dismissal. He paused at the top of the steps overlooking Dzerzhinsky Square. Was now the time to air his views with Shevchenko? He'd been invited hadn't he? He'd have to decide soon.

If the operation failed, Delnov would go down and Dolya with him.

Storm waited for what he estimated was another full hour.

There was still no sound from outside the cabin. Viktor had returned once with some water and allowed Storm to relieve himself outside in the snow. He had seized the opportunity to acquaint himself with the layout beyond the perimeter of the cabin, but there had been nothing to see except a narrow path leading away from the front door that seemed to disappear after a few yards.

Was Malin bluffing? Were he and Viktor nowhere near the cabin now, instead holed up some distance away? There was only one way to find out and he had to be sure. Viktor was his main concern.

The idea of escape had seemed ludicrous at first, but on further examination, as the hours dragged by and the isolation weighed on him, there seemed no other alternative.

Malin and Viktor would be back and he had nothing to tell them. Even if Charles or anyone was looking for him, he couldn't assume they knew he'd been taken out of the country. He was on his own. He would have to get by Viktor if there was even a chance he could make it to what he hoped was the safe refuge of the U.S. Embassy in Moscow. Malin's remarks implied he was at least near Moscow. How far? Which direction? He shoved these thoughts aside to concentrate on the task at hand.

He tried the door again, quietly at first then rattled it loudly. He'd already checked the windows. They were sealed or nailed shut and there was nothing to pry them open with to ensure a quiet getaway. He stood listening at the door for any answering sounds but there were none. Out the front window was only the pale moonlight on the snow.

He dragged the chair over by the door then poured the remaining water out of the heavy jug into the basin, weighing it in his hands. It was cracked in places but heavy and would serve his purpose. He raised it high over his head and hurled it as hard as he could through the window opposite the door.

The shattering glass pierced the eerie quiet of the forest like an explosion. Pieces of the jug scattered everywhere on the floor as it crashed through the window. He had to wait only seconds before heavy footsteps pounded up the path and onto the porch. Viktor.

Storm pressed against the wall near the door and waited, holding the chair above his head, listening to the key in the lock. The door burst open and Viktor lunged inside. He stopped, faced the broken window. Storm stepped from behind the door and slammed the chair against Viktor's head with all his strength. The big man groaned, stumbled under the impact and went down on his knees. He was stunned but not unconscious.

Storm was already out the door. He slammed it shut, twisted the key in the lock then yanked it out of the door and threw it as far as he could into the underbrush. He ran down the steps toward the path leading away from the cabin, blindly at first, crashing through branches, not caring about anything except putting as much distance as possible between himself and the cabin. Don't think. Run. Run. Run.

The path sloped downward and veered off to the right. As his eyes became accustomed to the shadowy moonlight, he could see it begin to rise in front of him until it was on a level higher than the cabin. He glanced back over his shoulder at the sound of Viktor crashing through the door, then a gunshot, booming through the stillness like a cannon. He caught a brief glimpse of Viktor's huge figure silhouetted on the porch, gun in hand.

Storm ran on up the path, but he'd gone only a few steps when he felt his foot catch on a low-lying branch and sending him sprawling into a clump of dense bush. He got up quickly, his face caked in snow and began to run again, but he knew the noise would have alerted Viktor and his footsteps would be easy to follow. His breathing was labored now and he could feel the blood pounding in his ears, the rush of adrenalin coursing through his body.

At the top of the slope, he found himself in a large clearing. He stopped momentarily. Which way? Before he could decide, he was suddenly blinded by intense, dazzling light coming from all sides of the clearing. Floodlights. He must have tripped some kind of alarm system. He could see one of the lights now, attached somehow to a tree limb near him.

Instinctively, he put up a hand to shield his eyes from the glare. He turned blindly to run toward the darkness when from behind, a pair of strong arms encircled his body and tried to wrestle him to the ground. He struggled to stay on his feet. Their two bodies twisted and turned in a sort of grotesque dance.

But he was no match for the superior strength of his assailant. He was thrown to the ground, pinned, unable to move. He tasted snow, felt the man's breath in his ear. Then, the voice, familiar, mocking.

"Still wanna play, eh, Storm?"

It was Garrison.

It was like some sick, practical joke, but played out in deadly earnest and he'd been its all too willing victim. His mind had rebelled instantly, refusing to accept the reality that one minute he'd been wrestling in the snow in what he'd believed to be a life and death struggle to make good his escape. Then abruptly the action was stopped, as if a director had shouted, "Cut!" The deception had been complete, convincing, and ingenuously planned and executed by a team of experienced professionals. He'd been at Langley all the time.

When he'd recovered from the utter shock and bewilderment and accepted the truth that the cabin and the forest were only on a remote section of the Langley complex—several hundred isolated acres protected by triple fencing and a grid of underground sensory alarms—the floodlights had been turned off and Major Garrison had helped him to his feet.

Only then had the principals come forward, introducing themselves, taking bows like actors with joking remarks or comments to help ease the tension. "You've got to admit we had you worried," Malin said, shaking hands with him. Malin it turned out was Stan Grabowski of the Soviet Affairs Desk.

Viktor's giant hulk belonged to Vic Lewis, formerly of Penn State University and Cleveland Browns professional football team. Lewis was now with the Plans Division. "Christ, Storm, I haven't been hit that hard since the playoffs in '76," he said, gently cuffing him on the shoulder and still rubbing his head where Storm had hit him with the chair.

Then Garrison, dressed in battle fatigues, almost sheepish, spreading his hands in mock surrender. "No hard feelings I hope, Storm," he said.

They had all retreated then, walking away to the waiting cars, leaving him alone with Charles, the director of this surrealistic drama, quietly apologetic saying gently, "I'm sorry, Christopher, but it was necessary."

Storm could only stare blankly at the procession. His mind was numb. He wanted to say something, scream at somebody, strike out, but he had been unable to do more than nod absently, take their offered hands and walk away quietly with Charles.

Throughout the ride back to the main buildings, he'd sat hunched in one corner of the rear seat, eyes locked on the blur of the landscape and raged in silence, his face a stolid mask. He was acutely aware, could almost feel Charles' searching looks from the seat next to him, gauging him, trying to predict his reaction.

Garrison rode in front with the driver, his jaw rigid in profile, staring straight ahead. Charles wanted something, some sign. Storm gave nothing but sullen silence.

He had truly believed he was in Russia. He had believed he was in real danger, the victim of a KGB kidnapping, a captured spy. And worse, he had been manipulated to believe. The force that had driven him to attempt escape had been quite simply a careful exploitation of his very real fear, a cleverly orchestrated test of his instinct for survival.

But yet, he saw clearly now, this test, this initiation, was his own rite of passage. He knew with a certainty that even now, his anger tempered, he had passed with flying colors. The friendly jibes by Garrison and the others had been genuine. There'd been no embarrassed silences, no awkward glances, no averting of eyes. Just a hand shaking camaraderie saying, "Welcome to the club, Storm."

Driven by fear, yes, but he'd shown initiative, courage, even daring in his attempt to escape and while not successful—it had been planned in advance—he had reacted to the situation as he was best equipped to do under the circumstances. The inner glow of satisfaction he felt spreading through him, causing his anger to subside even more, was undeniable.

In more practical terms, this elaborate testing proved beyond a doubt his earlier speculations about the real purpose of his mission—no, he could not put that name to it yet—was meant to be or had already become far more than a simple chat with his former lieutenant. He was now ready to meet head on whatever challenge lay ahead.

His original motives for acceptance—graduate school, money—now paled when placed alongside the force that would make him accept whatever it was he was to be assigned to do. His first reaction had been outrage of being tricked, made to perform like a guinea pig in some bizarre experiment, even if his performance had been in the prescribed manner.

He would continue now solely because if he did not, he would wonder about it for the rest of his life and the uncertainty would be intolerable. Even if he did back out now, he realized, he would probably be held in protective custody until the arrangements for Owens' return were completed. His own fate would be sealed.

In a week or a month, he would find himself back in his classroom with no way out. He had no illusion about his job and for the first time saw it clearly for what it was. He was not teaching; he was shoving English down the throats of one hundred, seventy-five teenagers in the properly prescribed manner and they were gagging on it, spitting it back at him with a rejection he found both alarming and sad. There was no going back there, ever.

Charles would have explained in intelligence parlance, the only failures were those of planning, of concept. His testing pointed clearly to one thing: to prepare for all possible eventualities. He had now confirmed himself beyond doubt a totally acceptable choice, however randomly that choice had been made originally.

He turned now to look at Charles in the darkened car. Almost as if he'd been reading his thoughts, Charles broke into a faint smile, put his hand on his arm.

"Hey, listen to this," Garrison said, calling their attention to the radio. It was tuned to a newscast.

"...and in a special address to the nation earlier today, the president acknowledged full responsibility for the failure of the rescue attempt to free the hostages in Iran. Several members of the rescue team were killed when one of the helicopters and a support plane collided on the ground in a heavy sandstorm in the Iranian desert. White House sources confirm that..."

"Goddamnit," Garrison roared, smashing his fist on the dashboard. "Who the fuck planned that one?" His jaw was rigid as he angrily snapped off the radio. Storm could only smile in wonder at his outburst. His hostility had all but vanished. Garrison probably regrets not having led the assault on the embassy, he thought.

Charles had said nothing, but his head was bowed slightly, his face, troubled, softly illuminated as the car turned into the main complex and stopped at the guard house. ID's were checked quickly; the car was waved through.

"Let me off here," Garrison said to the driver. He got out, nodded at Storm and Charles, slapped the top of the car with his palm and disappeared into one of the main buildings. The car continued on, finally stopping in front of Storm's quarters.

"Get your things together, Christopher. We'll be staying in town tonight." He paused, all business now. "The arrangements have been confirmed. We'll be flying to..." Charles didn't have to finish the sentence.

Storm packed quickly and took a last look around the room. As an afterthought, he grabbed the book of quotations off the desk and threw it in his bag.

He was back in the car in ten minutes. As it pulled away, he leaned back against the seat and closed his eyes, remembering George Dunne's admonition to find a way out. He had found one but he hadn't expected it to be like this.

He turned to Charles. "There's just one thing, Charles."

"Oh, what's that?" Charles looked at him inquiringly.

"You owe me a dinner."

"Don't worry, Christopher. There are a lot of good restaurants in Moscow."

Eight

One of the most closely guarded secrets in Moscow had nothing to do with espionage except in the most indirect way. The secret concerned a low, rambling two-story building just beyond the city's outer Ring Road. While its purpose was secret, its location was anything but as thousands of Muscovites passed the building every day.

There are no guards, at least none that are visible to the casual observer. They are present nonetheless—handpicked from the KGB's Ninth Directorate and the only men in the Soviet Union allowed to carry weapons near the Party rulers.

Anyone inquisitive enough to follow the long gravel drive from the main access road would be firmly turned away; enquires would be met by terse replies—ample warning to any citizen of Moscow about whatever is housed in the building is strictly off limits to the general public. To pursue the matter further would be inviting investigation and arrest, clearly illustrating one of Moscow's cardinal rules of survival: never go anywhere you're not expected.

Inside the seven-foot high wall, the gray building is surrounded by well-kept gardens, fountains and manicured lawns. There is an almost tranquil air about the place, like an exclusive club. Indeed to Moscow's privileged class, high ranking politburo members, KGB elite and their wives, it is just that. Recreation, however, is not its principal activity.

It began life as the Beria Clinic, named in honor of Lavrenti Beria, personally chosen by Joseph Stalin as the first head of the State Security Service. At that time it was the exclusive domain of the KGB. Its membership spread and expanded to include the Kremlin. It changed names a number of times as various leaders rose and fell out of favor. In recent years, it was known simply as The Clinic—Moscow's most selective and exclusive medical facility.

The staff is comprised of the cream of Moscow's medical

community. The doctors and nurses and other personnel are carefully screened, not only for their excellence in performance of their duties, but for their party loyalty and discretion, prerequisites for any important post in Moscow.

The Clinic has at its disposal the most modern, state-of-the-art equipment and facilities, including a small operating theatre for minor surgery. Premier Alexi Kosygin is reported to have had a boil removed from his backside some years ago. All rooms are tastefully decorated and furnished and include private telephones, color televisions, and if necessary, telex machines and other communications equipment.

When prominent party leaders or officials disappear from the public eye, it's more often than not for a trip to the Clinic. Only the highest ranking are admitted, usually for ailments no more serious than Kosygin's minor surgery, routine physicals or perhaps a much needed rest from the rigors and stress of Soviet political life.

The admittance procedures and restrictions were always strictly adhered to until a certain request was received at KGB headquarters. After careful consideration and review, the Director himself interceded on behalf of the requesting officer to break a long established tradition for the first time.

Colonel Vasili Delnov's request was granted, albeit with certain stipulations, and for the first time in its history, a foreigner—Robert Calvin Owens—was admitted to the Clinic.

It had been argued that Owens' "treatment" could be more properly conducted at the Serbsky Institute of Forensic Psychiatry, a facility of long standing reputation in administering corrective measures to those unfortunate Soviet citizens exhibiting political nonconformity. The principal technique employed by Serbsky's special diagnostic department is chemical therapy, mind shattering drugs such as aminazin, sulfazine and reserpine. With prolonged usage, such drugs render the patient incapable of muscular movement, soar the temperature or simply induce severe depression.

In Owens' case, however, secrecy was of the utmost importance. While the results at Serbsky are impressive, its rooms are crammed with political dissidents and leaks are common. Also, it was not anticipated that Owens would be a difficult patient. It was information, not a change of political thinking which prompted Colonel Delnov to request the Clinic. Finally, its location made it convenient to the city and the estate of *dachas* just outside Moscow. So in the end, the Clinic had won out.

A brilliant choice, Stefan Dolya thought, as his ZiL staff car turned onto the gravel drive and stopped at the guard post. Dolya received a respectful salute, the car was passed through without incident and moments later pulled up in front of the main entrance.

"Wait for me," Dolya instructed the driver. He went inside, nodded curtly to the duty officer and marched down the corridor to Owens's room, amused at the thought of the American occupying a room usually reserved for the First Secretary. It didn't matter, of course. At last report Brezhnev was in the best of health and in any case, Owens' stay would be short. No more than a few days, Delnov had predicted.

Dolya bounded up the stairs to the second floor, wrinkling his nose at the inevitable smells of disinfectant, ether and alcohol permeating hospitals. Delnov's sense of urgency and obsession for success was infectious, he decided, and now in the face of Shevchenko's shocking revelation, totally justified. Far more was at stake than a mere routine exchange.

Dimitri Zakharov's role had abruptly changed from that of a pawn on Delnov's chessboard, an attractive lure, designed to insure credibility for Owens' release, to the most vital part of the operation. Dolya frowned again at the maddening edicts bounding senior officers to the strict compartmentalization of the department, kept them from apprising their counterparts in other sections, often until it was too late.

How could they have known the very last possible choice to dangle before the FBI for such a gambit should be Dimitri Zakharov?

A sleeper case officer, Zakharov had gone undetected for years under his innocuous cover of trade official, but in reality he serviced scores of illegals in America.

And now, he was in the custody of the FBI interrogators. Years of carefully laid groundwork could be swept aside and destroyed in one swift stroke. Was this not an obvious example to argue for more flexibility in the department?

A shift in emphasis, yes, but now a shift in responsibility as well. Failure of the Owens-Zakharov exchange would now be viewed in quite different terms if it was unsuccessful or the Americans had even an inkling of Zakharov's true importance. Before Shevchenko's information came to light, Delnov's scheme would simply have been considered a daring effort with little loss.

Now failure, in addition to the loss of Zakharov, would certainly spell the end of D & D. Dolya shuddered inwardly as he pushed through the door of Owens' room. He didn't want to think about it. By this time tomorrow, everything would be well underway. He was anxious for the play to begin; there had been enough dress rehearsals.

The doctor's presence alarmed him immediately and Owens' inert form on the bed fueled his fears even more. The doctor turned as he came in, a tall gaunt man, who despite his age and height, stooped like an old man.

Dolya's eyes remained riveted on the bed. The covers were drawn back, the stethoscope slid over the exposed chest, the doctor's frowning face expressing concern. It was almost as if the cold instrument were on his own heart, searching for life.

"What is it? What's happened?" Dolya heard the tremble in his voice.

Dr. Sharin removed the stethoscope and straightened up. He shrugged helplessly it seemed to Dolya. "The drugs. I warned you we were working too quickly. He's lapsed into a coma. We've done everything we can for the moment."

Dolya's fear exploded into rage. "A coma? You better bloody well do more than that," he shouted. His eyes flicked to the other man seated beside the bed. "The information, Storm?" The man shook his head slowly. "Is there nothing..." his voice trailed off as he looked again at the doctor.

"We're trying," he said, but Dolya could read the fear in the man's eyes. "He was weak to begin with." He sighed and spread his hands in a despairing gesture.

Dolya looked at Owens. In his mind, he was gazing at his own demise. His voice dropped in pitch, became cold, hard.

"I don't care how you do it, but he has to be fully conscious by tomorrow. Do you hear me? Tomorrow afternoon." He was already reaching for the telephone. "Leave immediately. Both of you." The doctor and the other man hurried out, grateful to escape further wrath.

Dolya held the phone in his hand so tightly, his fingers went white. He stared at Owens. He wanted to grab him, shake him awake. How was he going to tell Delnov that Owens was in a coma? The sessions were due to begin tomorrow.

Storm and the others were arriving within the hour.

Delnov put down the phone and avoided the gaze of the man seated across from him. He was dressed casually in western sports clothes and smoking an American cigarette. His manner was relaxed, almost arrogant, totally at ease, unimpressed to be in the presence of a KGB Colonel. In spite of himself, Delnov felt a momentary stab of displeasure at the man's lack of deference, but quickly reminded himself that this was Dolya's sphere of influence and smiled instead.

"Problems?" the man asked. His eyebrows arched, but his expression was one more of amusement than interest, having overheard the conversation with Dolya.

He's so confident, Delnov thought. "A minor annoyance, nothing more. The idi...our medical consultant overdid it a bit with the drugs. Owens is indisposed for the moment, but Stefan assures me he will recover in time." He paused and gazed steadily at the man. Not a flicker of worry on his face. He wants it this way, Delnov suddenly realized. "Of course, it means your role will be even more important if Owens does not fully recover."

"Don't worry about me," the man snapped. "I can handle Storm with or without Owens." He stubbed out his cigarette in the ashtray.

Delnov flinched again inwardly at the man's insolence. His manner suggested, was it, yes, something more than arrogance. Contempt. It was to be expected, typical of Americans. Delnov had seen it before. Their complacency was maddening.

"Oh, I've no doubts," he said. "And of course it goes without saying, I'm, we are very grateful for your help in this matter." Delnov choked out the words. It took all his will to deliver them.

The man looked up and smiled. "You'd better be. I'm the one who's sticking my neck out, Comrade Colonel," he sneered, obviously enjoying Delnov's discomfort. "I'll probably win the Order of Lenin for you."

"We shall see," said Delnov. "If that happy occasion should arise you will be amply and suitably rewarded. In any case, you'll be safely back in America by that time, eh?" Delnov paused, trying to think of something more to say. "Well, I won't bore you with any last minute party rhetoric or..."

"No, don't. I've heard it all before."

"Yes, of course. Well then, there's nothing more is there? A drink perhaps? A toast to our joint success?"

"Suit yourself." The man shrugged and pointed to the drinks cabinet.

Delnov, seething inside, got up and poured them both a brandy. He knew he couldn't stomach much more of this, however important this man was. He had to get away from him. He returned with the drinks, longing for tomorrow.

"To tomorrow," he said, raising his glass. The man only nodded, ignoring the toast, merely sipping his drink. Delnov paused for a moment, swallowing the insult then downed his drink in a single gulp. He decided he needed an afternoon with Natalya. Yes, she could sooth his nerves.

He stood quickly and gathered up his hat and coat to go. At the door he stopped and looked back at the man once again.

He remained seated, raised his own glass mockingly to Delnov and smiled.

Part of him, as soon as the door of the aircraft was thrown open, wanted to remain in the comfort of his seat, securely strapped in, safe from whatever lay ahead. Several people were already getting to their feet, moving toward the exit, but he found himself unable to move.

"Well, Christopher, welcome to Moscow. No need to hurry," Charles said, as if sensing his uneasiness. "I'm sure we'll have a reception committee."

"No, it's okay. Let's go. I'm ready to stretch my legs a bit after this flight," Storm said, not meaning it. He forced himself to unbuckle the seatbelt and stood up to get his coat from the overhead rack.

He'd been subdued for most of the flight, staring out at the clouds, mulling over the past few days, trying to force his attention on the upcoming meeting with Owens. He tried to brush aside the premonition that something was going to go wrong. Yet it hammered at him, seeping into his consciousness with undeniable sureness. Even as they walked down the steps of the plane, he felt enveloped in an immediate sense of danger he could only relate to another arrival several years before in Vietnam.

After landing in Bien Hoa, just north of Saigon, he'd marched with the other newcomers—twinks the veterans called them—sweat soaked and edgy past a file of old hands headed for home. At Lai Khe and the Charlie Company barracks, he'd stopped before a huge sign emblazoned with the Big Red One of his Division and the Black Lion emblem of his battalion, steeped in tradition and honor on the battlefield since World War I. He'd dropped his bag and stared at the inscription above for a full five minutes: NO MISSION TOO DIFFICULT—NO SACRIFICE TOO GREAT.

He'd felt suddenly alone then, thousands of miles from home, his nineteen-year-old mind on a single thought. What have I gotten myself into?

Now, watching the sign for Sheremetyevo Airport grow larger as they walked across the tarmac, the feeling was the same. This time he was not alone, he reminded himself. There was Charles, they were being met by John Trask. Their arrival was anticipated, and of course, there was Owens. But he could take little comfort from the knowledge. The Viet Cong had been waiting as well.

He'd spent the last night in Washington in a hotel room,

talking until the early hours of the morning with Charles Fox, going over again and again exactly what was expected of him and what he could expect as well from the KGB.

He'd retired then, tossing and turning in a restless sleep, wrestling with the idea he was about to walk into the home ground of what was, according to Charles, the largest most ruthless intelligence agency in the world. By morning he felt like a man who awakens with a pounding hangover and discovers to his horror that somehow, in the previous night's drunken stupor, he's married the whore now sharing his bed.

The confidence, the elation of surviving his test, was false he realized, a creation of his own when confronted with the harsh reality of the present. A mere simulation, artificially contrived with margins for error. Here in Moscow there would be none.

"Smile, Christopher. We're being photographed about now," Charles said, his step jaunty, his manner relaxed, making Storm's uneasiness all the more obvious.

"What?"

"Routine, remember? Nothing to worry about. All passengers arriving on foreign flights are photographed. Bloody cold, eh?"

Storm nodded. Despite himself, he glanced about but could see no cameras. Inside the terminal, the change of temperature was comforting, the closeness of the crush of passengers reassuring. Many of the dark faces were Cubans he guessed, as they flowed along with the crowd to immigration and customs.

"Ah, there's John. He'll soon have us sorted out." Charles waved at a tall lanky figure a little in front of them. He was standing next to another man Storm guessed was about his own age. But his face was cold, hard-set eyes probing like twin microscopes.

Trask waved them over. "Hello, Charles," he said shaking hands. He turned to Storm, holding out his hand. "And of course, you're Chris Storm."

"Hi," Storm said, taking Trask's hand. His eyes flicked to Trask's companion.

"Charles, Chris, this is Major Dolya of the State Security

Services."

"Welcome to Moscow, gentlemen. I hope you had a pleasant flight," he said formally. Charles glanced about as if looking for someone else. Dolya caught his look and said, "Colonel Delnov has asked me to convey his apologies. Another matter has prevented him from meeting you as he had planned. Now, if you'll follow me I'll do what I can to ease your clearance through the formalities."

"That means there'll be no questions," Charles whispered to Storm. Their passports were handed over to the officials who eyed them curiously, but under Dolya's close scrutiny, they were stamped without delay.

Dolya led them outside the passenger lounge to a waiting ZiL sedan. The driver jumped out quickly and opened the doors. Charles, Storm and Trask were ushered into the back seat; Dolya sat up front with the driver.

"Your luggage will be brought along later," Dolya said as they pulled out of the airport onto the wide Leningrad Avenue for the drive into the center of Moscow.

"What are the arrangements, John?" Charles asked, once they were underway.

"You'll bunk with me at the compound. Chris, we've put you up at the Hotel Moskva. Nothing on for you today. Just relax. The hotel is close to Red Square. Maybe do a little sightseeing, huh?"

"Sure," Storm said, "sounds good." He felt a tenseness in his stomach and was not at all sure he liked the idea of being separated from Charles and Trask, but Charles had assured him it was for the best.

On the right they passed a huge reservoir. "The Kimky," Charles said, pointing to the dark gray water.

Dolya turned in the front seat, an amused expression on his face. "You are familiar with Moscow, Mr. Fox?" he asked.

"As a matter of fact, I am," Charles replied. "I'm sure Colonel Delnov must have mentioned it."

Dolya smiled. "Yes, of course, I'd forgotten."

Charles returned his smile. "Please convey my greetings to the Colonel. We go back a long time. I hope I'll be seeing him soon."

"Oh, I'm sure of it." Dolya's expression was icy. He turned his attention back to the road while Charles and Trask exchanged amused glances.

Storm took in the exchange, wondering what it was all about, but was soon absorbed in the unfamiliar city. An enormous football stadium slid past the window as they neared the center of town. Minutes later, the black sedan parked opposite the Hotel Moskva.

A second car appeared behind them. Dolya got out, snapped some orders to the driver of the second car and Storm's bag was taken inside. They followed Dolya into the lobby. While he talked with the desk clerk, Storm gazed around the foyer. It was deserted except for one man on the far side who was seemingly engrossed in a newspaper.

"A little local color," Charles said quietly, following Storm's gaze. "You'll be free to move about, but our friend there will be close by at all times I should think." Storm nodded, remembering Charles had said he would be under constant surveillance while in Moscow.

"Very well," Dolya said, turning back to them. "All is in order. I hope you find your room comfortable, Mr. Storm. Until tomorrow then, gentlemen." He shook hands all around, stopped just short of clicking his heels together and left.

"He's a cool one," Charles said as they headed for the elevator. A bellman led the way with Storm's bag.

"Yeah, Delnov's number two," Trask said. "The new breed of KGB. Moscow University, perfect English, very ambitious and ruthless. If everything hadn't been in order, he'd have had their asses."

Charles chuckled. "He or Delnov. C'mon, Christopher, let's see what your room is like."

They got off the elevator on the seventh floor and passed a matronly woman seated at a table at the end of the corridor. She was positioned so she could see anyone using the elevator or the stairs. One on every floor, Storm remembered.

The room turned out to be large and quite luxurious, with tall windows looking out over Red Square. Storm could see the domes and towers of the Kremlin and at the far end of the square what he guessed was St. Basil's Cathedral.

Turning from the window, he found Trask had dismissed the bellman. "Not bad, eh, Chris?" Charles seemed to be making some kind of cursory search of the room. Trask began to write something on a small pad he'd taken from his coat pocket. He looked at Charles, who just shrugged, then showed Storm what he'd written.

The room is probably bugged—no talk about Owens here, okay?

Storm nodded his understanding then Trask said in what he thought was an overly loud voice, "Okay, we'll leave you to it. Get some rest and we'll be back around seven for some dinner."

"Cheer up, Christopher," Charles said. "You won't be here long."

After they'd gone, he stood before the window again to gaze out at Red Square. There was a long line in front of the Lenin Mausoleum and he could just pick out the tiny figures of the guards.

A little sightseeing, Trask had suggested. Yes, maybe he should just go for a walk. Past the old bitch in the hall, past the inquiring glances of the desk clerk. Would he immediately reach for the phone? And at his heel, the man in the lobby. Or would someone else pick him up away from the hotel? Routine? Who were they kidding?

He stretched out on the bed and stared at the ceiling, but he knew he would not sleep. He was too keyed up. He could imagine the way athletes felt the night before a big game. The difference was after sixty minutes or nine innings they could retire to the showers. Games. The testing at Langley had been games.

He got up, drawn again to the window. He lit a cigarette and inhaled deeply, watching the people in the square warmed by the late afternoon sun. But it was alien, cold and uninviting. That's where it all had begun, Charles had told him. Robert Owens had made his initial contact right there in Red Square.

Well, it won't do any good to sit around here moping, he

thought. He grabbed his coat, locked the door behind him and walked toward the elevator. The woman at the table looked at him, but he ignored her quizzical stare and pressed the down button. When the doors hissed open, he turned and gave her a mock salute, then stepped inside.

Put that in your report: The American left his room at four twenty-six and made a rude gesture. He caught his reflection in the elevator mirror and noticed for the first time since his arrival in Moscow, he was smiling.

"I've got him," Eddie Waters said. "I can feel it."

"Who?" Richard Abrams had been only half listening to his old friend. He was still preoccupied with the previous night's tearful scene with his girlfriend, Monica. She was pregnant, didn't want an abortion and what was he going to do about it?

"The guy I've been interrogating," Waters said, looking up from his steak. He studied Abrams blank expression for a moment before viciously carving into the rare beef again.

They were at a small restaurant not from either the State Department or the FBI where they occasionally lunched together. They had known each other since law school and Waters was counting on an assist from his buddy to get to the bottom of the State Department's delay in releasing Zakharov for a trial date.

His own fishing expedition with the Russian had further convinced him he was hot on the trail of something much bigger, but Zakharov's trial date had to be locked up first. So far though, the lunch had been a failure. Abrams couldn't seem to concentrate. He wasn't getting the gist of Waters' appeal.

"Look, Rich, I know you're busy, but I really need some help on this."

"Sorry, Eddie. Lay it out for me again," Abrams said, sheepishly smiling at Waters. Besides Monica, there was the usual round of State matters to contend with and although months had passed, he was still bristling over his curt dismissal by the CIA on the Zakharov affair.

On further reflection, he disapproved entirely of the announced trade for the American defector. But an ambitious young man in the State Department didn't continue his upward climb by stepping on toes or chiding his superiors so he'd let the matter ride. Abrams was not a maker of waves.

"Okay," Waters continued. "We arrest what looks to be a minor Soviet trade official. Catch him in the act of receiving classified material. We can put him away for life and you guys are dragging your feet, keeping him under wraps. My old West Texas instincts tell me this guy is doing a lot more than selling ball bearings, so I checked him out further." Abrams was nodding in concentration. "Anyway, I put him in San Francisco about '74 or '75. What the hell was he doing out there? Then suddenly he turns up in New York? The Russians don't move people around like that."

Waters had decided not to tell Abrams it was more than his West Texas instincts driving him for Zakharov. An anonymous, special delivery letter with no return address, but instead the name and number of a retired bureau agent in Sonoma County. The agent had confirmed what the letter only hinted at: someone was helping him, wanting him to get Zakharov or just get some information. He was still puzzling over it.

Abrams sipped his wine and mulled over Waters' remarks. Something pricked his consciousness; however, it remained elusive, out of focus. "I don't know, Eddie. I've got my own problems, yet I'll look into it for you. There's probably some logical explanation unless the CIA are involved. *They* don't explain anything," he said frowning. "You tell me for instance, why they want to bring back an American defector and trade him for a top Russian? No questions asked."

Waters angrily sliced off another chunk of steak. "I don't know, but *my* Russian is not going to get away. I've got old Dimitri on the run now and..."

Abrams stopped, his glass midway to the table. "Did you say Dimitri?"

"Yeah, why?"

"Dimitri Zakharov?"

"You do know about it?"

It was Abrams who sighed now. "I won't have to do any checking for you, Eddie. Your Russian and mine are one and the same. You might as well throw in the towel. He's being exchanged for this defector I was talking about, Owens."

"Jesus Christ! When?"

Abrams shrugged. "Any day now. I'm surprised you haven't already got the word."

"Stop it. Delay it. Lose the paperwork, whatever. This clown is into more than buying information, I know it," Waters said, really excited now. The CIA link might explain a lot, but he needed more time.

"I don't think it's possible, Eddie. The decision has already been made. I don't like it either, and if what you say is true, well, it would be a shame to let a big fish get away for a traitor for God's sake."

"Exactly. Give it a shot, huh, Rich? Your best shot."

"What are you going to do?"

"I'm going to reel in Zakharov. If I can dig up enough they won't be able to let him go. Screw the defector. He can stay in Russia."

"Well, John, you're not living too badly here," Charles said, looking around Trask's apartment on the American Embassy compound. It was tastefully decorated and furnished directly from the States.

"It's humble but I call it home," Trask said, pouring them both drinks. They settled down into comfortable chairs.

"Well then, what's the drill?" Charles asked.

"Not the best," Trask admitted. "There wasn't much room for negotiation. Storm will be picked up and taken to the meet with Owens. They're using a *dacha* outside Moscow and we still don't know where they're holding him. I've got a couple of locals working on it. It's a joint operation all the way. We go in separate cars and return to Moscow after each day's session."

Charles nodded, immediately appreciating the advantage enjoyed by the Soviets. Owens could be withdrawn at any time or just not made available if things started to go wrong.

Storm, on the other hand, was exposed, vulnerable, and there wasn't much they could do about it except give him as much protection as possible. Still, if positions were reversed, they would have done it exactly the same way.

"How long do they give us?"

"Five days tops, less if we're lucky. What about Storm? How does he stack up?"

"We put him through some testing at Langley and he held up quite well, though he still seems edgy. That's to be expected, I suppose, given the circumstances. Still, I don't anticipate any problems."

Trask took a long pull on his drink. "We've got a lot riding on the young man."

"Yes, John, indeed we do." Trask looked up at Charles. The blue eyes were twinkling with amusement. Was that irony he detected in Fox's voice?

"Well, you know Delnov better than I do, Charles. What do you think? Will he try any funny stuff?"

Charles' eyes clouded over as the memories washed over him. Prague, the broken network, the Soviet tanks rolling into the city, crushing everything including some of Charles Fox's best people.

"Yes, John. We'll have to be on our guard. Delnov is capable of anything."

"So, Eddie, do we talk about San Francisco again?"

He already knows, the bastard, and he's flaunting it, Waters thought. He got me and he knows it.

The call from Richard Abrams had squashed any hopes he had of hanging onto Zakharov longer. Everything was in the works. There was no stopping the exchange now. He still felt if he could get Zakharov to talk. He sighed.

"No, Dimitri, we'll leave San Francisco. In fact there's not much point in going on is there?"

Zakharov was instantly on guard. "What do you mean?"

"You're going home, old buddy. The Moscow express."

"But why? I mean, I thought..."

"You're being traded, pal, for some creep defector. But

you know what? I think he wants to come home worse than you do."

Zakharov studied Waters closely for a moment, as if trying to detect some trick, some hidden meaning in Waters' words. He got up and walked over to the window. "This defector, he is American?"

"Sure. You don't think we'd trade for a..."

"His name. What is his name?" Zakharov turned, his voice trembling slightly, his face pale.

"Well, I guess you'll know soon enough anyway," Waters said. "Owens. Robert Owens."

Zakharov blanched for a moment, as if he'd had cold water thrown in his face. He smiled thinly, walked back to the table and lit a cigarette. The smile became a chuckle, then a raucous laugh, shaking his whole body until he was nearly hysterical.

Eddie Waters didn't know what to make of it.

The ride out of Moscow was entirely pleasant, Storm had to admit, as was the previous night's dinner with Charles and John Trask. They had eaten in the hotel dining room in an atmosphere of brightly lit opulence while the black suited waiters hovered about the table. Caviar, a ravioli-like dish that Charles said was Siberian, skewered lamb, rice, and at Charles' suggestion, they'd shared a bottle of Georgian wine.

Afterwards, they'd strolled out into the Moscow night, more for the privacy than the exercise, and discussed the arrangement for the first session with Owens. They virtually retraced Storm's steps from his afternoon exploration of Red Square.

He'd been approached several times about changing dollars on the black market and once a student offered to buy all his clothes. He'd just wandered about, getting a feel for the city, oddly exhilarated by the expanse of the great square.

Twice he'd caught sight of his tail, reflected in the frosty glass of the GUM department store and again while he stood with hundreds of others watching the guards at Lenin's tomb, discretely merging with the crowd. After two short walks,

Moscow seemed somehow less intimidating. He'd probed Charles for any sign of apprehension about the coming sessions and found none. If anything, both Charles and Trask seem preoccupied, almost bored.

Now, with the initial confrontation only minutes away, the uneasiness returned to plague him again. What if after all the preparation he wasn't able to positively identify and confirm Owens?

The car wound up into some low hills on a narrow two-lane strip penetrating a birch forest. It was colder here than in the city and there was snow everywhere, covering the ground, clinging to branches, as the last traces of winter hung on with ferocity. This was the landscape of Tolstoy and Pasternak, Storm thought. Not a meeting place for spies.

The car swung off the asphalt road onto a rough track running deeper into the forest. Another twenty minutes brought them to a clearing. A black ZiL was waiting. Across the clearing, Storm could see some kind of cabin, smoke curling up from its chimney. Dolya and another man, twice Dolya's bulk, got out of the ZiL.

"Delnov," Charles said as the car stopped. "Stay here for a minute, Christopher." He and Trask got out of the car to meet the Soviet contingent. Storm could hear their muffled voices. See their breath come in puffs, then Trask's signal for him to join them.

"Colonel Delnov, may I present Christopher Storm," Charles said. Storm's hand all but disappeared in Delnov's.

"I understand you are a teacher, Mr. Storm." Delnov's voice was naturally loud and boomed through the trees.

"Yeah, that's right," Storm said. Where was Owens? He was eager to get on with it and he disliked Delnov instantly.

"We appreciate you taking time off," Delnov said. He nodded to Dolya thus ending of the formalities.

"If you'll follow me," the major said, "I'll accompany you to the *dacha*." Storm's eyes flicked to Charles and found a reassuring look.

"We'll be nearby, Christopher." Storm nodded and started off with Dolya.

They were about a hundred yards from the *dacha*. "You'll

like our *dacha*, Mr. Storm," Dolya said, walking quickly, eyes straight ahead. Their feet crunched on the snow. "The word means simply country house. This one belongs to a retired General who is fortunately out of the country." He might have been a tour group of one, Storm thought, as he followed Dolya into the *dacha*.

Inside it was warm and cozy. Logs blazed in the stone fireplace and two chairs were arranged in front of the fire. Off the main room was a small kitchen. "Everything you will need is here," Dolya said.

Storm nodded. Everything, but Owens. He looked around the room. Near the back door were some worn boots and several heavy jackets hung on pegs. There were cooking smells from the kitchen. It certainly looked lived in but he wondered if it was all for effect.

"Where's Owens?"

Dolya looked at his watch nervously. "He'll be here shortly. If you need anything or wish to terminate the session, just pick up the phone and press the button. It's connected to another building nearby." Dolya paused, briefly looking around. He seemed satisfied. "Well, I think there is nothing more."

Storm stood by the window watching Dolya walk back across the clearing to join the others. Would they all just stand around out there, scuffing the snow while he tried to decide if the man he was going to spend the next few hours or days with was Robert Owens?

A few minutes later, he heard the sound of another car, doors slamming, then footsteps on the porch. The door opened and he saw Robert Calvin Owens for the first time in ten years.

Storm was flooded with childish relief upon recognizing Owens immediately.

Owens stood in the doorway for a second gazing back at him. "Corporal Storm, Company C," he said, shaking his head. He shut the door behind him and pulled off his gloves. "I didn't think I'd see you again."

Storm was unable to reply. Now that the moment was at hand he was speechless.

Owens walked over to the telephone, picked it up, checked the bottom and then set it down on the table again. He picked up the receiver, unscrewed the ear piece, looked inside, then replaced it and shrugged out of his coat. He dropped into one of the chairs in front of the fire, smiling at Storm's puzzled look.

"They promised me we wouldn't be taped and I like to be sure. Well, how's it going, Storm? They tell me you're a high school teacher these days. It took them long enough to get someone here, but I guess you'll do."

Storm was momentarily thrown. The face was the same, aged of course, ten years, maybe more. But the voice, the breezy manner somehow didn't fit with the unsure lieutenant he'd known in Vietnam. Nor was it the persona of a repentant defector.

He was prepared for the inevitable awkwardness of two strangers who have nothing in common but a briefly shared experience from the past. He had visualized a scenario in which they gradually became reacquainted, talked over old times and then finally got down to the business at hand. Yet Owens seemed almost irritated by his presence and Storm was suddenly struck with the notion he'd studied, learned his lines, but had somehow rehearsed for the wrong play.

Amused, Owens took in his stare, as if reading his thoughts. "Yeah, it's me alright. People do change you know." He looked away, then back again, not bothering to mask his impatience. "Well, you did come to identify me, right? So let's get started." Owens irritation seemed to grow with Storm's reluctance to speak because he simply didn't know where to begin.

"Look, Storm, didn't they fill you in on everything?"

"Well, not exactly. I mean, I don't know."

"This is just a formality for those clowns out there." Owens jerked a thumb toward the door. "We've got to make it look good for them, okay? But let's not waste a lot of time with dumb questions about who won the World Series last year." Owens managed a smile. "Anyway, it's been awhile since I've seen a ball game."

"I don't understand. I thought..."

"Oh c'mon, Storm. I don't know what they told you, but you must have at least figured out I'm CIA. Those aren't boy scouts out there. Look, I've got a headful of information I have to get back to Washington with what couldn't be written down. And all spies, contrary to popular belief, do not carry Minox cameras. I got some out with a dissident organization via Israel, but that route has dried up. So now, I have to go in person." He paused, trying to read Storm's expression. "You understand now? My head is crammed with vital information and I don't want it cluttered up with a lot of Mickey Mouse games."

Storm sat down, never taking his eyes off Owens, trying to recall voice inflection, attitude, but it was impossible, like distinguishing shapes in fog. It was what Owens was saying that bothered him. Something was terribly wrong.

"Wait a minute," he said, feeling a glint of understanding cut through Owens' remarks. "I get it now. Throw me off balance with this fast line of chatter and I'll be so convinced I'll forget I'm supposed to confirm who you say you are. Nice try, but you'll have to do better than that."

Owens sighed and rolled his eyes upward, exasperated, as if his patience was being tried by an obstinate child. He stood up and turned to face Storm in front of the fireplace. "Christ, who have they sent me? No, Storm, that is not it. Don't you know? Don't you really know?" He stared at Storm for a long moment, breathing deeply, as if realizing some final truth. "No, I guess you don't."

"Know what? What are you talking about?"

"What did they tell you?" Owens voice had grown quieter now.

"Just that you had defected and were coming back and they needed someone to verify your identity." Storm stopped, the realization taking hold.

Owens nodded. "Yeah, I guess it figures. Their need to know policy and besides it makes you more convincing."

"You mean it's...?"

"You got it. My defection was a setup, arranged from the beginning. Staged. Phony. Now do you understand? I've been a double agent all this time."

Nine

Eddie Waters picked his way along Constitution Avenue, oblivious to the lunch time crowd jostling and propelling him toward the Federal Building. He'd grabbed a quick sandwich and decided to bury himself in paperwork for the afternoon. A last ditch attempt to quell his depression with innocuous details.

Waters had made one final attempt to get Richard Abrams to intercede on his behalf, but it had been no go. Dimitri Zakharov was being returned to Moscow without delay and Waters was left with a briefcase full of virtually useless interrogation transcripts, and no doubt destined for the bureau's voluminous files, unearthed perhaps one day in the next century. Another iron-clad case which will never see a courtroom. Whatever else Zakharov had been involved in was lost forever.

Waters was still smarting from what he could only consider his failure with Zakharov. He was still haunted by the Soviet's almost hysterical laughter and parting comment. "Goodbye, Eddie," Zakharov had said. "It's been nice knowing you."

Waters stopped in front of the FBI Building and stared up at the sky. He wondered if Zakharov had already left. It was supposed to be sometime today. He shook his head and plodded up the steps, cursing the very bureaucracy he worked for.

"Excuse me, young man." A delicate hand touched Waters' sleeve. He turned and saw a small, rather frail looking woman with a lined face. "I'm looking for the FBI," she said.

"This is the FBI, ma'am," Waters said. He pointed to the huge letters over the entrance.

She seemed genuinely surprised. "Oh, yes, how stupid of me." Her face broke into a smile. "Well, I want to talk with one of the special agents." She said the words as if she'd been rehearsing them. "Do you work here?"

"Well, yes, but..."

"Oh, good. Isn't that lucky? I have to talk to someone right away." She gazed at Waters, her eyes pleading for assistance. They had the desired effect on Waters. He softened immediately.

"Well, there are hundreds of agents here, ma'am. Maybe we should check with information. They can direct you to the right department. I'll show you where it is."

"Thank you," she said, obviously relieved. She took Waters arm as they went inside.

Waters flashed his ID and vouched for the woman. A guard searched her handbag quickly and winked at Waters. Inside he guided her to the information directory.

"They'll take care of you here, ma'am. Just tell them your business and who you want to see, okay? Bye." He gave her a quick wave and escaped to the bank of elevators. Now what does she want with the FBI? he mused. Probably thinks they'll take her to see Efrem Zimbalist, Jr.

He got out on his floor and went to his office. "No calls, Julie. I'm bushed," he said to his secretary. He went into the small cramped office he shared with another agent. Its only good point was the view of the street below.

He dropped into a chair and stared out at the traffic for several minutes. He was about to start work on a stack of files when the intercom buzzed.

"Yes, Julie."

"Sorry, Mr. Waters, but there's a woman here to see you."

"Julie, I thought I told you no calls. I..."

"Yes, I know but she's insistent. Directory sent her up. She says she knows you. What should I do?"

Christ, the old lady. Serves me right for being a boy scout, Waters thought. He sighed wearily. He was trapped and might as well get it over with. "Okay, Julie, send her in."

Moments later Julie accompanied the old lady into Waters' office and settled her in a chair opposite him. "My," she said, looking around, "you certainly don't have a lot of room do you?"

From behind her, Julie winked at Waters and backed out of the office.

"No, I guess not. Now look, Mrs...."

"Well, I had to talk to someone didn't I? I didn't know anyone here, but you." She clutched her handbag tightly. "It's about my son, you see. He hasn't been home for some time now and..."

Why me? Waters thought . "Ah, excuse me, ma'am, but if your son is missing I think you want the police. They handle missing persons reports."

"My son is not missing. I know exactly where he is. Oh, here. This will explain everything." She took a small package out of her handbag and put it on Waters desk.

Waters gazed at the package for a moment. It was about three inches by five inches and wrapped in brown paper. He opened it and found what appeared to be a stack of postcards. Puzzled, he shuffled through the pack, but they appeared to be all the same.

"I don't understand," he said, wondering what bizarre incident he had let himself in for. There were forty or fifty cards in the pack, judging from its size and most contained the same message: a dutiful son's remembrance to his mother. He looked through them again, thinking he had missed something. Then his eye caught the post mark.

"These are from Russia."

"Well, of course they are," the old lady said. "That's where my son is. Oh, I forgot the letter." She took out a well-folded letter. It too had a Russian post mark. "That's why I came to the FBI," she said. "The police don't find missing persons in Russia, do they?"

"No, I suppose not," Waters said, wilting under her logic. He unfolded the letter. It was heavily creased from repeated readings. As Waters began to read, the color drained from his face.

He read it through, then scanned it again with growing incredulity. He looked up at the woman who seemed lost in thought. There was a sadness about her eyes he hadn't noticed before. "Who's Max?"

"What? Oh, Max was my son's dog. A beautiful

Labrador." She shook her head. A wisp of hair fell over her face. "He was hit by a car last year and I haven't had the heart to tell him."

"And you've been writing to him all this time?" Waters mind was reeling. It was incredible. Just walks in here off the street. He hardly heard her as she rambled on about the dog and the letters that came like clockwork.

"Sorry, Robert? And your name, your son's name is?"

"Owens. Mrs. Mildred Owens."

Storm guessed they'd been talking for over an hour now. Despite his initial misgivings, he had to admit he hadn't found a flicker of fraudulence about the man next to him who claimed to be Robert Owens. And why should there be?

Why? Why hadn't they told him what to expect? Instead he comes in and looks like a complete fool, parading his ignorance, confessing his total surprise. They hadn't needed him for anything more than a prop.

Storm had taken Owens' revelation like a sudden glancing blow that had rendered him defenseless, softened only by Owens' seemingly logical explanation. "Believe me, Storm," he'd said. "The less you know the better." He was probably right.

And now, their conversation, strained by the knowledge only Owens possessed, contained not the slightest suspicion, cast not the faintest doubt Owens was exactly who he said he was. So why am I withholding complete approval? Storm asked himself.

They had barely touched on Vietnam and Owens was incredible. Storm prided himself on his own memory, especially on Nam, but Owens must have total recall. He reeled off the names in Company C like it was only yesterday. What had he said earlier about a head full of information? Owens probably didn't *need* to write anything down. It was perfect, perhaps too perfect?

No, don't start that again. Was he Owens or wasn't he? Of course he was. Storm couldn't tell if the tiny fragments of doubts nagging him were due to real misgivings or were simply brought about by his anger rising and falling like a roller coaster. A response to what? A lack of trust? Humiliation? This was no good. He had to get away, get things in perspective, start again fresh.

His mind suddenly flashed on a college Shakespeare class. They were reading *Hamlet* and the professor had spent the entire first class hammering away at the first line of the play: "Who's there?" It was the key to the characters, he'd said.

The phone on the table broke the silence suddenly. Owens got up to answer it and after speaking in Russian for several minutes, hung up. He turned to Storm almost apologetically. "They suggest we call it a day and start again tomorrow."

Storm nodded, grateful for the reprieve. He wanted time to think, talk to Charles. "Where did you learn to speak Russian like that?" It had sounded flawless to Storm although he had no way of knowing. He was grasping at straws, he realized.

Owens shrugged. "Hey," he said. "I have been here five years." He indicated the door. "They want you first. See you tomorrow, huh?"

"Yeah, sure." Storm paused at the door. "Look, just for my own satisfaction, so I don't feel completely useless, let's talk about Nam some more, okay?" He watched Owens' eyes, assessing them for suspicion or reluctance, but found neither. "I mean you did say we have to at least go through the motions so we can't just sit here and stare at each other."

"Sure, why not? What specifically about Nam?"

"Oh, I don't know, the guys, how they're doing." He was stalling trying to dredge up some small point that would unquestionably prove Owens was genuine. He wondered if Owens was aware. "Hey," he said suddenly. "What about Julie and the Holiday Inn?"

Again Owens face was impassive. "Yeah, whatever. See you tomorrow then. Oh, and Storm, I'm...sorry about all this. I really am. You not knowing, I mean."

"Forget it. You're probably right. The less I know the better." But I do know about Julie and the Holiday Inn, he thought as he walked quickly back across the clearing, and Robert Calvin Owens, you had better know too. He glanced back once, over his shoulder. He could see Owens at the window watching his departure.

They were waiting almost as he'd left them. Delnov, towering over Dolya, Charles puffing on his pipe. John Trask and the embassy car were gone.

"John had to go back to the city unexpectedly," Charles said, before Storm could ask. Seeing Charles refueled his anger, although he realized suddenly he had never once directed it at Owens. "The Colonel and Major Dolya will drive us back."

Storm nodded, relieved the conversation on the return trip not only would be unnecessary but unwise, although he was betting they were eager for a first report.

"Did you find it strange to meet an old friend after so many years?" Delnov asked politely as they got in the car.

"We were never friends," Storm said, sitting in the back seat with Charles. Let them figure out what that means, he thought, as they pulled away and drove back to the main road.

The ride back seemed shorter until they neared Moscow. The traffic was heavy, but they had almost a clear way down the center of the wide boulevards in a lane obviously reserved for VIP traffic.

They pulled into the parking area near the hotel and Storm got out quickly. He wanted to avoid Charles, at least for the moment. Although the car was unmarked, he noted the hotel staff and passersby seemed to avoid coming near it.

"Wait a minute, Christopher," Charles said. He conferred briefly with the two Russians while Storm waited aimlessly under the portico. Then the car roared off, merging with traffic.

"Well, Christopher," Charles said.

Storm looked away, across Red Square. There was another long line in front of Lenin's tomb.

"He's as American as I am," Storm said.

He left Charles standing in front of the hotel and went to his room.

***

He had persuaded, pleaded, cajoled, even called in all his old favors but he'd made it. Just barely by the look of the boarding gate at Kennedy Airport. Eddie Waters flashed his badge at the attendant, along with his boarding pass and jogged down the now empty tube connecting the terminal to the waiting jumbo jet bound for Moscow. The last passenger was just passing a smiling hostess as he reached the door of the plane.

Again he held up his badge and boarding pass. The flight attendant went ashen-faced. Waters read her expression and it said, bomb scare? Hijack? She glanced nervously over her shoulder to the cockpit where the crew were doing their preflight check.

"No problem, Sue," Waters said, smiling as he read off her name tag. "You've got two men in first class accompanying a Soviet citizen and I have to see one of them. Sorry for the delay. Slight last minute change of plan."

Sue was visibly relieved. "Which one?"

"O'Hara. Could you tell him to come back here, please?"

She nodded and disappeared into the cabin and returned a minute later with a young, red-haired man in a dark suit.

"What gives, Waters? We're taking off in a few minutes."

"Not you, Kevin. You lucked out." Waters handed him an official looking paper, which O'Hara scanned quickly and looked up at Waters.

"Why the switch?" The disappointment in his eyes was clear to Waters, but that was the breaks.

"Search me," he said innocently. "I was just told to relieve you."

O'Hara's shoulders slumped. A trip to Moscow didn't come along every day. "Okay," he sighed. "Let me get my things." He left Waters to retrieve his coat and carry-on bag.

Waters glanced in the cockpit at the mass of dials and switches as the crew pored over the checklist. The pilot looked up at Waters and took off his headset. "Problems?"

"No, just a change in the detail accompanying the Russian." The pilot nodded and returned to his tasks.

"Some guys get all the luck," O'Hara said when he returned. "At least bring me a bottle of vodka, huh?"

"Will do. How's our boy?"

"Quiet, real quiet. You wouldn't think he was going home and beating a long prison rap. I'll never understand the Russians."

"Don't let it worry you, Kevin. Nobody does." O'Hara nodded almost sadly and started back up the ramp into the terminal.

"Will you take your seat please?" Sue had returned now and they were ready to get underway. "We're almost ready for takeoff. Your friend was in 4C."

"My pleasure, Sue, and you can bring me a tall bourbon as soon as we're up." Waters walked down the aisle, nodded to Karl Evans, the other agent assigned to the flight, and slid into his seat next to Zakharov.

"How you doin', Dimitri, old pal?" He smiled at the Russian as he buckled his seat belt.

Zakharov turned from the window in shock. "You?"

"Exactly. I couldn't let you go all the way to Moscow without saying goodbye now, could I?" Zakharov turned back to the window. The doors slammed shut and the giant engines whined to life.

With Robert Owens' letter to his mother, another piece of the puzzle fell into place. He began to understand Zakharov's laughter now. All he had to do was get Zakharov to confirm his suspicions.

Zakharov and Owens were connected. But how? Eddie Waters had about eight hours to find out.

Colonel Vasili Delnov rewound the tape on the small recorder for the third time, then pressed the play button. His eyes squinted in concentration as if the action would enable him to hear more clearly. He gripped his lighter tightly as the voice came over the tape.

"You got it. My defection was a setup, arranged from the beginning. Staged. Phony. Now, do you understand? I've been a double agent all this time."

Even with the poor quality of the recorder, Storm's sharp intake of breath was audible. It was followed by a long silence.

"Well, Stefan?" Delnov looked inquiringly at Dolya seated across from him. They were back in Delnov's Dzerzhinsky Square office. They had been reviewing the tape for over an hour, poring over each and every sentence.

"What is it you want me to say?" The tape assured Dolya, comforted him like a warm blanket on a cold night, but Delnov seemed to want more stroking, even if it was Dolya who could rightfully claim the success.

"The truth."

"I think there's no question. Storm's reaction is proof enough." He knew he was right. Sokolov's performance had been superb and Storm, being untrained, confused, had no reason to doubt him.

"Let us hope you are right, Stefan. On the whole, I agree, but as the Americans say, we're not home free yet."

Dolya started to protest. "But surely, I mean Zakharov is already on the way." He was fully confident that after one more session, Storm would make the verification without question. Hadn't Trask already ordered Zakharov's departure? The exchange would proceed as planned.

Dimitri Zakharov for Mikhail Aleksandrovich Sokolov. A better bargain could not be struck.

Delnov continued to shake his head. He ran the tape forward this time, stopping and starting it until he found a particular passage. "This last part bothers me," he said, depressing the play button. "Yes, here." They listened in silence to the last part of the conversation. "There," Delnov exclaimed. "This reference to Julie, the Holiday Inn. It's the first we've heard of it." He looked again at Dolya for confirmation.

Dolya masked his impatience. "Nothing to worry about. A girl, a hotel, Owens is conscious again and holding up nicely. Storm is just covering himself." Dolya was irritated. He wanted to get away. What did the man want? They'd done it. But yet, he felt a strange chill of apprehension gripping him, as if Delnov had voiced his own thoughts. Something could still go wrong. He found Delnov staring at him. His own resolve seemed to crumple under his gaze.

"You're right, of course. I'll see Owens tonight and determine the significance of the girl, the hotel. I'll take care of it."

Delnov smiled faintly. "Yes, Stefan, do that." He ejected the cassette and pushed it across the desk.

"Do we let them go outside?" Dolya asked, pocketing the tape. Fox had made the suggestion, arguing continuous confinement in the *dacha* would stretch already taut nerves.

Delnov frowned. "I don't like it, but we're this close; we can't afford to arouse suspicion at this point, can we?"

"No," Dolya agreed quickly, glad again it was Delnov's decision.

Delnov pushed his hulk back from the desk and stood up. "Study the tape again, Stefan. We must cover every possibility. We will make a token protest over leaving the *dacha*. Fox would expect at least that, then we will reluctantly agree. We can't monitor the session in the open, but..." He spread his hands.

"As you wish," Dolya said. There had been no other mention of Charles Fox and he was glad of it. A private feud would only hinder judgment.

They were, Dolya reflected, almost home free.

Charles stood gazing out over the gardens of the American compound. From the window of John Trask's apartment, he could just make out the guard post. The wide boulevard of Kutuzovsky Prospekt ran in front of the compound housing diplomats, embassy personnel and foreign newspaper correspondents. Charles raised his eyes from the traffic to the Hotel Ukraina across the boulevard.

"There's something I have to tell you, Charles," Trask said, joining him at the window. The radio was on in the background, playing music with the volume turned up high. "Zakharov is en route to Moscow with an FBI detail." Trask paused, trying to detect some flicker of interest, but found none.

"That's a bit premature isn't it, John? Or do you have that much faith in young Storm?"

Trask looked away. "They have a stopover in Frankfurt so we're not completely committed, but there's more to it." He paused again, yet still there was no reaction from Charles. Suddenly Trask realized Charles had known all along. "I don't have to tell you, do I?"

Charles turned to look at him as if for the first time. "What? That Owens' defection was arranged from the beginning? No, John. You don't. I must confess though I didn't know at first."

"How did you find out?"

"I always suspected it, but when I talked to the security man at Triton, Highlands, it became quite clear. He said, 'the only thing the Russians don't have is one of their own, right here in one of these companies.' That would be ideal, of course, if we could pull it off. You seem to have done just that. Owens' defection is staged. Moscow welcomes him with open arms and gives him carte blanche at Zelenograd, their own Silicon Valley. We have a man on the inside. Quite clever really, but I suspect getting him out again was your main concern."

Trask nodded. "There were contingency plans," he admitted, "but I'm afraid not very well thought out. We were counting on the Soviet's eagerness to accept a defector like Owens, but we got carried away. Getting someone out is always harder than getting them in." Trask busied himself with lighting a cigarette. "Look, Charles, I'm sorry about this. I told McKinley we'd never put it over on you, but he wouldn't listen. Convincing performances from all was the way he put it."

Charles nodded understandingly. "Don't be hard on yourself, John. You had no choice. I would have done the same in your place." He looked out over the courtyard again. "One thing still bothers me though."

"What's that?"

"That Moscow is willing to just let Owens walk away."

Trask shrugged. "We're giving them Zakharov. You know how they are about getting their own people back and Zakharov is certainly no loss to us. Owens is ten times more valuable."

"Still," Charles said, "they must have some safeguard. Perhaps Owens has been turned."

"No, I think that's a long shot. The main thing is we're getting Owens back, the real Owens. From what you say, Storm is already convinced. That's really why I okayed Zakharov's departure."

"Yes," Charles murmured. "The real Owens."

"What?"

"Sorry, John. Just thinking out loud."

Back in his room, Storm was surprised he'd heard nothing more from Charles. He'd eaten dinner alone and now that he'd gone over everything, he wanted to confront Charles. He'd decided to have one last go at Owens tomorrow and then let it go. He paced around the room for another fifteen minutes then left word at the front desk he was going for a walk. Charles could find him if he wanted.

He left the hotel and walked across Red Square. It seemed familiar now, he thought, pausing in front of GUM with other aimless wanderers to gaze at the great department store's shabby fashion displays. The queue in front of the Lenin Tomb had long since dispersed, leaving only the guards in front of the bronze doors. He continued walking across the square, past St. Basil's Cathedral, thinking again how it looked like something out of Disneyland. The wind was icy now as it swirled around the Kremlin walls. He regretted not having a heavier coat.

He paused on the Moskvoretsky Bridge to light a cigarette, then leaned over the railing to peer down at the dark, cold water. The occasional couple passed, holding hands, laughing, absorbed in each other, hardly giving him a second glance.

He wondered what Valerie was doing in Las Vegas, suddenly unable to imagine two more contrasting cities. Valerie, Danny, school, they would all have to be faced when he returned.

He turned away from the water and pulled up the collar of his coat around his neck and decided to start back to the hotel when he saw a bulky figure coming toward him. The bridge seemed suddenly deserted. He could hear footsteps on the pavement. The figure drew closer and stopped.

"Christopher?"

Despite himself, he set out a sigh of relief. I'm not cut out for this stuff, he thought.

"A bit cold for a stroll, isn't it?" Charles asked.

"For a minute I thought you were..."

"Ah, yes, your constant companion. No, he's waiting at the other end of the bridge."

With Charles at hand, Storm felt his anger rekindled. "Why didn't you tell me?"

Charles sigh was almost inaudible. "There's no reason you should believe me, Christopher, but I only found out myself tonight. Shall we go back? I think a brandy is in order."

They began to walk slowly back across the bridge. "What was the plan? Send me to identify Owens when you already knew it was him. He was right wasn't he? This is all just for the Russians' benefit isn't it?"

"Is that what he told you? Not entirely. We still wanted positive identification in any case," Charles said. "Your role is still important."

"Yeah, sure." He couldn't discard the feeling that somehow he had been cheated.

Charles stopped and looked at him. "You are quite sure, Christopher?"

"Like I said before, he's as American as I am." Storm turned away, avoiding Charles' gaze, as if he'd answered too quickly. He wasn't sure. Not yet. When he dared look at Charles again, he found only his gently mocking smile, making him think suddenly he'd gone too far. Goddamnit, it is Owens isn't it? he wanted to shout.

"We'll see again tomorrow, Christopher."

On flight 479 to Moscow, the lunch trays had been cleared away, coffee served and the curtains drawn across the windows. The cabin lights were dimmed and moments later, the feature film flashed on the screen in front of the yawning passengers.

At least two of them were not succumbing to the after meal drowsiness and dull drone of the jet engines. Eddie Waters was one and even he had failed to notice the other—a dark swarthy man two rows behind him and Dimitri Zakharov.

No one, in fact, had taken any notice of the man. He was merely one of the several Russians on the flight, but he was the only one trained and highly skilled in the art of assassination.

Eddie Waters also failed to notice the man slip into an empty seat behind him fifteen minutes after the movie had begun. Waters was too busy to notice anything.

Zakharov had been morosely silent since leaving New York and Waters had wisely elected not to press him. Not too soon. The Russian, he knew, was wary of his sudden and unexpected appearance and passed the time munching the tasteless meal, confining his answers to Water's innocuous questions with muffled grunts. Despite the length of the flight and the scheduled stopover in Frankfurt, Waters had precious little time. He had to know before Moscow.

He glanced at the Russian and found hooded eyes staring back at him. They both had headsets on but neither was interested in the film. "It's a good one," Waters said, pointing to the screen. He wanted to smile, but Zakharov's expression stopped him. "Might be your last look at western decadence," he joked.

"I've seen it," the Russian said curtly. "What do you want? Why did you come?"

Waters rolled his head on the seat toward Zakharov. "Well, Dimitri, the way I see it, we couldn't have a better place to talk for the last time, and anyway, it couldn't hurt to tell me now, could it?"

"Tell you what?" Instinctively the Russian moved his head closer to Waters.

Behind them, the swarthy man pushed the headphones up over his ears and leaned slightly forward to the gap in the seats.

"Well, for starters," Waters said, "why do you think it's so funny that you're being traded for Owens?"

"That, Eddie, is a long story," Zakharov said. He studied Waters in the dim light. "What difference does it make now? Your case is finished and I'm going free."

"Are you?"

Zakharov looked away. There would be denunciations in Moscow, even with Shevchenko's protection. By anyone's view, he had failed and failures were not tolerated in Moscow. But he had served well. With any luck, he would be retired or allowed to teach. There were many who could benefit from his experience, having played the game in America for five years.

Zakharov had been baffled by Delnov's order to court the Navy Lieutenant, Hopkins. Were Delnov and Shevchenko working together? He had never questioned it, not officially. Orders from Moscow were never questioned. He had simply carried them out and succeeded, perhaps too well. But he had never jeopardized or revealed his true mission. Would Moscow believe that? He had been in FBI hands for nearly two months. What did it matter what he told Waters now? He had been treated well and he liked Waters despite himself.

"This man you're getting back, Eddie, this Robert Owens. Be careful of him."

"Yeah? What do you know about Owens?" Waters tensed, all his senses alert.

"He's mine, Eddie. Owens is mine. I recruited him."

"So where do we begin?" Owens asked. Some of his confident manner of the previous day seemed to have dissipated. He watched Storm now almost suspiciously, on guard, as if he might be tricked into saying something he didn't want.

"Might as well stick to Nam," Storm said casually. He had searched his mind for some tiny detail, some long forgotten event that would leave no doubt whatsoever that the man he now shared a *dacha* with was the same he had shared the dusty trails and humid jungles of Vietnam with.

When he'd suggested Julie and the Holiday Inn, it had been a spur of the moment idea, popping into his mind unexpectedly, one of a thousand fragments that made up the Vietnam experience. Now, on further reflection, he knew deep down he didn't want this man not to be Owens. The further questioning he realized was only for his own satisfaction.

To throw Owens off guard, he even brought up the disastrous ambush when Owens called in mortar fire on their own unit and left them pinned down by friendly fire. But strangely enough, Owens seemed not at all timid about talking about it, accepting his guilt, his mistakes with an equanimity Storm found difficult to understand.

Storm had not mentioned Mike Savage's angry attempt on Owens, nor his own intervention. Finally, there was nowhere to go but Julie. They'd been talking for over an hour and the subject was nearly exhausted.

"So what about Julie?" Storm asked.

"What about her?" Storm turned away quickly to light a cigarette, trying to conceal his astonishment, behind a cloud of smoke. When he turned back, he caught Owens watching him, gauging it seemed to Storm, if he had made the correct response.

"Well, anything," Storm said.

"You are talking about the Julie in the Happy Bar, in Tachikawa?"

Had there been a Julie in a bar? Storm himself couldn't remember. There were hundreds of girls and bars just beyond the gates of the huge airbase in Japan who had welcomed thousands of GI's to and from Vietnam.

Storm smiled. "Was there any other?"

Owens seemed to relax immediately. "Yeah, she was really something, eh?" He shook his head. "I did some weird things over there. Christ, I was so drunk sometimes I can hardly remember. I remember Julie though. Everybody must remember Julie."

Storm nodded. He remembered, too. Blotting out the horrors of Nam with booze and pot was not unusual, it was the norm, especially if you were headed home. But Storm's Julie was not a girl in a bar.

"I wasn't thinking of that Julie," he said. "Another one. Can't put my finger on it though." He kept his face impassive.

Owens spread his hands. "Search me. She's the only one I can remember." He got up and went into the kitchen, returning with a beer. "What about the Holiday Inn? You mentioned that yesterday. I know at least one of those bars was named after the hotel chain, but I can't remember if it was in Tachikawa or Saigon."

"No, the bar was called the Hilton and it was in Saigon. I'm thinking of the Holiday Inn. Don't know why I can't get those two out of my mind. Julie and the Holiday Inn."

Storm was on sure ground now, but felt like a man trying to get his best friend to admit to something he already knew was true.

Owens sat down again. "Well, I guess I fail the test, right?" He smiled and handed Storm a beer.

Storm put down the bottle and stared at Owens. "Yes, I guess you do because there's no way you'd ever forget those two."

Owens looked around the room as if searching for something. Storm, puzzled, followed his gaze, but saw nothing.

"Wait a minute," Owens exclaimed. "Of course, now I know what you're talking about." His expression didn't match his voice. He was merely groping, Storm knew, out of his depth. He continued to speak rapidly, as if trying to impress Storm with his knowledge, like a student reciting for his teacher while knowing all the time he's answering the wrong question.

Finally Owens said, "How about a walk around the lake?"

The room was claustrophobic now, heavy with the odor of lies and deceit. They would be observed, naturally, they were told when Owens called for permission, but it was to be allowed.

Storm was relieved, but he could only guess at the man's motives, whoever he was. For Storm knew now as surely as he knew his own name.

This man was not Robert Owens.

Ten

The inflight movie was finished, the stewardesses were serving last drinks and coffee before preparing for the descent of flight 479 into Frankfurt. The passengers yawned, stretched, replaced shoes over swollen feet and joined the lines outside the lavatories.

The swarthy man had returned to his own seat. He was already formulating his plans for the one-hour layover in Frankfurt. After overhearing the quiet often tense monologue of Dimitri Zakharov, he had no doubts immediate action would be required once he'd reported to his contact on the ground. First, however, he would have to neutralize the other agent accompanying Zakharov. It was a minor annoyance, and one he could easily manage.

"More coffee, sir?" The stewardess tilted toward him invitingly, her face masked in an obligatory smile. He watched her name tag rise as her blouse stretched tautly over her breast. He hadn't been with a woman for a long time, he reminded himself. That too he would manage easily.

"Yes, thank you." He sipped the hot black liquid pensively and stared out the window. The rooftops of Frankfurt began to appear through the clouds. He wondered if an hour would be enough time. A delay would be most welcome he decided.

Once on the ground, he quickly spotted his quarry and led him to the bookstall in one corner of the noisy transit lounge. It was crammed with weary travelers and bored children, shouting above the snatches of conversation and announcements on the public address system.

At the bookstall, he bought a copy of the *Frankfurter-Zeitung* and retired to a far corner of the lounge, taking one of the empty plastic seats. Moments later, Oleg Lensky slipped into a seat near him.

"Trouble?" he asked, noting the newspaper. If the swarthy man had bought a magazine, Lensky would have ignored him.

He much preferred it that way. Lensky knew the swarthy man only by reputation.

"Perhaps," he intoned, seemingly intent on the sports pages. "Comrade Zakharov has become rather talkative with his companion. Moscow must be notified at once. Use your discretion, but..."

"I understand," Lensky said. "I'll return to the center now. Listen for a page—call for Herr Gruber."

The swarthy man nodded. Before he looked up, Lensky was already heading for the exit. He continued to scan the paper. The Moscow leg of the flight would be delayed now. He was sure of it.

"What's the matter, Karl? You don't look so good." Eddie Waters looked at Karl Evans with growing concern as the FBI man sipped from a bottle of mineral water and rubbed his stomach. Waters found himself with no appetite, but Zakharov was busy with a meaty sandwich and fried potatoes.

"I don't know," said Evans, grimacing. "Think it was the coffee on the plane. I should know better with my stomach." His face was nearly white. Suddenly, his eyes widened. "I'll be back in a minute." He rushed out of the coffee shop in search of the men's room.

"Your friend is not well?" Zakharov asked. He poked at the pile of French fries, arranging them neatly before spearing one with his fork.

Waters was intent on Evans disappearing figure. "Huh? Oh, he'll be okay. Just a little indigestion."

Waters wasn't worried. Not yet. Even if it was something serious he could handle Zakharov alone, although the detail specifically called for two agents. His mind raced backed over the conversation on the plane. If Zakharov continued the purge of his soul, as he called it, he would really have something to tell the CIA boys in Moscow. It might even change their plans about handing the Russian over. He guessed Zakharov's ramblings were probably only due to his belief the order was irrevocable. He glanced at his watch.

"Eat up, Dimitri. They'll be calling the flight in a few minutes."

At the counter, the swarthy man had watched Karl Evans hasty departure, satisfied the fast acting capsule had done its work and confident the FBI man would not be continuing on flight 479 to Moscow. About now he would be heaving his guts out and in another few minutes, pleading for a doctor.

He finished a slice of black forest cake, paid his check and wandered back into the lounge again to wait near the bank of courtesy telephones. He took in the departures board and what he saw made him breathe easier. Mentally, he congratulated Oleg Lensky.

Flight 479 was delayed one hour.

They walked from the clearing under Major Dolya's watchful eye, along a path through the birch forest. Snow clung to some of the branches; the lake was like crystal shimmering in the faint sunshine.

"The trail circles the lake," Dolya said, facing the two men. "It's a good hour walk, but of course..." His voice trailed off. It was not necessary to remind them that positioned around the lake at various points were several of his men.

Dolya left them, turning back toward the *dacha* after what seemed to Storm, one last cautioning glance. They would be alone but watched the entire time. They walked slowly at first, picking their way through the overgrowth on the trail, grateful for the fresh air, each wondering where or how to begin. A final scene which had to be played out to its conclusion.

It was Dolya who had conceived the Owens persona, carefully calculating as an untrained participant, his confusion would be compounded by a brash irritating manner. They had prepared well, draining Owens of all pertinent information about his service in Vietnam, first with simple interrogation, later with drugs, and finally, laboriously again when he'd recovered sufficiently from the near toxic doses. But in the end, they had misjudged Owens after all, discounted the possibility he would be capable of one final act of defiance.

"How did you know?" The voice was resigned, calm, seemingly undisturbed by the knowledge he had been stripped bare of an impersonation he knew had been doomed to failure from the outset.

Storm answered, keeping his eyes straight ahead. "Julie, the Holiday Inn." The lake was still frozen but in places aching to crack, split open and welcome the warmth of spring. Overhead, a flock of geese zoomed in nearly perfect formation.

"I thought so. Owens told me about the girl and the bar last night. I didn't believe him. It seemed a crude, last minute invention. He remembers you quite well, you know. Well, I can't blame him."

Storm pulled up short and turned. "You mean he's alive?" Once the realization had set in this man who now walked beside him was not Robert Owens, he'd assumed Owens was already dead. He had not allowed his mind to go beyond simply hearing a confirmation of his suspicions.

"Oh, yes, he's alive, although they almost killed him with the drugs. He's in a hospital near Moscow, a kind of special clinic for politburo dignitaries. The idea was to keep him available in case you brought up something unexpected, something we hadn't already covered, but it seems he was too clever for us. He's not well though. In fact, that's why he chanced everything." His eyes studied Storm. "He's dying. He just wanted to go home and die. Who can deny a man that?"

Storm nodded absently as they continued to walk along the path. What am I supposed to do now? he thought, digesting this new information . And why the suggestion for the walk? For what? To confess?

"What are they really?"

"What?"

"Julie, the Holiday Inn?"

"Julie was our main support base. Near Bien Hoa. Our company saw a lot of action from there. The Holiday Inn was just a patch of jungle. It had always been quiet and peaceful until we got there. Nobody who was there would ever forget either place or not know where they were."

Storm stopped to light a cigarette. They sat down on a large outcropping of rock near the edge of the lake. The ice was melting and the water gently lapped against the shore.

"Who are you really?" Storm asked.

The Russian stared out across the expanse of frozen lake, already cracking in places. "They were opposed to our being out here. In the *dacha* there are listening devices. Everything we've said to each other so far is on tape."

"Then why?"

"You have a right to know and it doesn't matter now one way or the other. I wanted to tell you something about myself, something I didn't want anyone to hear but you." He turned to look at Storm. "After I'm finished, it will be up to you to decide what to do."

Zakharov in tow, Waters found Karl Evans sprawled across two of the seats in the lounge, moaning and clutching his stomach. His face was pale, ghost white and he was sweating profusely. Several people had moved away, but they stared curiously from behind the safety of their luggage, assuming him to be drunk or possibly some kind of lunatic. His eyes were fearful as he looked up at Eddie Waters.

"Jesus, it's really bad, Eddie. You got to get me to a doctor. It's..."

He moaned again, his face contorting in pain as he doubled up on the seats. Zakharov stood quietly by Waters' side, watching grimly, his eyes darting around the lounge.

"Hang on, Karl," Waters said. He pointed to Zakharov. "You stay here." The Russian complied and sat down near Evans as Waters looked over to the Lufthansa desk. Two of the passenger agents were looking his way as a small crowd had begun to gather.

Waters went to the desk and flipped open his wallet, pointing to the FBI identification. "That man over there is my colleague. He needs immediate medical attention. Can you get an ambulance here? I want him taken to the American hospital in Frankfurt."

The agent's eyes flicked over Waters' shoulder at Evans. "Yes, yes, I'll telephone at once." Waters watched Evans and Zakharov as the girl spoke rapidly into the phone. "The ambulance will be here immediately," she said, hanging up the phone. "Do you wish...?"

"Thanks," Waters said, and hurried away. Evans looked worse. "Hold on, Karl. I'm sending you into Frankfurt, the American hospital, okay?"

Evans nodded. "Sorry, Eddie. Can you make it alone?"

"Yeah, don't worry about it," he said, gripping Evans' shoulder. He looked at his watch. Even with the flight delay, there wasn't time to ask for a backup from the embassy but he guessed he should call it in. The crowd around them was growing and he didn't like the idea of leaving Zakharov alone.

"Will Herr Gruber please pick up the white courtesy telephone? Herr Gruber, *bitte.*"

The swarthy man disengaged himself from the crowd of onlookers around Karl Evans and strode across the lounge. He picked up the phone, listened for a few moments and said, "*Ja, danke schoen.*" He hung up the phone and glanced at the departures board. There was more than enough time.

He waited until after the medical attendants wheeled in a stretcher and took Karl Evans away. Then he took a seat on the opposite side of the lounge where he could keep an eye on Waters and Zakharov, content to wait for the opportunity he knew would eventually present itself. The FBI man was clearly worried and Zakharov was getting more nervous by the minute.

He had to wait only ten minutes.

"My name is Mikhail Aleksandrovich Sokolov. It was shortened to Miki Sokol when I was in the States. It's not such an uncommon name there, especially in New York. Like you, I was an English teacher, plodding away in the provinces, no real future, until one day, something happened that changed my whole life."

Storm watched Sokol gaze out over the lake. The Russian seemed to have retreated into some inner world. Sokol. The name was strange to form, even in his mind. The physical resemblance to Owens was uncanny. He still thought of him as Owens, he realized, although his speech pattern had changed slightly as he got out of the role he had been groomed to play.

"I had an opportunity to buy a short wave radio." Sokol smiled. "How I wanted that radio. It's ironic if you think about it. I wanted to listen to the BBC broadcasts, the Voice of America. You know, improve my English. Instead, I end up...well, it was a foolish thing to do. I should have known." He spread his hands helplessly.

"I knew the radio was probably stolen, but I couldn't resist and it was alright for a while. I even began to congratulate myself on getting away with it, but of course one day, I had a visitor—a man from the KGB. He knew everything. Where I'd bought the radio, from whom, even that I listened to the BBC. I was petrified.

"I was taken to the local KGB office and told I was to be charged with crimes against the State. They had witnesses, a sworn confession from the man who'd sold me the radio, all the evidence. There was only one way out: their way, and of course, I took it. Gladly. The stories about the camps in Siberia are not myths. Of course they never wanted to punish me, they wanted to use me. I knew then I had been set up from the beginning. They never just ask you to do something. First they make sure they have the leverage to make you accept. Like the film, *The Godfather*, an offer you can't refuse. What I couldn't understand was why?" Sokol laughed grimly. "What had I to offer the KGB?"

Storm was struck by the similarity of their situations. Was his offer from Charles really any different? Didn't the CIA know in advance he wanted out of teaching, need money? He was deluding himself if he thought differently.

Further up the path, Storm thought he saw some movement in the brush. An animal or one of Dolya's men?

How easy it would be for them to be picked off here, dropped through a hole in the ice, into the freezing water. Sokol seemed unaware.

"I was ordered to Moscow for what I assumed would be my trial and sentencing, but when I arrived, I was met by another KGB officer and courteously taken to a luxurious hotel. I had never seen a room like that. He told me someone else would see me the following day. I had no idea what it all meant, but I hardly slept that night.

"The next day, two more officers came, one a general. They told me if I was willing to perform what they described as a great service to the State, my little indiscretion, as they called it, would be forgotten, erased entirely. I couldn't have been more surprised when they told me I was to be specially trained and sent to America as a deep cover illegal. America! I was a small town school teacher. An illegal? I didn't even know what the term meant at the time." He turned to Storm. "Do you?"

"I'm not sure. Enter the States illegally, I guess, like the Mexicans who come across into Texas and California."

"Ah," Sokol said. "But that's different. The Mexicans come to work, for a better life. KGB illegals come to spy, to wait for a call that might take years to come."

"And that's what you were?" Storm asked.

"Yes, but only after a great deal of training. The general told me it would be long and difficult, but if I succeeded, the rewards would be great. My parents would be given a new apartment and allowed to come to Moscow—the promised land. They left me then to consider their offer but of course there was no decision to make. By the time they returned the next day for my answer, my only concern was if I would be clever enough to survive the training. I accepted without reservation. Later, I came to realize that it was the KGB who had arranged the sale of the radio I was arrested for buying."

Storm picked up some pebbles and aimlessly threw them into the water, thinking again of his offer from Charles. Different, and for different reasons, but he had jumped just as eagerly. Was he really any different than Sokol? "I understand," he said. "I really do."

"No, you don't," Sokol said quickly, "but it doesn't matter. Thank you for the gesture." He looked away again, nodding silently before continuing.

"I was moved into an apartment in Moscow and my training began. Coding, surveillance, intensive English classes from agents who had already spent time in America, dress, social customs, even a woman to instruct me in the art of seduction American style. She also advised me as to the most suitable type of woman to become involved with if I found it necessary." He looked at Storm to see if he found that difficult to believe. "What I'm trying to explain is nothing was left to chance. C'mon, let's walk again," he said, glancing around.

They continued down the path weaving along the lakefront. The sky had darkened again, threatened. "After nearly two years of study there were examinations in all subjects. Oh, I enjoyed the life, I admit it. The apartment was comfortable, an old woman came in to cook all my favorite things, and by the time of the exams, I felt in debt. I was like a small boy desperate to prove myself to my tutors. The wait was agonizing. Finally, they told me I had passed in all subjects and was particularly good at acting, mimicking mannerisms. All that remained was one final, crucial test.

"I was completely outfitted with American clothes, luggage, even a copy of *Playboy* magazine was packed at the last minute. Then, I was flown to Copenhagen. For two weeks I lived the life of a well-off American tourist. On false papers of course, and by then the identity fit me like a well-worn glove."

He stopped again to look at Storm. "What do you know about freedom?"

Storm was taken aback. He had become mesmerized by Sokol's monologue. "Nothing."

"Let me tell you about freedom. Freedom means being able to go where you want, whenever you want. That's not possible in Russia. If a Russian wants to go from one city to another, he has to have a valid reason, travel permits. He can't just pick up and go. Can you imagine needing a permit to go to San Francisco for the weekend?"

"No," Storm admitted.

Sokol nodded. "How can I tell you how exciting, and yet at the same time, how terrifying it was during those two weeks." He flung his hands out to his sides and looked to the sky. "To wander about that beautiful city, going anywhere I pleased, yet knowing I was under constant surveillance. I drank in that freedom like a man dying of thirst. I was always worried though I would make some stupid blunder. I could hardly contain my elation and sadness when two weeks was up. But my parents were hostages, so I returned and their reactions told me I had passed again with flying colors. I was allowed one brief visit with my family. I was grateful for it because I knew it might be years before I saw them again.

"I left for America via Canada." He looked at Storm with an almost incredulous expression. "Do you know how easy it is to cross your borders?" he asked, smiling. "Incredible." He snapped his fingers. "Just like that and I was in the States. I had a carefully prepared life history, legend they call it, perfectly memorized so it was quite a simple matter to lose myself in New York City, get a job, rent an apartment and make friends.

"My only obligation was to send back what seemed to me innocuous information about America through prearranged contact points around the city. I also met periodically with another Russian. I never knew who he was, but I assume his job was to keep me honest. He brought me the odd bit of news about my family, and apparently, he was responsible for other illegals as well."

Despite himself, Storm broke in. "But you didn't have any qualms about what you were doing? I mean you say you were making friends. Didn't..."

"Keep walking," Sokol said. "Of course. I know you find it hard to comprehend, but remember this was my sentence: to live the life of a normal American citizen. If deceit was necessary, I was happy to practice it but you're right. There was also regret. You must understand the preparations for illegals are so thorough even some of the people you meet could be other illegals. You would have no way of knowing."

"So what happened?" Scores of questions were forming in his mind.

"Three years passed which is not unusual in this program. In fact, that's the idea. Completely immerse yourself in the American way of life until you're called upon. You begin to delude yourself you've been forgotten as the contacts become less and less frequent, but deep down, you know one day the call will come. They never forget, never."

Sokol reached down and picked up a stone and threw it into the lake. "I became quite a baseball fan, the New York Mets. I went to a lot of games, sometimes alone, sometimes with friends. But one game was an experience like no other I can remember. I stood with everyone else while the National Anthem was played. There I was, surrounded by thousands of every kind of Americans—clerks, lawyers, plumbers, doctors—and innocent or not, I was a spy in their midst. I looked down at the players standing along the base paths, their caps over their hearts, gazing out at the flag in center field, and suddenly, I was almost in tears. I knew at that moment I never wanted to leave America." A spasm of pain crossed his face and he sighed as if a tremor had passed through his body. "A few days later I was ordered back to Moscow."

They stopped again and Storm caught sight of a figure a few hundred yards from them. There was no mistaking it this time. It was not an animal, but one of Dolya's men. How many were there? Sokol followed his gaze and saw it too. He lowered his voice and seemed to hurry now.

"I couldn't understand it. I had done everything as they had instructed. I reviewed all my activities, but I could see nothing causing my recall on such short notice. The order was explicit. I was to leave my job, give up my apartment and return to Moscow immediately. What I wanted to do was just lose myself, but my family was still their leverage. They would suffer horribly if I didn't return and I knew I would be hunted down someday. So I came back to Moscow, not knowing what to expect. I couldn't have been more surprised at what I found.

"I was told in Moscow they were completely satisfied with my work so far, but now there was an opportunity for an even greater service. That was the first time I met Owens and I can tell you it was quite a shock. It was easy to see why I'd been singled out. You know they say everyone has a double somewhere in the world. It didn't take much to complete the likeness.

"When they told me the plan, I was terrified. I was sure it would never work no matter how well I was briefed, but Delnov, he was obsessed. Even with Owens cooperation I knew it would fail in the end and it seems I was right. I learned everything about him of course, but they couldn't rely on his truthfulness so they used drugs as well."

Sokol's face was cheerless now, his eyes downcast. "Owens is a very sick man and weakening more each day. If I had succeeded, I don't know what they would have done to him. No, that's not true. I know exactly."

He stopped again and turned to face Storm. "There's no reason for you to believe me, but everything I've told you, the only reason for all of it, is to convince you all I want now is to go back to America and pick up my life where I left off before I was recalled to Moscow."

"What about your family?" Storm asked, regretting the question as soon as it was out of his mouth. Sokol's eyes flashed briefly with pain. "I'm sorry," Storm said.

"No, it's alright. It's a fair question. My mother died six months ago. My father, well, he'll understand." Sokol paused, weighing Storm's reaction. "Do you understand what I'm saying? I have much to offer the CIA. It's up to you now."

"Are you saying you want me to..."

"Yes. Confirm me as Owens. You're the only one who knows any different. Once I come over, there's a chance Owens could be gotten out later."

He'd been half expecting something like this since they'd left the *dacha*, preparing himself, steeling his mind. Still when it came, it struck him like a fierce wind, an overpowering blow to his senses.

Sokol sensed his alarm and spoke quickly. "It's the only way. Owens is dying, he's doomed anyway. If I'm not confirmed, so am I."

Storm put up his hands as if to ward off a blow. "Can't I...why me?"

"You're the only one I can trust. The CIA is as ruthless in their own way as my people. They might make a deal, but not without getting your approval. The exchange has to go through and there's no time left. Zakharov's on the way."

"Exchange? Zakharov. Who is Zakharov?" Storm took a step backwards, as if distancing himself physically from Sokol to clear his mind.

"The Russian. He's to be traded for Owens—for me." Sokol looked at him strangely. "You didn't know there was to be an exchange?"

Storm shook his head. His mind was a turmoil of racing thoughts, fears, questions, disbelief.

Sokol looked at him impatiently. "I'll contact you, we'll meet somewhere when you decide. At least think about it. Where are you staying?"

"The Moskva, 715, but..."

Sokol nodded. "We'd better get back now." He put his hand on Storm's shoulder. "My life is in your hands."

Eddie Waters dialed the American embassy from one of the public telephones. Karl Evans had been taken away, moaning, grimacing in pain, the flight had been inexplicably delayed and now, Dimitri Zakharov, spooked by Evans sudden illness was about to clam up again.

He could feel it. Waters himself was dismayed by Evans unexpected attack of, what was it? Christ, he was in real pain. It had to be more than the coffee, but he was refusing to read more into it though Zakharov obviously was wary now.

As the phone rang in his ear, he glanced at his watch and the departures board. Twenty minutes until boarding. Zakharov stood quietly beside him, his eyes darting around the lounge.

Finally, the embassy switchboard answered. "I want to speak to someone in the political section," Waters said. "This is Special Agent E. Waters, FBI. I'm at Frankfurt Airport."

"Whom do you wish to speak to in the political section please?" It was the standard runaround, Waters knew. The CIA personnel were always hidden in the political section.

"Christ, I don't know. Anybody. This is an emergency." Waters still planned to make the flight, but he'd decided to advise the embassy about Evans.

Zakharov motioned to him and pointed to the door of the men's room next to the bank of phones. Waters nodded and watched Zakharov disappear through the door.

"If you'll hold the line, I'll see if I can connect you," the voice said. Waters gripped the phone tighter and endured several minutes of recorded music until the operator finally returned.

"I'm sorry, there's no one available in the political section. Do you wish to..."

Waters angrily slammed down the phone. Well, he had tried. Now where was Zakharov? Some of the passengers were starting to gather up their things and move toward the boarding gate. All he needed was to miss the plane because Zakharov was sitting on the can. He pushed through the door of the men's room and passed a dark, swarthy man on the way out.

There was a shoeshine stand just inside the door. Two elevated chairs with protruding footrests and an array of brushes, rags and polish in a wooden box, but no attendant. Waters pushed through the shutter-like doors and at first glance, the rest of the toilet was deserted as well. He saw only a row of wash basins and water splashed mirrors. Someone had left one of the taps running and absently, he turned it off.

"Dimitri?" he called. The Russian had to be in here. He hadn't seen him come out, but there was no answer except his own voice echoing around the tiled walls. The first tightness in his stomach began as he passed the wash basins and turned to the right, walking down the line of cubicles, his heart beating faster now. Open. Open. Open. Closed.

"Dimitri?" He pounded on the locked door. He started to call again when he heard the doors swing open and hurried footsteps. He walked back toward the urinals. Two men came in. One went to one of the wash basins and plopped down a small bag. The man took out a razor and an aerosol shave can and began to wet his face. The other man went directly to the urinals.

Waters did likewise, pretending to relieve himself, almost laughing at the absurdity of the situation. The other man finished quickly, wet his hands briefly under the nearest tap and ran out.

Waters went to one of the wash basins and began to methodically wash his hands, willing the other man to hurry up with his shaving. He glanced once in Waters' direction, smiled faintly and tapped his razor against the sink, continuing to shave carefully while he whistled some tuneless melody. Satisfied at last, he inspected his face for some tiny blemish.

"Attention please, flight 479 for Moscow is now ready for boarding at gate 26."

Waters stood, panic raging inside, roughly rubbing his hand under the blow dryer while the other man applied some after shave, carefully repacked his bag and left. Waters ducked into a cubicle next to the locked one and climbed up on the toilet seat to look down over the partition.

Dimitri Zakharov sat slumped forward, head bowed. He was, it seemed to Waters, on the verge of toppling over.

Waters quickly scrambled over the partition separating the cubicles, wondering how he would explain himself if anyone walked in at that moment. He dropped to the floor in front of Zakharov and pushed him upright. The Russian's head fell back against the tiled wall with a soft thud. The eyes stared back at Eddie Waters sightlessly.

Waters loosened his tie and leaned against the wall, closing his own eyes in anguish, beating his fist against the wall.

Barker, a short man in a wrinkled raincoat and thick glasses arrived forty minutes later. The area around the men's room was now cordoned off and two uniformed policemen stood nearby discouraging curious onlookers. Waters had left Zakharov in the locked cubicle and made another call to the American embassy.

He sat now, slumped in a chair, face in hands in a small office off the main lounge. Barker stood over him chomping on a cigar. "You really fucked this up, son," he said.

Waters nodded and ran his fingers through his hair. "How's Evans?"

Barker had come out from the embassy after Waters first call. "He'll be okay. Doc says it was some kind of fast acting poison. Not fatal though."

Waters stood up and looked through the window of the office as the stretcher emerged with Zakharov and rolled quickly away through the crowd.

"Well, I guess I'd better call Moscow," Barker said.

"What?"

"Someone's got to tell them we don't have anyone to trade now"

At the Lufthansa boarding gate, the swarthy man glanced back once over his shoulder, saw nothing to disturb him and handed his boarding pass to the smiling attendant.

"Have a nice flight, Herr Gruber," she said, tearing off the bottom half of the card.

"Thank you." He returned her smile and followed the other passengers down the ramp to the waiting plane, anticipating a pleasant week in Paris. He smiled again. He'd earned a holiday.

Eleven

The car seemed to have a will of its own as it hurtled through the twilight back to Moscow. Balking at the driver's herculean efforts to keep it on the narrow twisting road, the car at times threatened to defy gravity and careen into the thick birch forest as it slid from one side to the other.

Yet Delnov, looming over the driver like some ancient master of a galley slave ship, pounded on the dashboard, exhorting him to even greater speed. The urgency, transmitted to the driver's foot on the accelerator, permeated the car like a fog. Storm felt it immediately, saw it in the grim look of Delnov and the icy calm stare of Dolya when they'd returned from the lake, as if the walk had been some violation of the rules.

Sokol had been whisked away in another car as soon as they'd returned to the *dacha*. Missing were the bantering remarks that had been something of a ritual to the other sessions. Charles and John Trask were gone, returned to Moscow and Storm was curtly informed they expected him at the embassy. There was no explanation for the sudden change of plans nor the reason for the two American's absence. None of them could have known what Sokol had told him out in the icy air of the lake, so Storm steeled himself for some other unexpected event ahead.

Sokol's confession had left him stunned, stricken with apprehension. His mind was churning with the implications of the Russian's alarming proposal that he confirm him as Robert Owens. The satisfaction he'd felt in unmasking Sokol had been fleeting, evaporating, leaving in its wake an absurd scheme to deceive both the KGB and American intelligence. Was it a hastily contrived groping, designed to confuse him further or a desperate attempt to salvage failure? Storm could not decide which. He only knew what he'd seen in Sokol's eyes was the burning intensity of truth.

The Russian's chronicle had totally disarmed him, catching him completely by surprise. Sokol had laid himself bare, thrown himself at Storm's mercy with reckless abandon in what amounted to a simple plea for freedom, for life. Almost from the first words, he'd never doubted Sokol's sincerity, and even on further examination, he could not say exactly why.

If Storm believed him, he was now faced with an impossible dilemma. He did not want to play God, even a clumsy one who must grant life to one man, death to another. Was there any other option? Whichever direction he turned, he was faced with an alternative beyond the bounds of reason, incompatible with his own beliefs.

Now, the burden of choice had been passed to him alone.

To even consider Sokol's proposal meant he would have to confirm as genuine a self-confessed KGB spy. True, he could always reveal Sokol's identity later he rationalized, but he had no doubts as to the consequences that would come crashing down on him as a result of such an act. In any case, it would be after the fact. Sokol's return to America would be under false pretenses and the real Owens abandoned, left to die in Russia.

Yet in all conscience, he could not imagine himself simply revealing Sokol for what he was, a well-trained impostor, to be left in the angry hands of his KGB superiors. They no doubt had their own methods for dealing with failure. They would require a scapegoat; Sokol would be unanimously elected to fill the position. His confession made it clear there were no second chances with the KGB. Even with the planned exchange it was unthinkable the Soviets would suddenly admit their deception and willingly give up Owens.

And what of this, Zakharov, the other link in the exchange? His mind stumbled over the new name in the growing cast. Presumably he was a spy, being returned only in exchange for Owens. Once the trade was made, it was obvious the Soviets could never admit to the real Owens' existence.

Storm felt like an agonized Hamlet, flawed with the same indecisiveness as Shakespeare's greatest character. Whatever happened would be the result of his word and his word alone.

Unless it was somehow taken out of his hands, he could do neither.

His mind continued to wrestle with his choices as the car sped into the Moscow suburbs. They were slowed briefly by some road works which further agitated Delnov. He swore at the driver as the car slid by the construction site. Several husky women were part of the crew, manning shovels, spreading gravel, shoveling great mounds of dirt and carrying large buckets suspended across their shoulders on long poles.

The smell of hot tar invaded the car as the driver edged around the crew and turned onto a wide boulevard, eight lanes in either direction, dotted with militia men directing traffic. They were waved to the center and sped down the middle of the street past cartoon-like billboards praising the revolution and huge banners hanging from buildings—the early preparations for May Day.

They skirted Red Square and finally ground to a halt in front of the grillwork of the American Embassy. Storm was unceremoniously deposited without a word from either Delnov or Dolya.

At the guard post, he was stopped by the sentry. After several minutes of arguing and repeating his name and that of John Trask, he was allowed to pass. Inside, another Marine guard directed him down a long corridor to a single elevator. He pressed the basement button. When the doors opened, he was facing yet another Marine seated in from of a door marked: Authorized Personnel Only. All business, the guard picked up the phone and spoke his name. Nodding, he hung up, pressed a button on the desk which electrically operated the door. It sprang open suddenly to reveal Charles Fox, face drawn, expression haggard, silently beckoning him to follow.

They walked past an array of electronic equipment and Storm guessed this must be the heart of the embassy communications center. A few pale faces, tinged green by the glow of the light panels, glanced up as they walked by. At the end of the hall, Charles directed him into a small sparsely furnished office. John Trask was already there, jacket off, tie loosened, sleeves rolled up, looking as if he was about to interrogate a prisoner. Storm sat down and wondered what he was going to tell them.

"We've got a problem, Storm," Trask said, flicking a glance at Charles.

"Oh?" He tried to keep his voice noncommittal.

Charles lit his pipe and settled down in another chair. "I'm sure you must be aware, Christopher, there is much more involved here than merely confirming Owens' identity. Of course that's what you were brought here to do, but there was an additional phase we thought better to keep from you, at least until now." Trask looked at Charles, it seemed to Storm, to see how he was doing.

"You mean the Russian you're exchanging for Owens? Zakharov?" He caught both men by surprise. Charles eyebrows rose; Trask did nothing to hide his astonishment.

"You knew?" Trask asked.

"Sok...Owens told me today."

"I see," Charles said, recovering quickly. He and Trask exchanged looks, but Storm could not decipher their meaning. "Strange, but, well, in any case, as John says, we have a problem, particularly since your confirmation has been positive." He stopped and took the pipe out of his mouth. "I assume there's been nothing in today's session to change your mind."

Tell them. Tell them now, before it gets out of hand. "Should there have been?"

"No," Charles said, "I suppose not." He studied Storm for a moment and looked almost disappointed, Storm thought. "Unfortunately, we cannot complete our part of the exchange. We've had quite a disturbing signal from Frankfurt. Zakharov has died on us, quite unexpectedly of course."

"What?"

"A heart attack," Trask said quickly, cutting in before Charles could elaborate. He stared blankly at him but Storm knew there was something else, something they were holding back. He was sure of it, and if it hinged on his confirmation, then somehow he had to find the words to tell them.

"You would have lost him anyway."

"What do you mean?" Trask's head snapped up and Charles held himself completely still.

"I mean it's not Owens. The man I spent the last three days with is not Robert Owens." He slumped forward in his chair. He felt like a prisoner who had just talked to the enemy.

"Good Lord, Christopher, are you sure?" Charles asked.

"Who the hell is he then?" Trask had jumped to his feet.

"Okay, okay," Storm said. "I wasn't sure what to do. His name is Mikhail Sokolov. He's a KGB agent."

"He told you?" Charles leaned forward in his chair. Storm nodded.

"Well, I'll be a sonofabitch," Trask said. "Why?"

"We were walking around the lake," Storm said. Once started, the words spilled out in a rush. "He wants me to confirm him as Owens. He spent time in the States before, as an illegal he called it, and now he wants to go back."

Charles and Trask stared at him for several moments before Trask whistled softly and fell back in his chair. Charles got up and began to pace, twisting his pipe in his hands. "And Owens? He's..."

"No," Storm said. "He's alive, in a hospital somewhere here in Moscow."

Now, it was out of his hands.

"You have jeopardized my entire operation," Delnov raged. Stefan Dolya watched his chief, wondering how long Shevchenko would tolerate his outbursts. They had come directly to his office after the news of Zakharov's elimination had reached them at the *dacha*.

There would be no Dimitri Zakharov arriving as scheduled and there would be no exchange. A pity, Dolya thought in view of Sokolov's outstanding performance.

"Calm yourself," Shevchenko said, confidently seated behind his desk. "Do you think for a moment I would have undertaken such an action without the Director's approval? The fact that Zakharov was in the hands of the FBI for several weeks was bad enough, but he was spilling his guts on the plane. It became necessary to stop him."

"But why was I not informed." Delnov would not be placated. Dolya could already detect the note of defeat in his voice. Shevchenko had the Director's ear; Delnov did not.

"There simply wasn't time," Shevchenko said, spreading his hands innocently. "Surely you don't think I set out to deliberately sabotage your operation, Comrade Colonel Delnov?"

Shevchenko's mocking tone and address was too much for Delnov. "That's exactly what I think." He turned away and stared out the window.

Shevchenko shrugged at Delnov's broad back, removed his frameless glasses and rubbed his eyes. He's defeated too, Dolya thought suddenly, and it's a far greater defeat than Delnov's. But he will recover. Delnov, he realized, would not.

Dolya felt strangely relieved. It was out of his hands now. When the case was examined, he would be relieved of any responsibility. It would be Delnov who would face reprimands for failing to consult Shevchenko, losing a carefully conceived network of illegals and Zakharov's death. Delnov would have to answer for it all.

Delnov turned back from the window. "What am I to do now?" he asked. "The Americans are ready to trade. The man they brought to confirm Owens' identity is completely convinced."

Shevchenko put his glasses back on and leaned forward on the desk, clasping his hands in front of him. "That, Comrade Delnov, is your problem," he replied coldly. "I would suggest, however, you immediately prepare a detailed explanation for the Director to that effect. He left me with the impression your project is to be momentarily...suspended." Shevchenko smiled. "Now, if there is nothing further, I have my own work to do. You will excuse me, please."

Delnov blanched at the mention of the report to Andropov. There was nothing to be gained by ranting at Shevchenko. He turned on his heel and stalked out of the office without another word.

Dolya followed, but reluctantly.

* * *

An eerie silence had descended on the small office as the two intelligence men listened in rapt attention as Christopher Storm related his story of Mikhail Sokolov's confession.

John Trask, leaning back in his chair, fingers laced across his chest, Charles, packing, lighting and relighting his pipe—neither man had scarcely interrupted him—stopping him only now and again to clarify some particular point or other.

Storm was flooded with a sense relief. Even as he talked, he realized how foolish he'd been to even consider the Russian's plan. He was a total amateur in a field of professionals, relieved to pass the burden of decision on to its rightful place.

He found it difficult to measure their reaction. Once their initial astonishment had passed, their concentration was complete. He still had no idea how important Owens was and he could only guess at their interest in Sokolov.

It was nearly nine o'clock when the phone rang and Trask was called away to another part of the embassy. Storm was tired and glad for the respite. It had been a long day and recounting Sokol's story bit by bit had added to his weariness. They had drained him of every pertinent fact and impression of his meeting with the Russian.

"Well, Christopher," Charles said, "you've had quite an experience. There are very few people not in the business who have talked so freely with a trained illegal."

"I just wish it could have been different," Storm said. He knew he had done the right thing, but he was left with a bad taste in his mouth and the problem of what to do about Sokol was still unresolved. "What happens now?" He assumed his role in the operation was finished; he had already begun to think about returning home. With Zakharov dead, there could be no exchange and Owens was not his concern.

Before Charles could answer, Trask came back looking thoughtful, a small smile on his tired face. "Well, that was our friend Major Dolya," he said, answering Charles' inquiring look. "It seems they've decided a day off is in order. Doesn't want to strain the two of you." Trask shifted his eyes to Storm as he sat down.

"And time for them to come up with a plausible explanation about Zakharov's rather sudden death," Charles said. Both men seemed to have forgotten Storm was still present.

"I thought you said Zakharov died of a heart attack." Storm looked at the two men uncomprehendingly.

"So, I did," Trask said. "Look, Storm, I'm going to level with you. There was no heart attack. Oh, sure, it had all the appearances of a natural death, but it was deliberate, an assassination. Zakharov was killed by the KGB."

"But I don't understand. Why would they kill their own man?"

"We're not sure yet," Charles said. "We can only assume they were worried about Zakharov talking. It's possible he was involved in something we don't even know about, something very important to the Soviets."

"But why would they kill the man you wanted to trade for Owens? They can't pass off Sokolov without the exchange."

"True, which is probably the reason for the delaying tactics. They can't admit to any knowledge of Zakharov's death without making it obvious they were responsible. Don't you agree, John?"

Trask nodded. "Which still leaves us with the problem of Owens. We want him back, Storm. Sokolov's the only one who knows where he is and..." Both men looked at him expectantly.

Comprehension spread through Storm suddenly. "You want me to see Sokolov again?" he asked, already thinking of a thousand reasons not to, while admitting to himself not one of them was valid.

"Exactly," Trask said. "He trusts you, Storm. God knows he had no one else. He knows where you are, but he also knows you need time to think about his request."

"By now," Charles put in, "I think it's safe to assume he also knows Zakharov is dead, so he's got to act quickly. I think probably sometime tonight."

Storm felt the panic rising in him. When had they decided all this? The two of them were like a smooth working team, bringing him along, setting him up. He was supposed to be finished, going home.

"But what if he doesn't contact me? What if I don't hear anything from him?"

"If the man wants to come over as badly as you say, there'll be a contact," Charles said. "He's a professional, Christopher. He took a terrible risk confiding in you when he knew we'd evaluate everything you told us. The important thing is he knows where Owens is being held. Perhaps now we can force their hand. Of course with Zakharov out of the picture, we'll have to make some other concession."

"Suppose that doesn't work?" Storm could already see where this was heading and he didn't like the sound of it at all.

"Then," Trask said, "we try it another way. In exchange for Sokolov's help, we offer him asylum."

"Defection you mean."

"Alright, defection if you prefer. In any case, Sokolov doesn't have much choice. He's committed himself already."

"Do I have a choice?" Storm asked. He was bowled over by the ifs, the complications, the confusion. And Zakharov had been murdered, he reminded himself.

"Yeah, Storm, you have a choice," Trask said. His voice had taken on an edge. "You can walk out of here and go home, knowing you've condemned two men. Can you live with that?"

"Oh, come now, John," Charles said. "I think you're putting it a bit harshly."

"Am I? I don't think so," Trask said. Whatever concern Charles felt for Storm was not shared by Trask. "We need him. Sokolov laid his cards on the table. He trusts you and you want to just walk away."

Trask's words struck a nerve. He hardly knew Sokolov, but he couldn't forget those burning eyes, the naked plea. *My life is in your hands.* And Owens? Did he have any obligation to him? He'd saved his life once. Must he do it again? Yes, if he could. Trask was right. He would be responsible for both Owens and Sokolov if he walked away now.

"What do you want me to do?"

There was a collective sigh from both men. "You go back to the hotel and just wait," Trask said. "Have dinner, hang around the bar, wait for Sokolov to contact you. I doubt if he'll risk a phone call, but just be alert. Charles will be standing by and we'll take it from there. I'm a little too visible to be wandering around Moscow at night and we don't want Delnov or his crowd to suspect anything is up."

Storm listened, half alert, half accepting his murky form of penance. Obligation is the penalty of conscience, he decided, as Trask's voice, now devoid of any hostility, snapped off instructions in a crisp, business-like manner. Charles watched the proceedings in silence.

Storm's mood shifted through a scale of emotions like a wild roller coaster ride. He sought some rationalization to comfort him, but there was none. He had squandered his last chance to fold as surely as a poker player sees the final bet with his pockets empty.

He was in.

Supper was fish and a rice dish swimming in a watery white sauce, served by a black-suited waiter. There were only four people in the dining room. A boisterous German couple poured over maps and guides of Moscow and argued loudly, apparently over what sights to see. The other couple ate in silence as if they were strangers. Storm envied them. Their biggest decision lay with tomorrow's diversions. His had already been made.

He lingered over coffee and brandy before finally deciding, if any contact was planned, it wasn't going to be in the restaurant. He went to the desk, but there were no messages. The clerk, sensing his restless attitude, suggested an Intourist night club and offered a multi-colored brochure. "Moscow Nights" promised the traveler an exotic stage show by world class performers. The clerk added dollars could be spent there as the club was restricted for foreigners. Declining, Storm thanked him and headed for the bar.

It, too, was deserted. He took a table with a view of the foyer and ordered a brandy, feeling like a character on the late show. He signed the check and dropped a few coins on the waiter's silver tray. Taking this as perhaps a sign of affluence, the waiter continued to hover nearby.

Storm saw no one except his constant companion, who maintained his usual vigil in the lobby. A half hour later he gave it up. Maybe there wasn't going to be any contact, he thought. He went up to his room.

If he didn't hear anything from Sokol, it meant the Russian's performance out at the lake was just an act. Could he have been wrong about Sokol? He didn't think so.

Even the floor lady was indifferent. She took no notice of him as he passed down the corridor. Under bored, heavy-lidded eyes, she yawned into a magazine.

He opened his door and before he snapped on the light he felt the paper crinkling under his feet. The message had been pushed under the door. He scanned it quickly and his hopes fell. He went to the phone, dialed an outside line and called the number Trask had given him. Charles answered on the first ring.

"I hope I didn't wake you. I'm just going for a walk if you'd like to join me." He hung up, not waiting for an answer. He started out of the room when something on the bureau caught his eye. His few belongings were as he'd left them neatly arranged...too neatly. A quick once over was all he needed to confirm his suspicions.

His room had been searched.

Christopher Storm had one fleeting but vivid memory of the New York City Subway: old dirty cars, splashed with graffiti, ominous shapes lurking in the shadows, sleeping drunks and the threat of violence everywhere. The Pavolets Metro Station near Red Square was a study in contrast.

After meeting Charles, they walked hurriedly through the wind-whipped rain, past the guards at the Lenin Tomb, across the square and pushed through the double glass doors. Charles had the five kopek coins ready and they descended over five hundred feet to the lower level platform. The Metro stopped running at twelve thirty so it was not crowded.

A few soldiers crouched against the wall, their duffel bags nearby. Several couples strolled aimlessly past marble mosaic walls, seemingly oblivious to the murals of the revolution—huge panoramic paintings of Lenin rallying workers in vivid colors. The platform conductors were like the floor ladies in the hotels, burly women in dark blue uniforms, waving metal flags, rounding up stragglers, reminding this was the last train. Suspended over the track was a large digital clock, a beacon for the restless, counting off the minutes until the next train. Every three minutes at this time of night.

Charles and Storm moved toward the center of the platform. At the far end, Storm recognized the familiar figure of his tail, the man who had tracked his every step since his arrival in Moscow. Under a dark hat, he caught a brief glimpse of the man's face in the bright lighting of the station.

"I think our friend is a bit worried about now," Charles said, looking away. "He would hardly be expecting a nocturnal tour of Moscow and I don't imagine he's had time to call for help. It shouldn't be any problem losing him. Just follow my lead, Christopher."

Storm turned at the sound of the train approaching from the tunnel. The digital clock read: 00:18. The soldiers gathered their bags, the lovers shuffled toward the platform's edge to gaze hypnotically at the light streaking into the station. A pair of doors stopped directly in front of Charles and Storm, slid open for them to enter the train. The KGB man got on the last car but kept his head out the door watching them.

Charles hesitated for a moment then suddenly stepped out on the platform again and began to pat his pockets, as if trying to find his wallet. Storm had a glimpse of the KGB man, watching Charles's performance intently, trying to decide what they were up to. Should he stay on the train with Storm or get off with Charles. He decided on Charles but guessed wrong. As the doors began to shut, Charles wedged his way through as the whistle blew.

Too late, the KGB man got only his hands caught in the rubber facings of the doors. His face was already a blur as the train leapt out of the station. Storm saw him running back toward the entrance.

"Well, that wasn't too bad," Charles said, smiling and taking a seat. Storm chose to stand, gripping a handrail, his body swaying as the train picked up speed. Minutes later they paused at another station on the northeast line. Storm stared at the letters trying to make out the name. Charles met his eyes for a moment, signaling they would get off at the next stop.

The Moscow Metro may be beautiful, Storm thought, but subway travelers were the same the world over—no one looked at anyone.

At Komsomolskaya Station, Charles got to his feet and with the two soldiers, they left the train and walked quickly to the escalator. Storm had to hurry to keep up with Charles. Sokolov's note had been short, but precise. They would be met two blocks from the station.

They turned right out of the entrance. The street was deserted, but they'd gone only a few steps when they were joined by another figure. He stepped out of the shadows and whispered to Charles in Russian. Charles nodded and turned to Storm, pressing a finger to his lips. Russian only would be spoken until they reached their destination.

The man led them down a narrow alleyway behind a tall block of flats, one of a complex of several towering buildings. Only a few lights were visible in some of the windows. At the entrance to one of the buildings, the man stopped, said something further to Charles and disappeared into the darkness. Charles motioned for Storm to follow. Over a lighted panel, he pressed a button. There was a short buzz and the street door sprang open instantly. They walked up two flights of stairs and stopped before a door near the end of the second floor corridor. Charles pressed the doorbell button and inside they could hear the sound of a weak buzzer.

A bolt slid back and the door opened a few inches on a chain. An old woman with a gnarled face and snow-white hair, pulled straight back, stared out at them. Sokolov's face suddenly appeared behind her. The door shut again, the chain was taken off and they were admitted into the flat.

Sokolov led them from the tiny entrance hall into a small sitting room. It was crowded with ponderous, overstuffed furniture and lit by two small lamps. Dusty icons hung on the wall and a round table with a lace tablecloth took up one corner.

"Over here," Sokolov said, motioning them to the table. The old woman disappeared into the kitchen and Storm heard the scratching of a match. "Please sit down," Sokolov said. He brought cups and saucers and an ornate glass ashtray to the table.

He sat down and smiled faintly at Storm. There was no sense of betrayal in his expression only resignation. He turned his attention to Charles. "Now, Mr. Fox, please tell me what it is I must do to gain entrance to your country." Charles seemed momentarily taken aback by Sokolov's directness.

The transformation was slight, Storm decided, but he could see it nevertheless. In the atmosphere of the apartment with its heavy smell of cooked cabbage and musty furniture, Sokolov had shed the impersonation of Robert Owens like an actor who's removed his makeup at the end of a long running play knowing he will never play the role again. Sokolov was Russian again, down to his speech pattern, which had also slightly altered. A different person from the one Storm had known earlier in the afternoon at the lake.

"Christopher has told us quite a story," Charles began. "Am I to assume everything is true?"

"Exactly as I told it," Sokolov answered quickly. He seemed to take no offense at Charles' question. There was only a trace of anxiety in his face as he held the older man's steady gaze. "If there is anything I can do to further impress you of my..."

"No, that won't be necessary," Charles held up a hand. "Christopher was quite convinced and your actions put you in rather a difficult position to say the least."

Sokolov smiled again at Storm as if to say, you did the right thing to tell them everything. "For that I am glad," he said, turning back to Charles, "but as you say, my position is now difficult."

The old woman returned, shuffling in on floppy slippers, carrying a tray with a pot of tea. She set it on the table and wordlessly poured the dark liquid into their cups. She brought a bowl of hard-caked sugar from the sideboard, then disappeared again into one of the other rooms, shutting the door behind her.

"My old *babushka*," Sokolov explained. "She often took care of me when I was a child." He cast his eyes downward. "She knows nothing of my involvement with the KGB. She thinks I'm selling icons to foreigners." His smile was sardonic. "She wouldn't approve of that either, but it's better that way."

"Of course," Charles said, sipping his tea. It was strong and bracing. Storm and Sokolov both lit cigarettes and Charles began to fill his pipe. There was a strong air of expectancy in the room and Storm realized at once he was to be a silent observer to these negotiations.

"Our primary concern," Charles began, "is of course Owens. I presume you know Zakharov is no longer available and now...well, obviously there will be no exchange."

Sokolov nodded. "Delnov was furious. Zakharov's death was apparently ordered by a Colonel Shevchenko from the Illegals Directorate. Zakharov was Shevchenko's responsibility. By involving him in his own operation, he jeopardized Shevchenko's network. Everything is so strictly compartmentalized."

Charles looked thoughtful as he digested the Russian's words. "If we inform Delnov now that we know you were merely impersonating Owens..."

"He will simply know the knowledge could have only come from me."

"Exactly. And you're quite sure Owens is alive?"

"Yes, I saw him only yesterday. He is alive but weak."

Charles laid his pipe down and poured more tea. "Where is he?"

"At a private clinic for the politburo elite. Near the ring road."

"Strange, I'm not familiar with a hospital there," Charles said.

"Few people are."

"Would it be possible, feasible to reach Owens there?"

Sokolov seemed to hesitate. "No. No one has access to the Clinic except Delnov, Major Dolya and..."

"You." Charles caught a twinkle in Sokolov's eyes.

"Yes," Sokolov said after a long pause.

Charles got his pipe going again and stared at one of the icons hanging on the wall. Several minutes of heavy silence passed before he spoke again. "I'm sorry to put it to you this way, but our helping you will hinge on your cooperation in securing Owens' release. Once that is accomplished, I can assure you you'll be taken care of by our people, providing of course, you're willing to give us a complete picture of your activities in America and your training." From Charles' tone, it was clear this point was not negotiable.

"You strike a hard bargain, Mr. Fox," Sokolov said. He shrugged and smiled grimly. "I assumed that was to be the arrangement and I have little choice, do I? But to reach Owens, would require additional resources."

"That can be arranged," Charles said quickly.

Storm's mind was a whirlpool of confusion when he broke in at last. "Do I understand what you're saying? You're going to rescue Owens from this hospital? How?" He looked blankly at both men, who returned his look as if they had just become aware of his presence.

"At this stage, Christopher, there's no other alternative. The exchange is now impossible so we're forced to take some drastic measures if Owens is to be freed." There was a hint of condescension in his voice.

He dismissed Storm and turned back to Sokolov. "What I have in mind is still an exchange, at least a temporary one."

Storm was puzzled but Sokolov seemed to comprehend at once. "Yes, it could be done that way, but there is another problem."

"What's that?"

"Owens is being moved. When, I don't know, but it will be soon. I heard Dolya talking about it. Perhaps as soon as tomorrow morning."

"That complicates matters considerably," Charles said, glancing at his watch. Storm looked at his own. It was nearly one o'clock. "We don't have much time. The switch will have to be made before then." He paused, staring at Sokolov. "You understand the risk?"

The Russian shrugged. "At least this way I have a chance."

As far as Storm was concerned, they were talking in circles. What risk? What was Charles thinking? And was he to be a part of it?

"Good," Charles said. "Any suggestions? I mean you know the layout of the clinic."

"Yes, I've been thinking about it. There is a regular linen delivery service every morning between five and six, before the change of shift at the clinic. The guards take little notice of it. With a substitute driver..."

"Yes, yes, I see. We could make arrangements." There was excitement in Charles' voice, a quality Storm was seeing for the first time.

Storm sat as if in a fog. The words rushed by him without comprehension, but it suddenly dawned on him the obtuseness of the conversation was because of him. There was an urgency about Charles now and it drew him like a magnet, inexorably to a conclusion.

"I'll call you here," Charles said.

"Yes," Sokolov quickly scribbled a number and gave it to Charles who was already on his feet.

"I'll be in touch as soon as I've made the arrangements. Be ready to leave on short notice." Sokolov nodded. "C'mon, Christopher." He took in Storm's incredulous expression. "I'll explain later."

Dazedly, Storm got up and followed Charles to the door. Sokolov gave him one measured glance. The intensity was still in his eyes as he shook hands solemnly. "Thank you," he said.

Storm didn't know for what.

* * *

In the throes of defeat, Colonel Vasili Delnov resembled a pathetic wounded animal, oozing failure and self-pity like his own blood as his great plan limped toward its lame and impotent conclusion.

Stefan Dolya's loathing for his chief had steadily increased in the months they had worked together on the Owens project. Now, it had reached its zenith. Delnov needed a shoulder to cry on and he'd insisted Dolya accompany him back to his flat to join him in a dreary, vodka-inspired post mortem. In Dolya's eye, Delnov had sunk to new depths and never once had he accepted responsibility though it was a matter of record, he reminded himself.

"You know who is happiest tonight, Stefan?" he asked from behind bloodshot eyes. "Shevchenko. He was won at last. I am destroyed, Stefan. Utterly destroyed."

Dolya refused to answer, to be drawn into further participation. As Delnov's second, he was naturally affected just as he would have been if they'd been celebrating success. But now he was sickened by the display. His only hope in escaping was perhaps to divert Delnov to action, pierce his alcoholic fog with one last act of prudence.

"Shall I go ahead with the plans for moving Owens from the clinic?" He had hardly touched his own drink, but Delnov had not noticed.

Delnov waved a hand limply and let it drop. "What does it matter now?" He took another gulp of vodka and seemed to sink deeper in his chair, his words were slurred. His head rolled to the side. "Oh, I suppose. What do you think?"

Dolya was amused. The initiative was being passed to him. Now that it was too late, he was being consulted. "No doubt Owens will have to be eventually turned over to the Americans. But for the time being, it is perhaps more prudent to move him to a new location." Even as he spoke, his mind raced ahead. Suppose the Americans already knew about Owens being at the clinic. If Sokolov,...no, it wasn't possible. He studied Delnov through an appalling silence. The big man seemed to momentarily emerge from his stupor, comprehension spreading over his face.

"The walk around the lake!"

"It's a possibility. He spent over an hour with Storm and we have no idea what they talked about. But if Storm somehow managed to trip him up, Sokolov may have cast his lot with the Americans."

"Yes, yes," Delnov said, his eyes narrowing. "I never liked the idea of the walk." Dolya smiled as Delnov's face betrayed the remembrance it was he who had given approval. He simply ignored Dolya's smile. "They could be already making plans. But Sokolov? Do you think..." He pointed at the telephone. "Call him at once."

Dolya complied and dialed the number. He let it ring twenty times. In the stillness of the flat, the persistent tones were all too audible. "No answer," Dolya said unnecessarily, hanging up the phone. He took a perverse pleasure in Delnov's panic.

Delnov pounded the arm of the chair. "Move him, Stefan. Early this morning. If we were to lose Owens now..." His voice trailed off and he sank back in the chair.

Dolya left Delnov staring at his empty glass, mumbling about Natalya. She is the least of his worries, he thought. He would comply with what he was sure would be the last order from Delnov. He had already decided to take advantage of Shevchenko's interest.

Tomorrow, he would take up his offer.

It was Trask surprisingly, who objected. Jaw rigid, voice rasping from countless cigarettes and endless cups of coffee, he'd bored into Charles almost as soon as they'd returned from the meeting with Sokolov.

Storm had listened at first, exhausted and again feeling the impotent bystander. He'd dropped into a chair as the two men thrashed it out between themselves. He was amazed at his own lack of interest, resigned now at whatever lay in store for him. He nearly dozed off as the angry voices of Charles Fox and John Trask rose above him.

Robert Owens was still the primary concern. That above all else was the driving force behind downplaying Storm's role and it was having its effect on Trask. Weary of defending his own position against the onslaught of Charles' point by point proposal, Trask gradually weakened and finally caved in altogether.

Owens safe deliverance could be affected with Sokolov's and Storm's participation or not at all. That was how Charles had put it as they'd walked from the Russian's flat in search of a taxi back to the foreign compound.

Storm could see it now, all too clearly, despite the continuing urge to throw up his hands and simply walk away. But as Charles pointed out, could he just walk away now. Duty, obligation aside, his own situation had abruptly changed. His room had been searched, he could be picked up for questioning, denied leave of the country, even charged with spying and the Soviets would be entirely within their rights to do so.

There was little the U.S. government could do about it since they themselves were party to a conspiracy, an admission one of their own was already being held for precisely that reason. Sokolov would be exposed to whatever penalties failure imposed; Owens would be lost forever, and he would be left to dangle alone.

In addition, if the Soviets had even an inkling Sokolov had revealed the plan to substitute himself for Owens, they would have to take strong measures. Charles didn't elaborate on what those might be, but Storm could use his imagination. He already knew what had been done to Zakharov.

Grudgingly, he came round to the conclusion that Charles was right. This was the only way, although he also knew he was being used as insurance for Sokolov. His own involvement could be a guarantee against Charles' pledge to get the Russian out as well.

Storm had come full circle. He had come to Russia to affect Owens' release and now he was to be a hostage in his escape. And if they managed to pull it off? Well, that was another matter entirely. If he was to leave Russia at all, it wouldn't be the same way he'd arrived.

Trask's voice cut through his musings; his voice was tired but just as firm. "Have you told him yet?"

Storm opened his eyes to find both men studying him intently. Charles had apparently succeed in persuading Trask but his expression was troubled, the victory hollow.

Since the meeting with Sokolov, Charles' manner had changed from being a mild mannered consultant, passively agreeing to the various arrangements, to a decisive leader. The baton of command had subtly passed from John Trask and Charles now grasped it firmly.

"If you've been listening, Christopher, you know what we're up against. Despite what I told you, it's not too late to pull out and I'm sure John would advise you to do just that. We might be able to work out something." Charles spoke quietly. Storm heard the compassion in his voice as well as the doubt as their eyes met for an instant.

Storm had seen that look before in the eyes and faces of company commanders in Vietnam. Weary, burdened men, ordering patrols they knew had little chance of succeeding. It was a helplessness he sensed and realized Charles must have felt before on countless occasions when he'd asked less able men than himself to take those first tentative steps into the unknown.

His eyes flicked to Trask and were met by a steady gaze and a casual, almost off hand answer that belied his concern. "I'm not going to pretend the future of the world hangs in the balance," Trask said. "All I can tell you is that getting Owens back is vital to us, a matter of national security, whatever that means. Sometimes I think I don't know anymore." Trask paused. He glanced at Charles and Storm caught a slight nod of agreement. "What it boils down to is this: we've got one shot, but we need you along."

Storm bowed his head and sat motionless for several moments. It was impossible not to respond to such an appeal. He wondered if they knew the effect their words had created in him, reaching down inside him, feeding his mind and ego and heart like a meal for a starving man. Or had they simply spoken the words to evoke a desired response in him—yet one more subtle manipulation.

He raised his eyes again and searched their faces, finding nothing to either confirm or deny any such suspicion. It didn't really matter now, he suddenly realized, for he had doubts about everyone. Charles, Trask, Sokolov, even Owens. Everyone but himself.

"Well, I've come this far," he said. "I might as well see how it turns out." Trask's face remained a blank while Charles allowed himself a slight smile. "Are you two both crazy or does this really have a chance of working?"

"It has every chance, Christopher," Charles said. "You must believe that."

Storm wasn't sure why, but he did.

Twelve

The dawn was gray and cold and a light drizzle fell as the battered van swung into the drive leading to the grounds of the Clinic. Under a mountain of sheets, towels and hospital uniforms, Christopher Storm and Mikhail Sokolov huddled together and listened to the voices of the driver and the guard at the main entrance.

While the KGB trained illegals to penetrate America, U.S. intelligence did just the opposite within Russia itself. Finding Russians sympathetic to the cause of the West was not difficult. Getting them to work for western intelligence was another matter. But there was always a relative in Poland or Czechoslovakia, an old grudge against the State or simply revenge—all contributing factors to the network of locals scattered about the country and ranging from members of the diplomatic corps down to hotel porters.

The driver of the van, Anatoli Gubkin was such a man. Until 1968, Gubkin had been a loyal, faithful citizen of Soviet Russia, despite some of his doubts about certain Kremlin policies. The crushing invasion of Czechoslovakia had changed all that. He had relatives in Prague and had learned of their suffering, their humiliating defeat only after the fact. This didn't soften his resolve.

It had not been difficult to obtain information about the linen service, the daily, early morning deliveries to the Clinic. All was required was to substitute Gubkin for the regular driver. The stocky barrel chested Gubkin had listened patiently as Trask outlined what he was to do. He nodded with understanding, confidence and seemed to relish the idea once he grasped its purpose. Gubkin had inspected Storm briefly before their journey commenced and exchanged knowing looks with Sokolov. Now, as the van ground to a halt at the guard post, he wondered how the American would fair.

He rolled down the window of the van and eyed the guard ambling toward him. He looks tired, Gubkin thought, anxious for his relief, but there was wariness also at the sight of an unfamiliar face.

Gubkin shoved the clipboard toward the guard with a bored expression. All entries and exits into the Clinic grounds were initialed by the guards.

The guard scanned the inventory sheet and looked at Gubkin. "Where is the regular driver?"

"Fuck your mother," Gubkin said, slapping his hands on the steering wheel. It was the national expression of exasperation, not an insult. "The turd is sleeping off too much vodka and on a day like this, I get called," he said, glancing at the sky.

The guard wasn't impressed. "I've never seen you before," he said, handing back the clipboard. Gubkin carelessly flung it on the seat beside him.

"And you won't again if I can help it. Coming all the way out here, almost to the outskirts of the city and so early. My regular rounds are more to my liking. Breakfast first, I always say, but today..."

The guard cut him off. "Alright, old man, enough of your whining. Open the back." The guard was young, perhaps a new recruit and wary because of the earlier call. A KGB major was arriving soon and he didn't want anything amiss before his shift change. He stepped back from the door to let Gubkin out and unshouldered his rifle.

Gubkin jumped out of the van, muttering curses to himself, walked around to the back and threw open the doors. Inside, behind the piles of freshly laundered linen, Storm tensed. Sokolov touched his arm and they held their breath as Gubkin roughly pushed aside the stacks of sheets near the doors.

"What is it you think I have here?" He asked the guard querulously. "Here, look for yourself." He stepped aside as the guard poked though the piles of linen nearest the door with his rifle.

Through a narrow slit in one of the stacks, Storm could see the barrel probing towards him like a snake.

"Hey, careful with that dirty gun of yours," Gubkin shouted. "I'll have to take all this back if you keep that up." Gubkin edged closer to the guard. He was prepared to drop him although Trask preferred they gain entry without trouble if possible.

Satisfied, the guard stepped back. "Alright, old man, close the doors and be on your way." Gubkin slammed the doors and walked back to the front of the van. The guard returned to his post as Gubkin climbed in and started the engine. He slammed the gear shift and the tires spun on the slush and wet gravel. "Old man," Gubkin muttered to himself. "I'll show you old man."

He followed the curving drive past the main building. To his right, he could see the front entrance and an open parking area. He continued until he was past the building then turned to the right. At the rear, he reversed the van up to a small loading dock and shut off the motor. He tapped the wall behind him and got out, whistling softly to himself. He opened the two service doors and found the large, canvas basket on wheels just inside. He pushed it back onto the dock, opened the van's rear door and began to methodically stack linen inside the basket.

"C'mon," Sokolov said to Storm. They moved closer to Gubkin, crouching against the wall.

"Now," Gubkin whispered. "I'll stall as long as I can." Sokolov nodded and motioned for Storm to follow him. They ducked inside the clinic. Sokolov cracked open a door leading to the main corridor on the ground floor. At the far end, he could see the main reception desk. A guard with his back turned was bent over the desk talking to a nurse. Sokolov shut the door again and turned to Storm.

"Owens is on the second floor," he whispered. "The stairs are just across the hall. I'll go first." Storm nodded as Sokolov opened the door again and shot across the hallway. Storm followed seconds later just as the guard laughed and turned in his direction. They padded up the stairs to the second floor. Storm felt a twinge of nausea as he took in the hospital smells of disinfectant and alcohol.

At the top of the stairs, Sokolov stopped and peered around the corner, down the corridor. There were dim lights reflecting on the linoleum floors, but there seemed to be no one about. Sokolov motioned again and they crept down the hall, passing several doors. There was a desk in the middle of the corridor and no one was there. They both heard a cough, then a toilet flush.

"Night nurse," Sokolov whispered. "Hurry." They stopped in front of another door. "Here." They ducked inside and Sokolov carefully closed the door behind them.

The room was dark, lit only by the gray dawn seeping in the window. Storm could just make out the bed and next to it a small table and chair. His eyes gradually adjusted to the dimness and he crossed to the bed for his first look at Robert Owens in ten years.

Storm banked his knee on the bed as they got closer. Owens sat up suddenly. "Who's there?"

"Sokolov. Be quiet."

"What do you want?" Storm saw his head turn to him. "Who's that with you?" There was panic in his voice though he kept it low.

Storm moved closer as Owens' eyes sought him out. "Chris Storm." He put out his hand to touch Owens. "We're going to get you out of here."

Owens reached out and turned on a small bedside lamp. His eyes blinking, he peered at Storm. "Storm? What are you...?" Owens body was suddenly racked with a fit of coughing. It took several moments to control it.

Storm glanced from Owens to Sokolov. The resemblance was uncanny. They were like twins except for the pallor of Owens.

"How? I don't understand," Owens said, recovering from the coughing.

"They're moving you today," Sokolov said. "I don't know where but...wait. What's that?" They all looked toward the door. Voices sounded in the corridor, then footsteps coming their way.

"It's Dolya," Sokolov said. He pushed Owens back down on the bed and pointed to another door across the room.

"Quick in there." He motioned Storm to the door. They hurried inside and shut the door behind them.

The first thing Storm saw was the wire mesh screen covering the window. How were they going to get through that? There was a toilet, a wash basin and a walled-in shower stall with an opaque glass door. Sokolov opened the door. It seemed to Storm the catch made a horribly loud sound. They both got in the shower and pressed against the far wall. At the same moment, the room door opened.

They could hear Dolya and another man talking, then Owens. The voices were muffled, distant. Sokolov strained to listen, trying to make out the conversation. "They decided to move him within the hour, by ambulance," Sokolov whispered. Storm nodded his understanding, panic rising inside him. They would never pull it off.

Suddenly Dolya's voice grew louder. He was nearing the bathroom door. Oh, Christ, he's coming in here. Storm closed his eyes as the door opened. Dolya's heels clicked on the tile floor. There was a rustle of clothing, a zipper, then a stream splashing into the toilet as Dolya relieved himself. Storm held his breath until they heard the toilet flush, then water running in the sink. Dolya went back into the room and left the door ajar.

They could hear Owens clearly now, protesting over the move, his words punctuated with another fit of coughing. Moving Owens in an ambulance, in relative comfort would be bad enough, but alone with Storm, in the back of an old van? How would Owens survive that?

"I shall be back at seven to see to your removal," Dolya said. "You know, you should really see a doctor about that cough," he added, laughing. He said something else in Russian to the other man. Then the door closed and they heard the scrape of a chair. Sokolov shook his head. The guard was staying.

Sokolov gently pushed open the shower door. Inside the room he could see Owens, still stretched out on the bed, and next to him in a chair, one of Dolya's underlings. Sokolov pulled his head back inside the shower and shrugged at Storm. They had counted on getting there far enough ahead of Dolya to make the switch before he arrived. Now that would be impossible. Now what? Rush the guard?

Sokolov looked out again. Owens was sitting on the edge of the bed, looking to the bathroom. The guard was engrossed in a magazine. Sokolov risked an arm and pointed toward the toilet as he caught Owens' eye. Owens nodded and got up. He said something to the guard who grunted back and came into the bathroom, shutting the door behind him. Storm took several deep breaths for the first time in minutes, gratefully filling his lungs with air.

Owens started to speak, but Sokolov put a finger to his lips, motioned Storm out of the shower and began to strip off his clothes. Owens understood immediately and followed suit, taking off his hospital gown. In the harsh glare of the bathroom light, his face was pale and drawn. Obviously the drug therapy had taken its toll.

He gave Storm a quick searching look. He wonders if I'm capable of this, Storm thought, realizing what Sokolov had in mind as the Russian turned on the shower.

"You can't do this," Storm said, over the noise of the shower. "How will you get out?"

"It's the only way now," Sokolov answered tersely. He ducked under the shower to wet his body. A cloud of steam rose up around him and he seemed to disappear in the vapor.

Storm watched helplessly as Owens quickly got into Sokolov's clothes. Sokolov stepped out of the shower, grabbed a towel off the rack, dried himself quickly, then put on Owens' hospital gown. He wrapped the towel around his head, looking like a fighter headed for the ring. Storm reached in and turned off the shower. Sokolov looked at them both for a moment and mouthed, "Good luck."

Owens and Storm stood aside as he opened the door and went back into the room, hunching his shoulders in a slouch, forcing a cough. Storm heard the bed creak and then a slight moan. He mumbled something to the guard, but he seemed to take no notice.

Owens and Storm got back in the damp shower stall to wait for Dolya's return. Storm hoped Gubkin could continue to stall long enough for them to get back into what he now looked upon as the comparative safety of the van.

From the window of the employees' staff room, Gubkin had watched Dolya's car arrive. The driver remained in the car while Dolya and the other man had gone inside. Only Dolya had returned to the car which meant he'd left the guard with whom, Owens or Sokolov? Gubkin couldn't know if the switch had been made before or after Dolya's arrival.

He continued to linger over a glass of strong tea the old cleaning woman had fixed for him. He would have to move soon. She'd be returning any minute, wondering why he was still there. He had to get back to the van, but if the switch hadn't been made yet, he'd have to go to Owens' room and take out the guard. More time, more risk Dolya would return at any time. Gubkin sighed. His heavy face creased into a frown.

Anatoli Gubkin knew he was expendable. Trask's instructions were clear: Get Owens away with the least possible trouble, but if that wasn't possible, so be it. If necessary, Storm could drive the van, but getting past the guard post would be tricky even if there was a relief guard as Storm spoke no Russian. He sat for another few moments, then swallowed the remains of the sweet tea. He had made his decision.

He went out of the staff room. The canvas trolley was where he'd left it in the corridor. It was now piled high with dirty linen. The one clean set he placed near the top of the pile. He pushed the trolley down the corridor to the elevator and went up to the second floor. Still no one about. It was too early for the patients to be awake and the night staff hadn't yet been relieved. Their replacements would be arriving soon.

He stopped the trolley in front of Owens' room and knocked lightly, then opened the door. The guard looked up and dropped his magazine. "What do you want?"

Gubkin eyed the guard and smiled. "It's not what I want, comrade," he said, pointing to the trolley. "Clean linen for the distinguished patient."

The guard waved him away. "Not here. He's being moved."

"But, comrade, if they're not changed, I'll be reprimanded," Gubkin pleaded.

"Oh, alright," the guard said, after a moment's hesitation. "Leave them with me, old man."

Gubkin took the neat stack of sheets from the trolley. He spun quickly and shoved them in the guard's face. Before he could react, Gubkin's powerful arm shot out like a piston and smashed into the guard's neck. There was a slight groan then the man sank to his knees. Gubkin caught him and silently lowered him to the floor. He pulled the trolley inside and shut the door.

Sokolov bounded out of bed and together, they dragged the guard across the floor. They heaved him on the bed and began to strip off his clothes. Sokolov took off the hospital gown and pulled it over the guard's body. They turned the man on his stomach and pulled the bed clothes around him. Sokolov jerked his head towards the bathroom door and began to dress in the guard's uniform. Gubkin went for Storm and Owens.

Sokolov was nearly dressed when Gubkin returned with the two Americans. He found what he was looking for in the pocket of the guard's jacket: a red, KGB identity card.

Gubkin motioned Storm and Owens into the trolley and covered them with a pile of sheets. He opened the door, checked the corridor, then signaled to Sokolov. All clear.

Gubkin swiftly retraced his steps down the corridor to the elevator, pushing the now heavy trolley in front of him. At the loading ramp, he began to throw the soiled linen into the back of the van.

Storm and Owens were nearly uncovered when an ambulance careened around the corner and backed in alongside Gubkin's van. He stopped his loading to watch with natural curiosity as the two attendants wheeled a stretcher out of the back and went into the Clinic.

"Now," Gubkin called to Storm and Owens.

They climbed out of the trolley and dived into the back of the van under a pile of sheets and laundry bags. Gubkin threw the rest of the sheets over them, slammed the doors and got into the van. He wanted to get away before the switch was discovered in the hospital room.

He turned the key to start the engine, but just then the service doors flew open again. The attendants emerged pushing the stretcher out to the ambulance. Gubkin pulled away smiling to himself, noticing the form strapped on the stretcher under a blanket. The attendants probably didn't even know who they were picking up. He gunned the engine and headed for the guard post.

Sokolov was nearly downstairs when he saw the ambulance attendants wheel the gurney onto the elevator. On the ground floor, he walked along the main corridor, keeping close to the wall. He was almost to the reception desk when he heard footsteps and Dolya's voice. He pushed open the nearest door and found himself in a storage room. He listened at the door as Dolya's heels clicked by sharply then faded altogether.

He ducked out of the storage room and continued down the corridor, past the reception desk toward the main entrance. The nurse looked up and gave him a nod of recognition. He passed her without stopping and bounded down the front steps to Dolya's car, having forgotten the driver would be waiting. It was too late to back up.

"Change in plans," he said, opening the door. "Major Dolya is riding in the ambulance. Let's go." The driver hesitated, momentarily confused.

"But the major, he said..."

"Come on," Sokolov pressed. "The major is in a bad mood. You don't want to make him angry do you?" He restrained himself from looking back to the Clinic entrance. Dolya could come out any second. The driver took what seemed an agonizingly long time to start the car and pull away.

As they rounded the drive, they cut directly in front of Gubkin's van. At the guard post, they were waved through without a second look.

Gubkin slowed to let the staff car pass and caught a glimpse of Sokolov in the front seat with the driver. He watched enviously as it passed the guard post and disappeared down the drive. He didn't anticipate any problems as he braked and felt for the clipboard for the guard to initial.

The guard stepped out of the shelter and peered in at Gubkin. It was a different guard. Gubkin cursed his luck. They must have already made the shift change. He started to question Gubkin when a horn sounded behind them. Gubkin looked in the rear-view mirror and froze. It was the ambulance.

"Better hurry, comrade," he said to the guard. "I think we have a VIP back there." He leaned out of the window. "I heard it was the First Secretary."

The guard flinched and straightened up. "Get this van out of the way," he shouted, already looking toward the ambulance, concern spreading over his face.

Gubkin gave him a mock salute and gunned the van forward, heading for the main gate and the access road to freedom. He banged on the wall behind him to signal Storm and Owens they were clear. He checked the rear-view mirror once more and suddenly began to laugh.

Major Stefan Dolya was sprinting for the ambulance, waving his arms and shouting.

Even as he ran for the ambulance, Dolya knew he was too late. He'd found Owens' room empty, the guard gone and when he'd recovered his senses enough to run back downstairs, his own car and driver were also gone.

He skidded to a stop behind the ambulance, his mind only vaguely registering the name on the linen van receding in the distance. He was only interested in the ambulance. He flung open the doors and jumped in the back, startling the attendant. Dolya pushed him aside and clawed at the form on the gurney. Ripping off the blanket, he turned over the lifeless form and stared into the face of his own guard.

An almost primeval scream came out of his constricted throat. "Imbeciles," he raged, stomping out of the ambulance. By then, the guard had come around to the back of the ambulance. "And you," Dolya shouted. His face was red and contorted; his eyes blazing. He grabbed the guard by his coat. "Who was in that van?"

The guard shrank back in terror. He'd expected perhaps a State leader in the ambulance, not a maniacal KGB major. "Only...only the driver from the linen service," he stammered.

"What linen service? Think, man, think," Dolya shouted.

"I don't know. The regular one I guess."

Dolya threw up his hands and looked toward the sky, darkened now with more rain. He started back to the Clinic, then remembering his car was gone, reversed himself and climbed into the front seat of the ambulance with the driver.

"Drive, idiot," he shouted. "Use the red light and siren, to Dzerzhinsky Square."

"And the patient?" the driver asked tentatively.

Dolya looked at him incredulously. "Fool! The patient is dead, and if you don't drive you will be, too."

If we don't find them, Dolya thought, so will I.

The mammoth Leningrad Station off Komsomol Square was swarming with early morning travelers. It seemed to Storm as he pushed along brushing hundreds of bodies and half supporting Owens, everyone in Moscow must be going somewhere. He glanced at Owens shuffling along beside him. Both of them were dressed in rough baggy workmen's clothes and both wore a cloth cap pulled low over their eyes.

They blended in well with the crowd, but Owens was weak and Storm had to all but carry him as they were propelled along by the wave of humanity toward the station concourse. The huge crowd was strangely comforting to Storm, now that they were on their own. But as he eyed the militia men, casually patrolling, his confidence began to ebb. How were they ever going to find Sokolov?

Storm had been relieved when Gubkin told him the Russian made his escape in Dolya's staff car. Engine idling, Gubkin smoked nervously while he and Owens quickly changed clothes in the back of the van. Their narrow escape from the Clinic, just seconds ahead of Dolya, was a stroke of luck the burly Russian didn't want to press further. He had dropped them near the station and made one final check of their false identity papers and travel warrants Trask provided.

"Show them without hesitation," Gubkin had grinned. They got out of the van and disappeared into the Komsomol traffic. By a little after seven, Storm and Owens were in the station. Plenty of time for them to catch the Leningrad train if Sokolov made it. They couldn't do it without him.

By now Storm knew a city-wide search was well underway. A scouring of Moscow that would leave no avenue of escape unchecked. The airport would be swarming with extra KGB personnel, road blocks would be set up around the city, checkpoints erected at Metro stations, even the U.S. embassy would come under close scrutiny.

But no one, if John Trask and Charles Fox had calculated correctly, would anticipate a further penetration into Russia. The Leningrad train was their best hope, their only chance of eluding the massive dragnet—but only if Sokolov arrived in time.

Owens was weakening by the minute and Storm couldn't chance a word of comfort, not here in the thick of the crowd unless he wanted to give away his total ignorance of Russian. Along one wall, Storm caught sight of some wooden benches and an empty space. They broke free of the swarm and squeezed in between two families of noisy, darting children, rushing amid a pile of cardboard suitcases tied together with bits of twine. A group of soldiers sprawled on duffel bags and everywhere there was the noxious odor of stale cheese and bread, harsh cigarette smoke rose like a cloud and mingled with the steam of the great locomotives.

They sat down and Owens was immediately racked with another fit of coughing. Several faces turned their way as he held a handkerchief over his mouth until his body calmed. He reached in his pocket for a small vial of pills.

"I need something to drink with these," he whispered to Storm. His face was pale and ashen, his eyes watering.

Storm looked around. He didn't like the idea of leaving Owens even for a few minutes. If anything happened, without Owens to do the talking, he would be dead. Trask had cautioned him that travel papers were routinely checked.

Where was Sokolov? Across the way, he spotted a refreshment stand and decided to chance it. Owens needed reviving or he would be completely useless.

A young girl sold juice in paper containers to the impatient crowd. Storm eventually pushed his way to the front of the line and without speaking, held up one finger and handed the girl a five ruble note. Her eyes widened. The drink was only a few kopeks, he realized too late, and she was obviously asking him if he had something smaller. He shrugged and smiled.

She was pretty, not more than eighteen or nineteen, he guessed, with dark eyes and hair. He was suddenly overcome with loneliness and frustration. He wanted to speak to her but he could not. She handed him the drink, said something and smiled back at him. He returned her smile, shrugged and walked away as more people crowded around the stand.

Owens was dozing when he returned, head slumped forward on his chest. Storm nudged him gently awake. He handed Owens the drink and began to scan the passing faces for Sokolov, realizing even if he were already in the station, he would never find him in this mess.

He looked again at Owens. The drink and pill seemed to have roused him somewhat. He sipped the juice and gazed at Storm with grateful eyes. "You know we haven't had time to talk," he said, keeping his voice low. He followed Storm's gaze. "Don't worry about Sokolov. He'll make it."

Storm shook his head. "I don't know how he'll find us in this mess even if he does. Look, will you be okay? I'm going to have a look around."

Owens nodded slightly. "Sorry I'm not more help. Watch yourself."

Storm got up and moved off, back toward the main entrance, looking for some central point, a kiosk, an information booth, anyplace Sokolov might be waiting for them. They were stupid to not have arranged something, but Storm realized everything about this journey would be improvised.

Moving against the stream of the crowd, he found the going difficult. He noticed several militia men, but no one gave him a second look as he pushed through the oncoming tide of travelers. The din of a thousand conversations filled his ears.

He'd almost made it to the front when he heard a loud voice behind him. It couldn't be Sokolov, not like that. He continued on. The voice called out again. Faces were turning toward him. The voice was calling him. He stopped and turned around and met the cold eyes of one of the militia men. His hand was outstretched to Storm. By the simple act of going in the opposite direction as the crowd, he was suspect, drawing attention to himself. The man wanted his papers. He barked something again at Storm and the people around him moved aside, not wanting to be associated or contaminated.

Storm's eyes flicked over the policeman. He was hemmed in by people on all sides. He could possibly lose himself in the station, but he would have to get away first. The policeman moved closer. Storm reached in his coat pocket for the travel documents. Even if they passed inspection, suspicion had already been aroused by his hesitation. There would be questions.

Storm felt his face flush as the policeman took his papers and shook them open with a flourish. He couldn't control the sudden beads of sweat appearing on his forehead. The policeman looked up from the papers and said something to Storm. A question? A minor detail? From the tone of his voice, it was obviously an inquiry of some sort. Storm stared blankly, not knowing how to respond or reply. His mind refused to work. A quick nod, a shrug? Even the wrong gesture would give him away.

The policeman spoke again, obviously irritated now, taking Storm's silence for insolence. Militia men were not accustomed to having their questions ignored.

"*Da*," Storm said. Yes, remembering the only word of Russian he knew. Then, another voice, familiar, surging out of the crowd around him that had remained to see the outcome of his encounter.

Storm and the policeman both turned in the direction the voice had come from and saw Sokolov, pushing people aside angrily, waving a red plastic card. He was dressed in an ill-fitting suit and dark tie. As he came closer, the policeman didn't need a closer look to see the card Sokolov waved was KGB identification. The change that came over him was immediate.

Sokolov was brusque, explaining quickly but with authority. Without another look at Storm, the policeman returned his papers. Sokolov made a few more terse comments, the policeman gave him a quick salute and they were on their way back into the station concourse.

Sokolov kept silent until they were well clear of the area. Storm felt the adrenalin subside, his heartbeat begin to slow. He had almost bolted, crashed through the crowd like a wanted fugitive suddenly discovered. Exactly what I am, he reminded himself.

"That won't work more than once," Sokolov said. "I told them you were a suspected drug dealer and I had you under surveillance."

"Thanks a lot," Storm said.

Sokolov managed a brief smile. "Now, we've drawn attention to ourselves." They stopped in front of a wall of glass windows. Before them, lines of people waited for tickets. It seemed everything in Russia was a line.

"You wait with Owens while I get the tickets. We've got to get on the train as soon as possible. Wait fifteen minutes and then go to track five."

Storm nodded and Sokolov joined one of the queues. Storm weaved his way back through the crowd, looking for the refreshment stand as a marker to the benches where he'd left Owens. He stopped suddenly. Had he made a wrong turn? No, the girl was still selling drinks. This was the place. The two families were still there. He stared at the empty place beside them.

Owens was gone.

Even as he took his seat near the end of the long polished table, gleaming in the overhead light, Colonel Vasili Delnov realized he was to be a witness at his own post mortem.

He might as well strip himself and lie naked on the table to await the precise surgical incisions. Eyes puffy, face sagging, he folded his hands and kept his head bowed after one swift glance at Shevchenko seated opposite him, a study in casualness as he inspected his fingernails. Major Stefan Dolya was on Shevchenko's left. Eyes straight ahead, hands clasped together tightly, he was in obvious discomfort in Delnov's presence, having already changed masters.

Delnov raised his eyes over the head of Shevchenko to the portraits of Lenin and the other heroes of the revolution that lined the wall of the conference room. They seemed to look down on him with disapproval, but strangely, he could think only of Natalya. Too late, he realized, he loved her, and now she too would be lost.

The door behind Delnov opened. He flinched inwardly as it was slammed and the Deputy Director of the Committee for State Security walked in the room. The deputy's heels clicked across the parquet floor and stopped at the head of the table. He dropped a file folder on the table and sat down. The rimless glasses were halfway down the bridge of his nose as he bent his small body and began to study the file before him. Delnov could only take solace that his ruin was to be at the hands of Andropov himself.

"Well, gentlemen," the deputy spoke at last. His voice was soft yet seemed to pierce the silence like a shout. "The initial alerts are underway, thanks to the foresight of Major Dolya, so we can do little more at the moment. I suggest, however, we review the major points of this rather fascinating situation." He paused looking around the table, but his expression invited no comment. His eyes were cold, ball-bearing hard and reflected a ruthlessness just beneath the surface.

"Colonel Delnov, suppose for a few moments we simply review the entire operation. It will perhaps better enable us to understand how we have arrived at this rather curious turn of events." His voice was icy now and floated across the table to Delnov like a freezing mist.

Stefan Dolya realized at once the Deputy's intention. The KGB's obsession with secrecy, its organization of strict compartmentalization was as much to blame for the failure of Delnov's operation as his misguided zeal. It was often difficult to reconstruct what happened when something went wrong. At Delnov's expense, it seemed the deputy was going to do just that.

"An American, Robert Owens," the deputy began, "employed in a highly technical position, denounces America and ostensibly comes to our attention as a defector. He manages to continue this charade undetected for several years, while at the same time he is in effect still a loyal American passing information on a regular basis through numerous channels. Eventually, he is discovered and the flow of information is stopped. Partially, I might add, Colonel Delnov, because of your efforts. On this point you are to be commended." The deputy allowed himself a chilly smile.

"At your request, Colonel, a rather bizarre scheme is suggested, designed to humiliate the Americans and at the same time penetrate an area of technology within their own sphere. And, no doubt," he added, again turning to Delnov, "to bring glory on yourself. A questionable plan at best, but be that as it may, it wins reluctant approval. One of our deep cover illegals is recalled and coached, I admit, remarkably well by Major Dolya, acting under strict orders, of course, to impersonate the spy, Owens. Am I correct so far, Colonel?" The deputy's eyes bored into Delnov, who barely managed a nod.

"Good, I wish to be entirely accurate." He smiled around the table and got confirmation of his good wishes from Shevchenko and Dolya, warmed by the passing credit he was receiving from the deputy director.

"The next phase," the deputy continued, "is to arrange an exchange—the bogus Owens for one of our own comrades who has unfortunately run afoul of the American authorities. At that particular moment, however, our representatives in America seem to be on their best behavior. In short, there is no one available for such an exchange. It is at this point, the case takes its bizarre turn. In your infinite wisdom, Colonel Delnov, you contrive to manufacture such an exchange by literally offering the Americans—on a platter is the way I believe they describe it—one of our own. Dimitri Zakharov, a loyal and trusted member of our organization whose unfortunate demise can also be added to your list of responsibilities."

Delnov's head snapped up. This was more than he could endure. "If I am permitted, sir, it was not I who ordered..."

"Silence!" The deputy's voice, suddenly shrill and high pitched, rang out. He placed both hands on the table as if to rise. "You are *not* permitted." Delnov gave a brief shrug and noted the faint smile on Shevchenko's thin lips.

The deputy's anger passed and he continued in the same quiet, calm voice. "Comrade Zakharov's elimination became a necessity when it was revealed that he was a vital cog in our illegals operations. Had you consulted with Colonel Shevchenko before, instead of after the fact, it could perhaps have been avoided altogether. As you correctly calculated, however, the Americans rose to the bait and the trade was arranged. Sokolov's performance was apparently sufficient to convince the American Storm, but unfortunately, not before Zakharov's arrival."

He turned to Delnov, like a snake about to strike. "And now," he said, "you will please explain, Colonel Delnov, how we have reached the present situation whereby Owens, Storm *and* Sokolov have seemingly vanished from Moscow."

Delnov felt all eyes on him. His throat was constricted. He had been stripped, blamed for everything. He raised his head slightly. "I'm...I'm not quite sure," he began. "I was just informed of the situation only..."

"Not quite sure?" the deputy said incredulously. "Again, Colonel, correct me if I'm wrong, but is it not true that you were in charge of this entire operation, including the security. Is the responsibility of the three men in question—one of them attached to this very department—not entirely and unequivocally your responsibility?"

Delnov seemed to cringe with every word. "I...I, it is as you say, and I intend to use every possible means at my disposal to rectify this unfortunate situation."

"Unfortunate?" the deputy rose to his feet. He was a full foot shorter than Delnov, but he seemed to tower over him.

"Am I to now understand you to imply that this incredible fiasco is simply a matter of bad luck?" The deputy raised his fist and smashed it down on the table.

"I didn't mean to imply I was not at fault," Delnov said weakly. His voice was little more than a hoarse whisper.

The deputy sighed and was suddenly calm again. His voice was like that of a judge passing sentence. Shevchenko and Dolya were merely interested spectators.

"Colonel Delnov, you will, as of this moment, consider yourself under house arrest and confine yourself to your quarters. The matter of your official reprimand will be taken up with the director when he has personally had time to review the case." The deputy closed the file.

"But the arrangements for the search?"

"Colonel Shevchenko will assume command of the search operation with the very able assistance of Major Dolya. Between the two of them, perhaps they can clean up the mess you have made on our own doorstep." Shevchenko and Dolya nodded solemnly to the deputy. His inference was not lost on either of them. They could go as easily as Delnov if they failed.

"But sir...I," Delnov began a feeble protest but he knew all was lost.

"You are dismissed, Colonel," The deputy's voice was once again cold and hard edged.

Without a further word, Delnov stood up. He ignored Shevchenko and glanced at Stefan Dolya. The young major felt his former chief's eyes, but he could not look up. He was shaken inwardly and surprised by his lack of satisfaction at witnessing the destruction of the man he thought he had come to loathe. Delnov marched out of the conference room and closed the door softly behind him.

Delnov's departure was followed by several moments of silence, broken only by the hiss of Shevchenko's butane lighter when he lit a cigar. Finally, the deputy spoke.

"Well, Colonel," he said turning to Shevchenko, "any speculation at this point?" His voice had softened, as if he had expended his supply of wrath on Delnov.

Shevchenko took a long time to answer. Was it genuine reflection or posturing? Dolya couldn't tell and he realized suddenly, he was faced now with a new personality to fathom, a new chief and master to anticipate. His own survival would depend on it.

"I'm sure you'll concur, Comrade Deputy, that at this point recriminations would be a waste of time. However, I think we can safely assume this to be a CIA operation instigated by their resident at the embassy, John Trask. The role of Charles Fox is at this point, unclear."

"But Fox has left the country already, has he not?" The deputy turned to Dolya for confirmation.

"Yes, sir. On the morning flight to Copenhagen."

"Mmm. And that puzzles me," Shevchenko said, "as well as their little escapade this morning. I confess I'm a bit confused as to what they hoped to gain. Their escape can only be regarded as temporary. They can't possibly hope to simply fly away, as it were, nor can they take refuge in the embassy. The Americans would surely not expose themselves to an incident of diplomatic proportions. The increased surveillance and checkpoints was the only proper, sound action. We must cover the airport as well as the foreigners' compound."

"Very well, Colonel. What else do you suggest?"

Shevchenko shrugged. "I'm afraid given the existing circumstances, there is little else we can do except wait and see which way our rabbits run." He raised his hand in a gesture of helplessness that was not lost on the deputy. Even if he failed to recapture the fugitives, he had successfully steered the blame to Delnov.

"Very well, Colonel, you will proceed as you see fit. You have complete authorization from the director. I would remind you, however, with that authority comes the director's wishes for a swift and decisive conclusion of this entire affair."

Shevchenko held the deputy's steady gaze. "Of course, that goes without saying. I shall keep you informed as to our progress."

Shevchenko and Dolya got to their feet as the deputy gathered up his papers and left the room. Shevchenko sat down again immediately. Dolya remained standing to await instructions.

"I want a command center established immediately, Stefan, and photos of these men distributed city-wide. I will also require constant communications with all positions and checkpoints. You heard the deputy, Stefan. We have full authorization. See that we use it accordingly."

"Yes sir, I'll arrange it immediately." Dolya restrained himself from saluting and started for the door.

"And, Stefan, I also want complete, detailed road and railway maps—all routes out of Moscow."

"You don't think..."

Shevchenko smiled darkly. A hint of condescension crept into his voice. "I simply want to cover all possibilities. We must not fail, Stefan. You understand that?"

"Yes, of course." Dolya answered automatically. How many times had he heard the exact words from Delnov?

For several minutes, Shevchenko sat alone at the huge table. Why had Fox left? That was bothering him. And why Copenhagen? It would come to him eventually, he knew. For the moment, he was satisfied. The rules had been laid down. It merely remained to play out the game.

Mikhail Sokolov, Robert Owens and Christopher Storm would be taken dead or alive, whichever was the most convenient. At a minimum, they would not be allowed to leave the Soviet Union.

Charles Fox had only just managed to escape the net over Moscow which was tightening by the minute. His departure had been duly noted, but had not brought about any problems and he was not detained. The airport personnel had not been instructed otherwise and since he was not a regular member of the embassy staff, there had been no reason to question his exit from Moscow.

Charles knew, however, his destination would be reported. If the KGB ran true to form, he would be put under routine surveillance once he was on the ground in Copenhagen.

Unmolested but watched nevertheless. An unavoidable annoyance.

If John Trask played his role convincingly, Moscow would buy the story that Charles was simply disassociating himself from the Clinic escape. Yes, they would understand, at least long enough for him to continue on to Helsinki and make the necessary arrangements there.

It all hinged, this contrivance of his, on Sokolov, Owens and Storm making the train and traveling undetected several hundred miles through the interior of Russia, losing themselves in Leningrad long enough to board yet another train and survive for the rendezvous in Finland. A tall order for even a trained, resourceful operative, which granted Sokolov was. Owens was another story. Experience yes but weak now, dying Sokolov had said, with a terminal illness. Could he survive such a journey? He would slow the others, perhaps even jeopardize their safety. Yet it was Owens who was the least expendable of the three. But Storm? The question hung before him like an irritating cobweb that couldn't be brushed away. Resourceful, courageous, combat experienced, Storm was all that, but he was confronting an enemy he had little knowledge of. The battleground was not a steamy jungle in southeast Asia, but all of Soviet Russia, which could unleash the resources of the largest intelligence agency in the world to find and capture the three men.

He realized, even as he felt it, the sharp twinge of regret was merely an acknowledgement of the inevitable complications of amateurs. The idea had come to him simply and wholly, and now he felt himself effortlessly drawn to its conclusion. Risk? What did it matter now since everything was in motion?

He was suddenly awash in feelings he hadn't expected. Guilt? No, simply concern. His long-held notion of himself was that of a detached expediter of men. And yet, with a rush of surprise, he felt continually pulled back to concern for Christopher Storm. He did not consider his motives, but left them at the bottom of his mind, an undisturbed well, clearly accessible, but for now, distant. He had a personal obligation to Storm. However subtly done, he had pushed Storm into his present position. He and he alone was responsible and he wondered if he had not made a horrible mistake.

He shook off the pleasure or humor as he took refuge in the one, small compartment of bitterness he kept securely locked away. The victory was hollow; the satisfaction was there nonetheless. Delnov was finished at last. He would never recover from this. Charles was not a vengeful man, but there was something undeniably satisfying in the knowledge that the man who had smashed his network in Prague and halted his own active career was now surely disgraced beyond redemption in the eyes of his superiors. Charles at least had not had to suffer that indignity. With Delnov's fall, came his successor.

Whoever assumed command from Delnov would naturally think the escape route would be by air and wait them out. Eventually, he would figure out what Charles had in mind. By then it would be too late.

They must make the train.

On the ground, Charles brushed aside any remaining doubts and made his way to the Finn-Air desk. The connections were good, fortunately, and he had only an hour to wait for the Helsinki flight. Doubling back was an added nuisance, but it would further confuse Moscow and perhaps give them precious extra time. It was necessary, unavoidable and hadn't he spent most of his life doing the unavoidable?

He went into the bar and ordered a large gin and tonic. He lit his pipe and inspected his fellow travelers with deceptive casualness.

It took him only ten minutes and half a drink to spot his tail.

Down a sharp flight of stairs into a room warm and close. Dirty mirrors, air heavy with the stench of urine and sweat from countless bodies, water splashed everywhere in tiny puddles.

At the entrance to the toilets, a burly woman perched on a low stool and collected coins in the lid of a cardboard box.

Through gold-flecked teeth, she joked with the men as they passed and snarled at those who failed to tip her.

Storm located Owens by the sound of his dry, hacking cough, inside one of the cubicles. While he relieved himself and stalled at one of the wash basins, Owens emerged at last, face drawn, pallor deeper than before. He bent over a sink and splashed water on his face then gazed into the cracked mirror above him. Storm caught his eye and pointed to his watch. Owens nodded and smiled a shrug of apology.

He walked ahead of Storm in a slow shuffling gait. At the top of the stairs, Storm took his elbow and guided him like a blind man toward the platform. He saw Sokolov waiting near the ticket barrier scanning the crowd for them. He thrust tickets at them and they joined the rush to the waiting train, waving tickets at the guard as they passed the barrier. It was almost too easy, but there would be a closer inspection once the train was underway.

They boarded behind a large family and some soldiers struggling with luggage and duffel bags and followed Sokolov to a cramped compartment. There was barely room to turn around. A single lamp flickered overhead and two fold down bunks were attached to the wall above the seats. A ceiling speaker, already blaring a continuous stream of party propaganda, hung from one wall. Sokolov called it entertainment for the passengers. It could be turned down, but not off. Storm was suddenly reminded of a similar box in his Las Vegas classroom and felt an unexpected wave of home sickness wash over him while they stowed their bags. Owens collapsed immediately on one of the bunks.

"Our papers will be checked once we're out of Moscow," Sokolov said. "Just remember to let me do the talking. As far as anyone is concerned, you're being taken to Leningrad for questioning." The stolen KGB card would keep intruders at a distance.

Storm nodded, the fatigue taking hold. He slumped on the worn seat and stared out at the dirty, rain-streaked window. A sharp piercing whistle blew on the platform. Doors slammed shut. A cloud of steam wafted past the window, obliterating the people left on the platform and the train lurched forward and slowly began to move out of the station.

The steam and noise of the strain stirred his hopes briefly as they picked up speed. Leningrad was nearly twenty-four hours away. For the moment, they could relax, safe as one can be, on the run from the KGB on their home ground.

Storm slept.

Thirteen

Dolya found Colonel Shevchenko in the eighth floor officers' canteen having a late breakfast of bacon and eggs. He sat at a table alone. As Dolya made his way across the crowded dining room, he was acutely aware of the interested glances and surprise his arrival brought forth. By now everyone knew of Delnov's firing. The fact that Dolya had survived made him a man to be reckoned with. He enjoyed the feeling as he slipped into a seat opposite his new chief.

Shevchenko was crunching on a slice of toast, smeared with strawberry jam. "You will eat something, Stefan?" A waiter appeared as if by magic with a fresh pot of coffee.

"No, nothing," Dolya said. The waiter was waved away and Shevchenko plucked another slice of toast from a metal rack and cut it into squares. The crumbs littered the white linen tablecloth and Dolya began to sweep them into three neat little piles.

"You have news I take it?" Shevchenko's eyes sought his with a hungry expression, ready it seemed to gobble up the tiniest morsel of information. As yet there had been no report from the Copenhagen residency regarding Charles Fox's arrival. Shevchenko was getting impatient.

"They've found the car," Dolya announced.

Shevchenko's eyes ignited slightly. "Ah, the one appropriated by comrade Sokolov. Yours I believe, was it not?" He smiled faintly. "And the driver?"

Dolya flushed, but ignored the slur. "Unharmed. He was locked in the trunk of the car and his clothes and identification were stolen. The car was found in the Lyublinsky district. The driver is being brought in for questioning." Dolya poured himself some coffee.

"Mmm, Lyublinsky," Shevchenko murmured, swallowing the last square of toast. He pictured the area in his mind. A collection of small shops and businesses amid tall blocks of workers flats. "Are we to assume now Sokolov is on his own?" He dabbed at his delicate lips with a white napkin.

Dolya gripped the corner of a sugar packet between thumb and forefinger, swinging the packet in an arc. "I think...no, we cannot assume that," he ventured. Shevchenko's eyebrows, narrow strips of white, rose slightly, inviting Dolya to continue.

"Owens is ill—seriously ill, and Storm, as far as we know, speaks no Russian. Even if they managed travel documents, there would be checks, questions. They would need help." He risked a glance at the Colonel to gauge his reaction to his theory. He stopped the swinging sugar packet and tore off a corner.

Shevchenko smiled benignly. He liked this young officer. Delnov had been a fool not to delegate more responsibility to him. "Exactly how I see it," he beamed. "But where would this help come from?"

"I don't know. Unless—" Dolya poured the sugar in his coffee and placed the torn piece into the now empty packet and crumpled it all into a ball. He had no more to offer.

Shevchenko was disappointed. He had reached the same conclusion. For perhaps the first time in his career, he was baffled. There was not a trace of them anywhere. All international flights left from Sheremetyevo and there had not been a single suspicious sighting. He had pored over maps, rail and bus schedules, but nothing seemed to look remotely promising. No reports from the train stations or the scores of roadblocks that had been doubled and clamped around Moscow like a vise. There were a number of false alarms, but they were hardly worth mentioning. Everyone, it seemed, wanted to get in on the act.

It was impossible they could have gotten away. Therefore, they were still in Moscow. But where? The KGB relied on unpaid informers and three strangers in any block of flats would certainly arouse suspicion. Perhaps they had split up, each going in a different direction. One could travel alone easier than in a group. Storm, at least, would not survive militia checks on his own. Yet every minute they stayed in Moscow decreased their chances of escape and Sokolov, he reminded himself, knew exactly how this security apparatus worked.

No, all his instincts told him they were already gone—deeper into Russia. The answer was there somewhere, tantalizingly close, but just out of his grasp. He continued to puzzle over the departure of Charles Fox, despite the report from their embassy informer.

Apparently a violent argument had taken place between Fox and John Trask, spilling into the corridors, embarrassing secretaries and other staff arriving for work, ending with Fox storming out of the embassy and leaving on the first available flight.

When contacted through routine channels, Trask had flatly denied any knowledge of the escape at the Clinic and had even pleaded, though not very convincingly, to have Storm turned over to the American authorities when and if he was found. There was no mention of the exchange or of Charles Fox.

But he wondered now, was the argument genuine or simply staged for the benefit of the informer they undoubtedly knew was there? A case of reverse disinformation?

"And the search of Storm's room?" Shevchenko's mind snapped out of speculation and back to the present.

"His things were removed by embassy staff this morning, but there was nothing," Dolya said, startled after the long silence.

Nothing. Nothing. Nothing. Shevchenko sighed. The word echoed in his brain. Even the linen van turned up nothing. One looked like another and hundreds of similar vans made deliveries and pickups to various places all over Moscow every day. The regular driver had simply been ill.

The waiter cleared away the dishes and Shevchenko lit a small cigar. He was almost irritated by Dolya's presence, which seemed to underline their lack of progress thus far.

A messenger shortened their awkward silence. He glanced around the room then came to their table and handed Dolya a folded slip of paper. Shevchenko was grateful for the interruption. Dolya read it in haste, aware of the Colonel's interested gaze.

"A militia man reports a KGB officer stopped him from checking the papers of someone. He says the KGB officer might have been Sokolov."

Shevchenko expelled a cloud of smoke. Another false sighting no doubt. "Where?"

"Leningrad Station."

Something clicked in his mind, like a tiny tumbler in a combination lock, dropping almost silently into place. Leningrad Station. The Red Arrow Express, commuter trains, the Siberian workers train—even Sokolov wouldn't survive that—locals stopped at every hamlet between Moscow and Leningrad. It was probably another false lead, but it would at least keep Dolya busy for a while.

"Investigate it yourself, Stefan," he said. "I'm going back to the center. I'll question the driver when he's brought in and find out why we've had no report from Copenhagen yet." He said it lightly, but in fact, he was hoping the call would provide some clue or eliminate Charles Fox from the picture entirely. It was a nagging irritation, continually thinking about Fox. His apprehension was growing now since the search was slipping away. "Yes, go yourself. We don't want to overlook anything."

Impossible. Two Americans. One seriously ill, the other speaks not a word of Russian and Sokolov, one of his own in possession of the coveted red, KGB identity card. Perhaps the militia men did see something at the train station.

Fox, Copenhagen, Leningrad. What was the connection?

The train had just left Kiln, some eighty kilometers from Moscow, when Storm was awakened by a knock on their door. Owens was out like a light on the padded wooden bunk, getting some much needed rest. When Storm opened his eyes, he saw Sokolov already on his feet.

The expected check of their travel papers had as yet not occurred and this was probably it. Storm started to get up but Sokolov motioned him back and mimed for him to pretend to be asleep. Storm hunched down in the seat and pulled his cap over his eyes. Sokolov took his papers and Owens' and opened the door.

The conductor was an old man in a shabby uniform and carried a large leather wallet. His badge was shiny though. Probably polishes it every night, Sokolov thought.

"Yes, what is it?" Sokolov said gruffly, rubbing his eyes as if he'd been asleep.

"Your papers and theirs, too." He looked past Sokolov and indicated Storm and Owens.

"These are my friends and we're all very tired as you can see. Here, I have their papers." He thrust them into the conductor's hands.

He scanned them briefly. "Well, it's irregular but..." He handed them back without another word and Sokolov shut the door. Storm breathed a sigh of relief and sat up. Owens had not wakened.

"It can't be that easy," Storm said. He had expected a major confrontation.

"It usually isn't," Sokolov said. "We were lucky. Some of them can really be nasty about it. I'm glad though. I didn't want to use the KGB card unless it was absolutely necessary. How about something to eat?"

"Yeah, I'm starved," Storm said, realizing he hadn't eaten since the night before. "Let's go."

"No, you stay here. I'll bring something back. We don't want to press our luck."

Storm nodded, disappointed but knew Sokolov was right. He wouldn't even know what to order.

"Don't expect much," Sokolov said. "This isn't the Super Chief. There's bound to be a buffet car though. I'll get some sandwiches and something to drink."

"Anything," Storm said, locking the door behind Sokolov. He leaned against the seat and lit a cigarette, watching the landscape flow by. Great plowed fields stretched endlessly under a canopy of dark sky. If circumstances were different, he might be enjoying a lazy train ride through the Russian countryside.

"Looks a lot different than Nam, eh?"

Storm looked up at the bunk opposite him. Owens had raised himself up on one elbow and was staring out the window. He fought off another coughing fit. It passed quickly and Storm noticed some of his color had returned, but he was obviously in some pain.

"Thought you were sleeping," Storm said. He was unable to rid himself of the picture of Robert Owens he had carried with him since Vietnam. That Owens could have handled whatever lay in store for them. But the thin body and sunken eyes facing him now was another man. "Anything I can do?"

Owens shook his head and dropped back on the bunk, staring at the ceiling inches above his face. "No, no one can do anything, Storm." He rolled his head toward Storm. "Funny, eh? I mean with this cough you'd think it would be lung cancer, but then I don't even smoke."

"What are you talking about?"

"You know anything about multiple sclerosis?"

"Multiple...no, nothing." he said, trying to keep his voice steady.

Owens smiled grimly and swung his legs over the side of the bunk. "I know a lot about it now. I had all sorts of tests run, everything I could get my hands on. At first, I thought it was my eyes. I started getting these headaches, dizzy spells, blurred vision, that kind of thing. But an optician ruled that out. My eyes were perfect. I had some other test then. Brain scan, spinal tap, the works. The Russians have some excellent medical facilities; I'll say that for them. Anyway, it was eventually confirmed. MS. Attacks the nervous system and beyond arresting the disease, there's no cure. Rest, lots of it will buy you a few years, but then..." He stared into space.

Storm felt at a total loss. Owens' illness had been hinted at, but nothing like this. He suddenly remembered Sokolov's words as they'd walked around the lake. *He's dying. He just wants to go home to die.* No wonder he wanted out, no wonder Fox and Trask wanted him out. "How long have you known?"

"Almost a year, but even the extra time doesn't matter much now."

"What do you mean?" For some reason Storm knew Owens wasn't talking about his recovery.

"It must be the drugs they gave me. I can't figure anything else." He looked down at Storm and tapped the side of his head with his finger. "All that information that's supposed to be up here? The reason Washington wants me back so badly, the reason we're going through all this, leaving Russia by the back door. It's all for nothing."

Storm felt a shudder go through him. "Why?"

"My memory. It's gone. Since I woke up in the Clinic. I can't remember a thing."

Sokolov had to walk through four cars to reach the buffet. The compartments were crammed with families spilling out into the corridors. Doors were open, children ran about playing over the loud roar of conversation and singing. Some people had even changed into pajamas for the long journey.

The buffet car was crowded with men pushing around the bar to gulp glasses of vodka, wolf down sandwiches or sip strong tea. Sokolov finally managed to edge his way through the mob and bought several cans of juice, some sandwiches and a small bottle of vodka. As an afterthought, he bought a tumbler for himself.

"Mikhail?" The voice came from behind him. He felt himself jostled as the voice edged closer. "It is Mikhail, isn't it? Mikhail Sokolov?" He turned to look at the gaunt face, the beginnings of a smile curling around the full lips, the dark questioning eyes. "You do remember me?" Another push and the man was at his side.

Of course he remembered. There was no way he could ever forget this man. At the first sound of the familiar voice, his impulse had been to ignore it completely, but this man couldn't be fooled into thinking he'd been mistaken. Not Karpov, Vladimir Karpov.

Sokolov forced a smile. "Of course, Comrade Karpov. How could I forget?"

Karpov's smile was full now, wreathing his face. "I was sure it was you, but you seem, I don't know, somehow different. Your face is, well, changed." The sharp eyes probed and searched Sokolov's face like a surgeon, looking for flaws, demanding an explanation. His voice dropped suddenly. "You are going to visit your family? I seem to remember they live near Leningrad."

Sokolov gave a slight nod, his mind working rapidly. Of course Vladimir Karpov would wonder at his presence on the train bound for Leningrad when he knew Sokolov had trained for an assignment in America. But a family visit was a plausible excuse he mentally thanked Karpov for. "Correct as usual," he said.

Karpov seemed relieved. "And your work? It is going well?"

"Yes, very well." He couldn't stop himself from nodding his head.

"Splendid, splendid," Karpov said. "I'm very glad. You were always one of my favorite pupils. Come, let us find a table, or better still, join me in my compartment. We can talk. I want to hear about your travels."

"Well,..." Sokolov began. This was madness. He had to get away from Karpov. Of all the people to meet now. He would want to talk well into the night. There would be too many questions to answer and could he withstand Karpov's scrutiny for several hours? But he couldn't avoid him either. A brushoff would arouse greater suspicion.

"I see you are not traveling alone," Karpov said, curiously eyeing the drinks and sandwiches on the bar. His eyes shifted to Sokolov as he waited for an explanation.

"Oh, these." Sokolov felt like a character in an American situation comedy. "They...some fellow travelers. They weren't feeling up to making the trek to the buffet. I offered to bring them something."

Karpov laughed. "I can't say I blame them. I missed the Red Arrow. Good. You are free then. You must join me. I insist."

"Well, if you're sure. I don't want to impose," Sokolov protested lamely.

"Nonsense," Karpov said, clapping him on the shoulder. "It will be good to talk with an old friend. We can keep each other company. I'm in the first class carriage, third compartment. I at least managed that."

"Fine. I'll just take these things back to my friends and join you later if it's alright."

"Excellent." He placed both hands on Sokolov's shoulders. "It's really good to see you, Mikhail." He stepped aside to let Sokolov pass. "Don't forget, third compartment," he called.

Sokolov stopped in the vestibule and let the cold air wash over him, listened to the sound of the wheels on the tracks beneath his feet. He knew if he didn't appear within a reasonable time, Karpov would come looking for him. There was no way to avoid it. He'd have to think of something before they arrived in Leningrad. He glanced back through the glass. He could see Karpov talking with the barman. He'd have to warn Storm. He sighed and began to make his way back through the train.

There were enough complications already and now this.

Dolya was elated.

The militia men at Leningrad Station had positively identified Sokolov as the KGB officer who had interfered with his check of another man's documents. Dolya's high spirits were only somewhat dimmed by the policeman's reluctance to identify Storm as the second man. He had seen no third man at all. Still, pinpointing Sokolov was something. The first real break they'd had.

He burst into the Command center, excitedly in search of Shevchenko. The Colonel was seated at a long table, poring over maps and reports logged by the hastily recruited staff. There were several telephones on the table and a number of men manned computer terminals linking the center with the numerous road blocks and check points around Moscow.

Shevchenko looked up and caught Dolya's eager expression. "I have news also, Stefan. Here, look." He thrust a typed page into Dolya's hands. "The report from Copenhagen residency. Fox had only stayed long enough to catch another flight to..."

"Helsinki?" Dolya exclaimed, scanning the report.

"Exactly." Shevchenko was clearly excited as well, but Dolya failed to see the reason for the Colonel's liveliness. "Don't you see? If Fox were merely removing himself from the game, he would have flown straight to New York or Washington. Not Helsinki. What business would he have there?"

"There's an American Embassy there," Dolya said, still unsure. He had yet to see the connection. "There might be a perfectly logical explanation."

"Of course there is." Shevchenko seemed to seize on this unimportant fact, but its significance escaped Dolya. "Fox is planning something from Finland. I'm sure of it."

"But what can he do from Finland? We share a common border, but it's well guarded. What could he hope to accomplish?" Dolya was still puzzled.

"Yes, but not everywhere, Stefan. Not everywhere." Shevchenko was smiling now, obviously enjoying this display of his own mental prowess. "First, what does our militia man say?"

"It was Sokolov, no question about it. He identified him from the wire photo."

"And the others?"

"He couldn't be sure. The other man might have been Storm, but he saw no one else, no Owens," Dolya said.

"Never mind, that's not important. What *is* important is Sokolov and possibly, no probably, Storm were both seen at Leningrad Station, obviously preparing to travel. Owens could have been anywhere nearby. That proves it."

"What?"

Shevchenko shuffled through a pile of maps and pulled one out. It was a railway map of the northern sector and included the southern tip of Finland. "Here," he said, stabbing at a point on the map with his finger. "This is where they will cross." Dolya leaned closer to examine the place on the map.

About sixty miles north of Leningrad between Luzhaika and the Finnish city of Imatra, the railway line crossed the border between the two countries. There was no fence, no coils of barbed wire and the guards were old, veterans of the regular army. Given the relations between Finland and the

Soviet Union, they were decidedly lax. Across this point on the frontier came petty smugglers with coffee, butter, foreign currency.

On the main road, a car would be taken apart at the check points, searched for false compartments, men hidden in spaces hardly big enough for a suitcase. But a train? With the right papers, at an undermanned border post, the three men could glide into Finland and leave the train at any point en route to Helsinki, avoiding the Finnish authorities altogether.

Dolya looked up from the map, his mind racing ahead. Involuntarily, he glanced at his watch. Shevchenko was beaming. He had solved the mystery but he hadn't prevented the escape. Not yet.

"How do we stop them?"

"The Red Arrow Express arrives in Leningrad early this evening," said Shevchenko. "I've already alerted our people there to meet the train, but I think they are on the slow train. More opportunities to get off if they have trouble. Fortunately, that makes it easier for us. We can board some men along the way, even before they get to Leningrad."

Dolya was nodding in agreement as he traced his finger along the route, suddenly aware that everyone in the room was listening. "Contact Kalinin," he said to one of the officers manning the battery of phones. "Tell them to board two men," he looked to Shevchenko for confirmation and got a nod, "on the Leningrad train."

"Excellent," Shevchenko whispered, rubbing his hands together. "Our three friends will have a surprise in store for them."

"Sir." The officer on the telephone had stopped talking and was holding one hand over the mouthpiece.

"What is it?" Dolya asked.

"Kalinin reports we already have a man on that train." He glanced at a pad in front of him where he had scribbled a name. "A Vladimir Karpov. He called from Moscow to say he would check in at Kalinin on the way to Leningrad."

Shevchenko and Dolya looked at each other and grinned. "Fortune is with us, eh, Stefan? Tell the boarding party to contact Karpov first. He may have already spotted Sokolov.

We don't want to cause a major incident looking for the others until we're sure they're all on the train."

Shevchenko turned to Dolya. "It's quite ironic, isn't it?" Dolya could only agree.

Vladimir Karpov, First Department, Illegals Directorate had been Sokolov's training officer.

The train hurtled along the rails into the night. The sway and rhythmic sound of steel on steel coupled with generous quantities of vodka had lulled Karpov into a pensive mood. Between them, they had managed to almost finish the bottle Karpov had produced to celebrate their reunion.

Sokolov had managed to hold his own drinking down until Karpov's consumption was almost double his own. He wondered now if Karpov had been aware as the train slowed and approached Kalinin.

Karpov blinked as the station lights splashed in the window of his compartment. He stood up and stretched, his mouth gaping open in a great yawn. Maybe he would want to sleep after all, Sokolov thought, as the train lurched to a halt.

"Come, Mikhail. We have a few minutes here. Let's get a breath of fresh air."

Sokolov followed Karpov's example, making a great show of his sleepiness. "No, I think I'll turn in," he said. "The vodka has made me sleepy and I want to be rested when I arrive in Leningrad. I'm afraid I can't match you when it comes to vodka."

"A pity, Mikhail. The night is still young. We could talk some more." His disappointment was genuine and Sokolov had a momentary pang of regret at the deception. "You can rest in Leningrad can't you?"

"Well, you forget. I haven't seen my family for a long time and there is also a certain young lady whose acquaintance I wish to renew. She is in the best of health and expects the same of me."

Karpov threw back his head and laughed heartily. "Well, I can't begrudge you that. Yes, save yourself for the little wench, but I shall be up late if you change your mind. I'm picking up some reports from a courier." He glanced out the window briefly. His eyes grew serious. "It's been wonderful to see you again, Mikhail. It really has. I'm sure your work will not go unrewarded," he added. "Well, I'd better hurry or the courier will miss me. In the morning then, perhaps?"

Sokolov stood up and the two men shook hands solemnly. "Yes, in the morning, before we leave the train." Karpov left and Sokolov ducked back into his compartment and turned off the light. He had already seen them. Two men in topcoats and hats. They were not anxious relatives meeting weary travelers.

He peered out the window. The platform was nearly deserted now. A cold wind blew papers across the tracks. Seconds later, Karpov's wobbly frame emerged from the train and stepped down onto the platform. He was immediately approached by the two men. They talked rapidly for a few moments and from his gestures, Karpov was obviously protesting. Then his head turned sharply toward the compartment window. He doesn't believe it, Sokolov thought, but he knew what the two men were telling him.

At the sound of the whistle, the two men split up and went in opposite directions, obviously boarding the train at either end. Karpov was left alone on the platform, suddenly a forlorn figure, staring at the train. Sokolov left the compartment and rushed back to Storm and Owens.

"Get away from the window," he said to Storm as he closed the door.

Storm turned. "What's the matter?" Owens was asleep.

"We've been spotted," Sokolov said, snapping off the light. "They know we're on the train. Probably the militia man at the station in Moscow."

Storm nodded. "My fault. What do we do now?" He stumbled as the train lurched into motion and began to pull out of the station. He'd hoped Sokolov had come to tell them he'd managed to ditch his former teacher.

Sokolov sat down. There was one way that just might work, he thought, remembering Karpov's warm reception, his obvious disbelief on the platform.

"They won't try anything on the train, at least not until they're sure we're all on, but there'll be a complete search in Leningrad. We've got to avoid them and I've got to get rid of those two who just boarded. Stay in the compartment and keep the door locked. There shouldn't be any more checks tonight."

"How are you going to get them off the train?" Storm asked.

"I'm not sure, but I've got an idea."

Storm took in Sokolov's grim expression. The odds were against them from the beginning and now, getting shorter all the time. Whatever idea the Russian had, Storm didn't think he wanted to hear about it.

Fourteen

Phil Rogers looked more like an insurance executive than an intelligence officer. The Helsinki station chief sat listening to Charles Fox, wagging his head, rubbing his pointed chin and chain-smoking menthol cigarettes. His eyes occasionally flicked to the telex message from John Trask in Moscow on his desk.

The telex was strengthened by a signal from Langley advising him to give Charles whatever assistance was necessary. But there was always a catch phrase: authorization within reason. Translated it meant if anything went wrong, Rogers would be burned, not Charles, so it was still he who would make the final decision.

"Dammit, Charles, you're asking too much. You know Finland's position regarding Moscow. They're no great fans of the Kremlin, but they like things nice and quiet around here and so do I." He got up and poured them both coffee.

"I'm not suggesting the Finns mount an operation in downtown Helsinki or even violate the Soviet border," Charles answered sharply. He'd already wasted over an hour trying to convince Rogers he was not some crazy old man hatching a hair brained scheme. "We're talking about an isolated area of lake country and foothills, a frozen wasteland if you like, and I'm not suggesting we do anything until they're safely on the Finnish side of the border. A helicopter is..."

"And that's another thing," Rogers broke in. "What makes you think the Finnish Air Ministry is going to authorize the use of a chopper and one of their pilots for this? I certainly don't have anyone who can fly a chopper."

Rogers sipped his coffee and both men lapsed into silence to clear the air and calm down. "You really think you can pull this off?" Charles' answer was more silence and a cold stare.

Rogers sighed and picked up the phone, glancing toward the window as he dialed the Finnish Air Ministry. Heavy wet snowflakes drifted down across its surface. "They're expecting heavy snow by morning you know. You might get refused because of the weather and...Hello? Yes, this is Phillip Rogers, U.S. Embassy. Can I speak to the minister please, it's urgent. Yes, I'll wait."

He held his hand over the receiver. "You know what's really funny, Charles? You don't even know for sure if they're going to be on that train."

"Oh, they'll be on it," Charles said. "They have to be."

Sokolov knocked lightly on the door of Karpov's compartment. "*Da?*" He opened the door and found Karpov staring listlessly out at the night as the train rushed relentlessly toward Leningrad. There was no sign of the other two men, but Sokolov knew they would be at opposite ends of the train waiting for Karpov's instructions.

"Mikhail?" Sokolov shut the door. Karpov's eyes never left him as he sat down opposite. Both men stared in silence at each other for several moments. Finally, Sokolov spoke.

"How much do you know?"

"Everything, nothing, I..." Karpov flung his hands toward Sokolov. "I didn't want to believe it, Mikhail. I still can't believe it. You, a...traitor?"

"What did the two men tell you? The ones who boarded the train?"

It seemed to take great effort for Karpov to form the words. "That you and two Americans were attempting to escape. You will all be arrested in Leningrad. The Americans, at least the one called Storm, may be released eventually, but you, Mikhail Sokolov, you will be tried and sentenced."

"That's all? That's all they told you?"

"That's all? Isn't that enough?" Karpov said savagely. He paused for several moments and then said, "And to think I trusted you, looked upon you almost as a..." His voice trailed off sadly and he stared out the window again. Sokolov could see the pain and disappointment in his eyes reflected in the window.

"You really believe that of me?" Sokolov asked.

"What else am I to believe?" But even as he spoke, Sokolov saw it, the faint glimmer of hope that there was some mistake.

"What are their instructions, the other two?"

"They are to do nothing until I give the word. Not until Leningrad unless it becomes necessary. But I will, Mikhail, believe me I will."

Sokolov smiled to hide his relief. He lit a cigarette. "Of course you would, but it won't be necessary. Those two are local goons. Moscow wouldn't have told them."

"Told them what?" Despite himself, Karpov was showing interest.

Sokolov managed a convincing sigh. "It is you who disappoint me, Vladimir Karpov." He watched the surprise spread over the older man's face. "Yes, there are two Americans on this train and yes, they plan to escape our borders, but, they only *think* I am helping them. I'm under orders to play along, prevent them from doing something stupid until we get to Leningrad. Those two goons are just the kind of thing that could panic them." Karpov's surprise had become confusion now, but the spark of belief suddenly grew brighter in his eyes. He wanted to believe.

He listened in mute fascination as Sokolov related his recall from New York to impersonate Owens, the escape from the Clinic. Nearly all of it. The determined set of Karpov's face softened somewhat, but then clouded over when Sokolov came to the news of Dimitri Zakharov's death. When he spoke at last, it was with restrained excitement. "An incredible story, Mikhail. Incredible. And you say it was Colonel Delnov who masterminded this ingenious plan. But what happened?"

"The American who was sent over to make a positive identification of Owens managed to trip me up—with Owens help of course. With Zakharov's death, the exchange was ruined, but the Americans still wanted Owens. They contacted me through Storm and offered me asylum in America if I would help them rescue Owens." He laughed mirthlessly. "It's not such a tempting offer. I've lived in New York."

Karpov seemed to ignore the remark. His eyes were alive now, wary, suspicious, calculating. "A very convincing story, Mikhail, but why does Moscow not know of your double role?"

Sokolov leaned forward. "There was no time to get word to them about the escape. Naturally, they assume—the search command—that I'm on the run as well. I confess I'm puzzled that Delnov hasn't informed them."

"All plausible, Mikhail, but how do I know it's..."

"The truth? All right, I turn over Storm and Owens to you. They'd never be found without turning the train upside down and searching every compartment. They're not wearing signs saying 'we're the Americans.' They have travel papers, Russian clothes, they blend in very well and Owens is fluent."

Sokolov couldn't help thinking maybe this was all for the best. What difference did it make anyway? Owens was dying and Storm had not really done anything to be construed as a serious crime. Both governments would make a lot of noise, but in the end, Storm would probably be released. And he himself could always claim he had been forced to go along with the escape plan.

He met Karpov's eyes again and saw the suspicion had nearly dissolved, replaced with, yes, anticipation. Karpov was already beginning to see himself as a hero of sorts. "The important thing is for you to get those two from Kalinin off the train. Let them report to Moscow that you've been alerted and have contacted me." Sokolov paused and shrugged. "If you think it's necessary, call Delnov, verify my story." He leaned back against the seat. There was nothing more he could say, but from Karpov, not a flicker of reaction. He seemed fascinated with the mechanics of the escape.

"Mmm. Was there no plan once you reached Leningrad?"

"We were to be met by members of a dissident group and taken separately in cars to the frontier. You see that's why Moscow wanted me to follow through on this. It's a chance to break up a dissident group as well."

"Yes, yes, I see," said Karpov thoughtfully. Sokolov knew he was considering his options. He straightened up suddenly.

"Very well, Mikhail. First I will talk to the Americans then I will decide. I will instruct the Kalinin men to leave the train only if I'm satisfied. Understood?"

"Fair enough," Sokolov agreed.

The only alternative was to kill Karpov.

Christopher Storm paced about the tiny compartment, occasionally pausing to stare out at the dark night rushing by. The train's heating system, if it had one, was obviously not working and the wet snowflakes blowing against the window told him it was going to get worse not better. He shivered and pulled his coat around him and tried another swallow of the vodka Sokolov had brought back earlier. Where the hell was he? Jesus Christ, of all the people to be on the train, Sokolov had to run into someone he knew.

He stood up, lit another cigarette, crushed it out half smoked, lit another, sat down again, listening to the voice repeating in his brain. The compartment was stifling. Except for a couple of furtive trips to the toilet, he hadn't been out of it since they'd left Moscow.

He glanced up at Owens sleeping peacefully on the bunk above. He hadn't stirred since their brief conversation. The confession of his loss of memory seemed to act like yet another drug. Owens had seemed almost apathetic about their situation. Given Owens' condition, he could understand it, but at the same time it irritated him.

Perhaps it was Owens' attitude, Sokolov's absence—closeted again with his former instructor—or simply the gnawing sensation that they weren't going to make it. Whatever the reason, he realized he'd begun to toy with the idea of giving up the whole, insane idea of escape.

True, he'd participated in the abduction of Owens from the Clinic, but up to now what had he actually done except ride a train with false travel papers? How much illegality did that constitute in Soviet Russia? Perhaps too much, he thought, remembering Solzhenitsyn's accounts of the Siberian labor camps and wishing he'd never read them. Maybe they'd make an example of him. Or was there still time to simply surrender to the authorities in Leningrad? Anything short of that would simply compound the situation.

But what if Charles was right? What if they could pull it off? Would it be worth it now knowing all the precious intelligence Owens was wanted for was perhaps lost permanently? Langley would no doubt love to have a crack at Sokolov, but they still had to get across the border. Wouldn't they be better off quitting now before they were committed beyond return?

"Getting to you?" Storm jumped at the sound of Owens' voice in the darkened compartment. He hadn't realized Owens was awake.

"What?"

"The pressure, the waiting." Owens raised up slightly on the bunk.

Storm sighed and sat down opposite. "Yeah, I guess it is. I've been wondering what we're doing here, whether it's all worth it." He could see Owens resting his head on his hand, his elbow on the bunk.

"For me, it always goes back to Nam. Everything. You haven't mentioned it, but I'm sure you haven't forgotten the time I blew everything and got that kid killed."

"Yeah, I remember I think." Storm was glad Owens couldn't see his face in the darkness; the memory was vivid.

"Well, I never forgot," Owens said. His voice had taken on a faraway quality as if he was voicing deeply buried thoughts for the first time. "You must have wondered how I got into this."

"Yeah, I guess I did," Storm said. He had assumed Owens volunteered for his assignment in Russia.

"They didn't make me, nothing like that, but I grabbed it. For me, it was a chance to make up for what I did in Nam," Owens continued. "A rare opportunity, they called it, to do a great service for my country. But I never saw it that way. For me it was redemption for that kid, all the others. All I had to do was pretend to be a defector. If I put myself in danger and survived, well, then it would be all right. At least I had done something."

Storm knew exactly what Owens was talking about and he

realized suddenly they could not give up. Here, on a train hurtling through Russia, he was guided by the same lesson he had learned in the rice paddies of Vietnam. Survival, but not at the expense of your buddies. In Vietnam, he had taken his turn at point, pushed into an exposed area of jungle, crawled up a hill under fire—not for his country or any belief in the war, but for his buddies. Men he had lived with, laughed with, suffered with, loved and watched die before his very eyes. And he realized now, he had suffered the same fate as Owens: the guilt of survival. He had come back; others had not. That's what the dreams were all about. Owens and Sokolov were not buddies in the same sense, but they had been thrown together nonetheless and told to survive. If he walked out now, alone and survived, he'd never rid himself of the feeling of desertion.

A soft knock on the door interrupted his thoughts. He froze. A guard? Documents check? He glanced at Owens motionless in the bunk. It was late enough for pretending sleep to be reasonable. Ignore it?

Silence broken only by the clatter of the wheels on the track. Then another knock and Sokolov's voice.

Storm expelled a huge breath and unlocked the door. He stood aside to let Sokolov in, surprised by the other man with him. He shut the door and turned on the light. He looked questioningly at Sokolov. "Who's this?" he burst out, instantly regretting the blurted words.

Karpov stood like an uninvited guest for dinner, eyeing him curiously. He nodded to Sokolov who said, "It doesn't matter now, Storm. It's no good. This is Vladimir Karpov, the teacher I told you about." He said it with almost an air of apology. "I had to tell him. They know all about us."

Storm tensed. Here it comes at last, he thought, crashing down like an avalanche. "Tell him what?" There was something strange about Sokolov's expression.

"Look," Sokolov said, "I was never going to go all the way with you. The idea was to penetrate the dissident group in Leningrad, the ones who were going to get us across the border. Do you understand? The dissidents." He shrugged. "Sorry, Storm, but I have a job to do, too. You believed my story about wanting to go back to the States so easily. Well, I told you I was a good actor."

Storm nodded dumbly, a genuine look of disbelief crossing his face, his mind racing ahead. He could see Karpov was following Sokolov's remarks, but what was he talking about. There was no dissident group in Leningrad, not that he knew of, and they were taking another train across the border into Finland, not a car. He kept his eyes on Sokolov, aware too of Karpov's eyes and abruptly, Sokolov's real intent.

"So you're turning us in. Is that it?"

"I'm afraid so," Sokolov said. Storm saw the flicker of relief in his eyes that he understood. "That was always the idea. You're new to this game, but there's one rule you better learn. Never trust..."

Storm pushed Karpov aside and dived for Sokolov. He caught him around the waist and they crashed into the seat, rolled onto the floor. Karpov was almost as quick. He grabbed Storm by the shoulder and pressed the barrel of his gun to the side of Storm's head. "That's quite enough, Mr. Storm," he said.

Storm released his grip on Sokolov. Karpov waved him to the seat and backed up toward the door, glancing at Owens stirring in his bunk, but he said nothing. Sokolov got off the floor and glared at Storm.

"Now, Mr. Storm, Mr. Owens, let's see where we are. I can quite understand your outburst at Comrade Sokolov, but any further stupidity will simply make your position worse than it already is."

"When did you start carrying a gun?" Sokolov asked. He seemed surprised to see Karpov armed.

"My own precaution, Mikhail, and for you a fortunate one, eh?" Sokolov rubbed the back of his head where he had hit the floor.

"Now, Mr. Storm, from what Mikhail has told me you have unwittingly become involved in this situation. The matter of Mr. Owens is still to be considered." Karpov flicked a glance at Owens lying on the bunk.

Owens lay back down and stared at the ceiling. "You can't do anything to me that hasn't already been done," he said.

"That remains to be seen, but you," he said turning again to Storm, "were in fact authorized entry to the Soviet Union. You have violated our hospitality, but your position is relatively clear. When we arrive in Leningrad, you will be returned to Moscow and the matter will be sorted out by my superiors, providing of course you remain cooperative."

"I don't have much choice do I?" Storm said sullenly.

"No, you do not, but to resist will only make matters worse."

They all felt it now. The train had begun to slow. "Ah, another stop, I believe," Karpov said. "Mikhail, you will remain here with the prisoners while I attend to the other matter we discussed. Naturally, I shall have to contact Moscow." He handed the gun to Sokolov and hurried away as the train lumbered into the station.

Sokolov shut the door and shoved the gun into his pocket. "Not bad, Storm," he grinned, rubbing his head. "I wouldn't want you really mad at me, though."

"Sorry, guess I over did it. What happens now?" Owens sat up in the bunk and seemed not at all surprised by Sokolov's actions. Storm realized Owens had never once doubted the Russian.

"Karpov will get rid of those goons who got on in Kalinin, but if he calls Moscow we're dead. My whole story will be blown. I can't let him make the call."

"How will you stop him?" Storm asked, already knowing. His eyes were drawn to the gun outlined in Sokolov's pocket.

"Don't worry I'm not going to shoot anybody unless I have to. Keep the door locked till I get back," Sokolov said, leaving the compartment.

Storm glanced up at Owens.

"Well, in for a dollar?"

Sokolov stood on the steps between the two cars of the train. A short way up the platform, he could see Karpov and the two KGB men in heated conversation. Their voices rang out along the platform, but were muffled by the wind enough to make them garbled. Snow was falling heavily now and already accumulating. He watched another few moments, but it was clear Karpov had overruled them. The two men angrily stomped off toward the exit.

Karpov stood watching their departure and glanced back once in Sokolov's direction. Then he began to walk across the platform toward the station office. In a town this small, it was no more than a wooden shack. A light shown through the window and Sokolov could just make out an old man in the streaked window, drinking tea, trying to stay warm. The few passengers that had ventured outside were already returning to the train as Sokolov stepped down on the platform and followed Karpov.

He stopped just outside the office. Through the glass, he could see Karpov talking rapidly with the old man and pointing to the telephone. Sokolov took out the red KGB card and drew the gun. Karpov and the old man both looked up as he opened the door. The old man froze; Karpov paled.

"Sorry, Vladimir," Sokolov said, as he shut the door behind him.

Several minutes later, he left the station master, mouth gaping open and sprinted for the train. It had already begun to leave the station. He ran alongside, but it was picking up speed. He slipped once on the ice and managed to regain his footing. He jumped for the handrail, swung up onto the train just as it cleared the end of the platform.

Storm reached out and pulled him aboard. "Problems?"

Sokolov was breathing hard. "Not now. All we have to do is get past the welcoming committee in Leningrad."

Somehow, Storm felt sure they were going to make it now.

Fifteen

When the call finally came, it split the silence that had engulfed the Moscow Command Center like a shrill alarm, jangling already frayed nerves and adding to the tension of every man in the room. The operator lunged to silence it like a man diffusing a bomb.

Since Novgorod residency's report two hours earlier of Vladimir Karpov's contact with Sokolov, there had been no additional news. A positive sighting of at least one of the fugitives confirmed Shevchenko's theory, but he had been enraged to learn the Karpov had taken it upon himself to order the two men off the train. Only the promise that Karpov himself was due to report in had deadened his resolve to discipline and officially reprimand Karpov. The man was an instructor, not a field officer and had no right to take such action.

But Karpov's call had never come. Already in a growing state of apprehension, Shevchenko had plunged into a frenzied fury of nervous activity. Hopping up and down from his chair like a yo-yo, everyone in the center watched him with wary eyes, dreading they might be the next to bear the brunt of his rage. Pacing, sitting down, pacing again, ordering coffee sent in, only to let it go untouched, then berating the orderly for serving him cold coffee, smoking cigar after cigar and occasionally stopping to scribble furiously on the pad before him as some thought, some minute point flickered through his mind.

When the quiet became so maddening that Shevchenko himself was aware of his own footsteps on the parquet floor, he'd stopped in mid-stride and shouted in the face of the embarrassed glances confronting him. "What are you all staring at?" he demanded. When no one answered and all eyes lowered, suddenly engrossed in busy work, he'd grabbed a huge book of train schedules and flung it against the wall.

Watching him, Dolya sympathized with his growing frustration, but like the others, he waited silently, holding his own feeble suggestions in check, which on reexamination seemed futile, pointless and would only serve to infuriate Shevchenko further. The ringing telephone promised relief.

The operator nodded, listened and wrote quickly on a pad in front of him. Finally, he slammed down the phone. He looked at Shevchenko standing over him, his face white with fear.

"Well?" Shevchenko said, clenching and unclenching his fists.

The operator's eyes darted to Dolya who had risen from his chair, as if for support. "It's Chudove. They received a call from the train station a few minutes ago. The prisoner is making a fuss and the station master wanted to know what he should do."

"What prisoner?" Shevchenko's voice had dropped to a whisper.

"Karpov. He was handed over to the station master by a man he claims was a KGB officer. They've released Karpov. He's flying back to Moscow to report personally."

"Then he'll be flown to Siberia," Shevchenko said. He turned around and slumped in his chair, staring for several moments at the operator as if he disbelieved him. Finally, he motioned to Dolya to join him at the table. "Comrade Sokolov is becoming too clever, Major Dolya, and it seems everyone working for us is a fool." He slammed his fist on the table. "Listen to me, Stefan. Here." He jabbed his finger at the map, at the Finnish border. "I want both points covered—the road and the train crossing between Imatra and Luzhaika. There's a division garrisoned at Vyborg."

Dolya nodded, staring at the Colonel's manicured finger, realizing both their careers would hinge on stopping the fugitives at this desolate spot on the Russian frontier. "Isn't it still possible they'll be picked up in Leningrad? As far as we know, they're still on the train."

Shevchenko was already shaking his head. "That could be bungled as well. We'll follow through of course, but I suspect Sokolov has something planned to skirt Leningrad. We must be sure, Stefan." His eyes locked with Dolya's. "You will fly to Vyborg immediately and take charge of the train border crossing point. I'll alert the highway frontier. They appear to be crossing on the train, but there could be some other alternatives so we must assume either are possible."

"I'll leave at once," Dolya said, rising. "There's no way they can get through."

"If they do, we might as well go with them," Shevchenko replied.

"The pilot's bitching about the weather," Phil Rogers said. "See for yourself."

Charles peered through the glass enclosure at the medium range helicopter on the pad outside. The howling wind rattled the windows and snow was swirling around the chopper nearly obscuring it from view.

"You don't have to go, Phil," Charles said.

Rogers answer was a grin. "You don't get away that easy, Charles. I gave my word to the Air Minister I'd tag along. I signed for that baby."

Charles didn't know or care how Phil Rogers had managed it, but they had the helicopter and a reluctant pilot. He would be glad to have Rogers along as well. "Well, let's go then."

They opened the door of operations and were instantly buffeted by the near gale force winds. Charles could feel the cold even through the heavy parka as they fought their way across the slippery tarmac.

The door slid back and the two men scrambled aboard. Charles climbed into the passenger seat next to the pilot, who had already begun his preflight check. He was a young, chubby-faced lieutenant with a brush mustache and a mop of blonde hair. He put on the headphones and glared at Charles with undisguised hostility. Seconds later, the turbos began to whine and above their heads, the rotors commenced a slow turn, slicing the wind and snow.

"Got your skis?" the pilot shouted over the howl of the rotor blades and the wind.

Charles smiled and nodded, giving the pilot the thumbs up

sign just as a heavy gust of wind slammed into them, and it seemed to Charles the craft was going to tip over. The helicopter righted itself and the rotor blades whined in protest as the clumsy machine tilted off the ground. The pilot's hand gripped the stick tightly and Charles could nearly feel the strain in his own arms.

Then suddenly, as if catapulted off the pad like a rocket, the ground disappeared below them and they were hurtling through the sky over Helsinki. The pilot turned them inland and set an easterly course for Imatra. As they cleared the city lights, the expanse of tundra lay below them like an immense white canvas, broken only by clumps of forest and the occasional dim lights of an odd dwelling.

For the first hour, it was difficult to see anything with the snow swirling about them in the darkness, but as they neared Imatra, the snow and wind subsided and on the eastern horizon Charles saw the first glimpse of sunrise.

The windshield wiper blades ceased their monotonous sweep across the glass as the pilot banked over a lake. Below, Charles could see a herd of caribou bolt and stampede across the snow at the strange intrusion.

The pilot looked questioningly at Charles and pointed to a throat microphone. Charles adjusted a headset and listened to the pilot's voice, small and tinny in his ears. "How close you want to get to the border checkpoint?"

Charles unfolded a map and pointed to a spot he had marked earlier. "Just where we're out of sight, but near enough to give us visibility of the area," he replied.

Ridiculous, thought Charles. He was already listening for trains.

Storm braced himself against the door on the platform between the first two cars as the train crunched to a halt with a clang of metal and the couplers ground against each other. Leningrad.

As in Moscow, the station was crowded. The brightly lit platform was immediately a mob scene as doors flew open and the train emptied its mass of passengers, dragging suitcases, boxes, pushing impatiently toward the barrier.

He glanced at Owens, leaning on the other wall, eyes closed, seemingly asleep. The rest of the journey had rejuvenated him somewhat. He was less pale and the coughing fits had been less frequent, but he would need all of his reserves now.

Bluffing the waiting KGB team was the only way they'd make the connecting train, Sokolov had said. He was banking on the wire photo of himself being unclear enough for a positive identification. The crowd and the stolen KGB card should do the rest. But now that they were actually here, Storm wasn't so sure.

The train belched a great cloud of steam as Storm put his hand on the door handle. He saw them as the steam cloud cleared. Four only? He'd expected more. They were pushing people aside as they fought against the tide of arriving passengers, eyes searching and finally seeing Sokolov moving their way, waving the KGB card, a hat pulled down over his face.

There was a hurried conversation as Sokolov pointed to the far end of the train. The four men began to shove people out of the way as they hurried off. Sokolov began to follow, then managed to disengage himself from the swarm and hung back looking for Storm.

"Okay, let's go," Storm said. He threw open the door and stepped down onto the platform with Owens following close behind. They quickly melted in with the crowd and worked their way to the barrier, clutching their tickets. The guard scarcely looked at them as they pushed past. Storm turned and found Sokolov at his side.

"Hurry," he said. "As soon as they find the compartment empty and me gone, they'll be back here and put out the alert."

They dashed down the stairs to the lower level. Sokolov, Storm knew, feared the slowness of the train. They might miss the connection for the Helsinki Express, but they were in time: seven minutes to spare.

They slowed and walked past the barrier and boarded the second car. Storm glanced back once, but there was no pursuit. The train, however, could always be held up, delayed, searched. If it left on time, they had a chance.

As they found an empty compartment, doors slammed, a whistle blew and the train began to move forward. Owens was out of breath and had gone pale again. He collapsed on the seat while Sokolov continued to watch out the window as the train picked up speed and cleared the station yards, emerging into the canals of Leningrad. Storm's euphoria was quickly shattered by Sokolov's grim face.

"Too easy," he said.

"What do you mean?"

"This place should have been crawling with KGB. I think they let us through," Sokolov said.

"But why?"

"Who knows? Less of an incident at the border. They must have known this was how we'd try to leave. All they have to do is wait for us at the frontier. Well anyway, let's get changed. We don't look like Finnish tourists."

Storm had nearly forgotten the extra clothes. They broke open their bags and quickly changed into sports clothes and ski jackets, while Storm's mind raced ahead.

The original plan had called for them to stay on the train until it crossed the border into Finland. Charles would pick them up on the other side. But if what Sokolov thought was true, they'd never get beyond the check point. Owens roused himself long enough to change then sat down again and closed his eyes. Storm and Sokolov faced each other realizing they had come to the same conclusion.

"Any chance of the train being stopped before the border?" Storm asked.

"Not likely. It's only sixty miles, but they'll be on full alert. There will probably be an army waiting for us there."

"So we leave the train, right?"

"I don't see any other way," Sokolov said. Both of them looked at Owens, wondering if he could survive a jump from a moving train. Owens felt their silence and opened his eyes.

"You two do whatever you think best. I'll just slow you down."

"No," Sokolov said. "There's a grade near the border. The

snow is thick up there." It was true. Leningrad was blanketed with snow, and in the country it would be even heavier.

"Either we all go or we all stay on the train, agreed?" Storm said.

Sokolov nodded.

Owens hesitated. "Okay, you win, but I think you're both nuts."

"I just hope Fox is waiting," Storm said.

Charles stood on a rise in front of the trees, straining his eyes through the binoculars at the check point below. The helicopter was behind him, out of sight with the pilot inside ready to go on Charles' signal.

There was an almost ethereal quiet, broken only by Phil Rogers pacing in the snow behind him. Charles could see the customs shed on the Russian side and two guards smoking. It didn't appear they had been alerted yet, but it was too much to expect they wouldn't be very soon.

"Anything doing?" Rogers asked, stopping near Charles to look down.

"No, not yet...wait a minute, yes. Replacements by the look of it. Here, take a look." He handed the glasses to Rogers and turned away, feeling the disappointment seep through him. Something had gone wrong if they were expected on the train, but at least the presence of the soldiers meant they were on it.

Rogers adjusted the glasses. There was a flurry of activity at the check point as two troop carriers pulled up and deposited what looked to be twenty or thirty soldiers. "Who's the tall one?" Rogers asked, handing the glasses back to Charles.

"Major Dolya, I believe. He must have flown in from Moscow to run the show." Charles dropped the glasses and turned away.

"They'll never get through, Charles," said Rogers quietly. We don't know if they're all on the train anyway."

Charles ignored Rogers and swept the glassed down the track. Around a sweeping curve, a gentle grade led up to the

Russian side of the border crossing. A sloping embankment led off from the tracks. He mentally marked the spot where he would jump from the train if he were on board. Down the embankment, up the other side, through the trees and across.

If they could avoid the troops long enough, the chopper could pick them up and they'd all have lunch in Helsinki. He had no doubts they would be fired on and he would be helpless to do anything until they were safely across the frontier.

He turned to look back at the helicopter on the other side of the trees. The pilot sat inside, smoking in boredom. Once they were airborne, the noise of the chopper would carry all the way to the border. It should be a simple pickup, but it was complicated by the fact that they couldn't afford to give away their position until the last minute.

"I know what you're thinking, Charles, but I can't allow it," Rogers said.

Charles only glanced coldly at Rogers and zoomed in on the border post. He could see Dolya clearly now, his breath coming in puffs as he barked orders to the soldiers armed with AK-47 assault rifles. Anyone on that side of the border was fair game and the Finns wouldn't do anything but stand and watch.

"Listen," Rogers said. He turned his head, straining his ears. Charles heard it too. The low, mournful wail of a train whistle, chugging up the grade. Charles put down the glasses and gazed steadily at Phil Rogers.

"Don't fight me, Phil," he said. "We're going to get them off that train."

Standing between the cars at the tail end of the train, Storm could feel the icy air leaking through between the cars. They'd jammed the locks on both doors so nobody could get to them, but they'd also cut themselves off from getting back inside. There was only one way off the train now. Out the door and into the snow.

Owens sat on the floor, arms clamped tightly about him, as if gathering his final reserves of strength. Sokolov pulled the window down and let in an icy blast of air.

"Alright, the grade is coming up." He ducked his head back inside. His face was red and snowflakes were stuck in his hair. "You first," he said to Storm. "Owens and I will follow. Get up the other side of the embankment and make for those trees."

"I don't know," Owens said. "I still think I'll just slow you down." He got to his feet unsteadily. "It's better..."

"No," Storm and Sokolov said, almost together. They looked at each other and grinned.

What a strange alliance they made, Storm thought. "You'll be warm and dry before you know it," he said. But he heard the doubt in his own voice, saw it reflected in Sokolov's eyes. He looked out the window again, feeling the train slow as it began to struggle up the grade. He couldn't find words and what was there left to say anyway.

Sokolov pushed the door open and Storm climbed down on the metal step, clinging to the hand rail and hung for a moment staring down at the white ground flashing by below him. He tried to estimate the train's speed, but all he could think of was it was going too fast to jump.

The embankment below the tracks, covered with snow appeared soft and inviting, but it could be hiding a multitude of hazards—rocks, tree stumps. He shut these thoughts out of his mind and crouched lower on the step. The wind clawed at him, threatening to pull him off the side of the train. He glanced up once more at Sokolov and Owens, their faces framed in the doorway, then he picked a spot mentally and pushed off.

A rush of cold air hit him in the face. He felt himself being thrown backwards. He put up his arms for balance, waiting for the shock of impact. He hit the frozen ground at an angle, crunching into hard packed snow. The momentum from the train and wind blew him backwards, then he was tumbling down the embankment, out of control, over and over. Patches of sky, snow, train, sky, snow, train. Instinctively he tucked his knees up and put out his arms to slow his descent. Finally, he came to a halt, face down near the bottom of the embankment.

He lay motionless for a moment, stunned and nearly insensible, checking his limbs, but there was no pain, only the incredible cold. The light gloves were all they had and felt like metal shackles on his hands. He pulled himself up on hands and knees and slowly got to his feet, shaken, but if he could believe his senses, unhurt. He'd made it.

The opposite slope rose above him to his left. It was much steeper and higher than it looked from the train. Over the top were the trees. Ahead of him he could see the last car of the train disappearing around the bend. No sign of Sokolov or Owens, but he assumed they had jumped further along and were temporarily out of sight.

He began to climb at an angle up the opposite slope, digging his hands in the snow for support, feeling the icy wetness penetrating his clothes. He was nearly halfway to the top when he caught sight of Sokolov and Owens, further ahead and below him. Sokolov was crouching over Owens lying face down in the snow. Sokolov saw him and waved him down.

Storm worked his way across the face of the embankment to a point just above the other two, then jumped in great leaps through the drifting snow until he reached them. Owens was not moving and his arm was twisted at a grotesque angle behind him.

"You okay?" Sokolov asked. There was pinkish snow on his face. A cut from a tree branch or rock, Storm guessed.

"Yeah, I'm alright." He glanced down at Owens. Sokolov turned him over gently and Owens moaned. "His arm."

"Broken. We'll have to drag him up over the slope. Can you walk?" he asked Owens.

"Yeah, I think so, but my arm," Owens answered weakly. He held it to his side protectively and struggled to his feet with Storm and Sokolov supporting him.

"Okay, let's make for the trees up over the embankment. If Fox is here, that's where he'll be," Sokolov said.

It was slow going up the slope. Half carrying Owens, who stumbled and fell every few steps, moaning in pain. They slipped in the snow, clawing their way up the face of the embankment.

Suddenly a sharp whistle knifed through the air. They were less than halfway up the embankment. "Train's at the check point," Sokolov said, breathing hard. It was clearly visible now, perhaps a half a mile away, but Storm could see them clearly.

Soldiers.

"There," Charles shouted. "Halfway up the embankment. Looks like one of them is hurt." He squinted through the glasses again.

"Which one?" Rogers asked. He stood next to Charles. He could see three speck-like figures outlined in the snow.

"I can't tell. Can't see their faces." Charles swiveled the glasses back toward the check point. The soldiers were fanning out along the tracks in a wide arc and headed for the embankment. Some of the passengers were off the train, huddled together in small groups.

"We can't do anything until they're across, Charles. You know that." Rogers watched in fascination as the three figures struggled up the slope.

"Yes, yes, I know." Through the glasses, Charles felt the impatience and frustration grip him. He could see some of the soldiers shouting and pointing toward the embankment. They've been spotted, no doubt about it and the gap would close quickly.

Charles turned to the helicopter and signaled the pilot, who was watching him through the glass. Charles waved his hand in a circular motion and instantly the whine of the turbos began. "Come on, Phil. We can at least buzz the troops, cause a little confusion."

They turned and ran back to the chopper. "We'll need the rescue winch to pull them up," Charles said, his mind already hurtling ahead.

"Yeah, yeah," Rogers shouted. He yelled something else, but his voice was drowned out by the roar of the helicopter engine. They scrambled in and slid the door shut as it lifted off and left the cover of the trees.

"Buzz the check point," Rogers shouted to the pilot, but

even as he gave the order he knew they would be too late.

The first shot was a surprise when it came, kicking up snow a few feet in front of them. Storm felt a cold spray on his face. He could hear the soldiers shouting now, distant voices below them. Instinctively, they flattened on the ground.

"C'mon," Sokolov said. "A little more and we'll be in the trees." They crawled the rest of the way, slow agonizing feet at a time, dragging Owens who had mercifully passed out. The rifles echoed like canons now, throwing up sprays of snow all around them.

Then another sound. A helicopter. Storm looked up and saw it clear the trees above them, then bank sharply and zoom down toward the soldiers below them.

"Fox," he shouted, watching as the chopper flew in low, down the embankment, scattering the soldiers. Some of them dived in the snow and a few got off hurried shots as it swooped over their heads and banked into another turn to make a second pass. Trailing from the chopper, Storm could see a long cable. Sokolov saw it too.

"Rescue winch," Sokolov shouted to Storm. He raised up slightly and reached for Owens, but jerked his hand back like he had touched fire. He was thrown, twisted back and felt a sudden searing pain in his shoulder. He saw a red stain spread over his arm and spill onto the snow. He lay back for a moment, staring at a patch of sky, his vision was suddenly filled with the chopper directly overhead, lowering to them, the cable snaking down.

"C'mon," Sokolov shouted. He grabbed for the harness attached to the winch cable. Storm's vision blurred as he pulled Owens with his good arm and watched Sokolov buckle Owens into the harness. He signaled the chopper to pull him up. Through a haze Storm could see Charles' face peering down at them. Owens dangled like a rag doll, winding and twisting slowly upward.

"You next," Sokolov said, turning to Storm. "I'm going to hold them off for a bit." He took the gun out of his pocket—Karpov's revolver. "Tell Fox to pick me up on the other side of the trees."

Storm nodded and watched Sokolov scoot back down the embankment, finding cover where he could. He heard two shots from the pistol, like cracks, and saw the soldiers flatten in the snow at the returning fire.

Above him, the winch cable and harness was lowered, dancing in the wind. He felt the snow beat around him, thrown up by the prop wash of the chopper. The cable seemed to take forever to reach him. His shoulder was throbbing now, his legs frozen like lead.

He grabbed for the harness with his good arm, missed and fell forward in the snow. He was losing consciousness. He could feel it coming, feel himself slipping away. He wanted to just stay where he was and lie there in the snow.

A voice above him. "Get up, Christopher, get up!" It was Charles, leaning out the door of the chopper.

He struggled to his knees and thrust his good arm through the harness, managed to get it over his head. He felt it tighten around him and lift him off the ground. He spun in the air for a moment, dangling, then he was a few feet above the trees. He looked down, saw blood dripping onto the snow, Sokolov below, crouching behind a tree, looking up at him, firing at the soldiers.

Then, he blacked out for a few moments, his head falling backwards.

When he opened his eyes, he could see Charles, arms outstretched and the face of another man behind him. Up and up the winch drew him closer to the safety of the chopper. Then he was at the door, arms reaching for him.

He didn't hear the sound of the terrible blow that struck him in the side, smashing him against the side of the helicopter. The door was an open hole, he was falling inside the dark tunnel, blackness all around him.

Sixteen

He awoke as always, aware of the bed under him, the strong smell of disinfectant in the room. The first time he thought he was back in the clinic. But this time was better, easier. He heard clearly, a soft chime.

"Doctor Klein, report to surgery. Doctor Klein."

He opened his eyes slowly. He was fully encased in white. Bed, gown, even the tube that caused the tiny pin prick of pain in his arm. It rose upwards to a metal stand that held a bottle. Clear liquid flowed out of the bottle, back down the tube, into his arm. The tiny pain meant—life.

He turned his head and saw Charles perched on a chair beside the bed. He looked like a client waiting to see his attorney. Confident, assured, his impeccable attire, perfect as usual, right down to the camel hair topcoat folded over his knee. The anxious face staring down at him from the door of the chopper was now once again, calm, concerned, but amused as well.

Charles smiled. "Well, how are they treating you, Christopher?"

Storm managed a smile of his own. "I guess I'll live, huh?" His right shoulder and arm were in a cast. He could feel a strange warmth in his side, taped tightly with heavy bandages.

"Oh, you'll do far more than that. The doctors tell me you'll be up and about in a couple of weeks." Charles adjusted the coat in his lap. Storm wondered if Charles ever got dirty.

"Sokolov? Did he..."

"Yes, as a matter of fact he did. You won't remember of course, but we picked him up on the other side of the trees. He's fine."

"And Owens?"

"A neighbor of yours actually. Just down the hall. Shock, exposure, a badly broken arm, but..."

"Yeah, I know. He told me on the train." It all seemed ages ago now. How long had he been here? Days? Weeks? "Where am I?"

"Bethesda Naval Hospital, Maryland." Charles arched his eyebrows. "There is one small point bothering me, Christopher. I wondered if you knew."

"What?"

"Well, you were a bit naughty about Owens, Sokolov I mean." Storm turned away to face a blank television screen. "You said, I believe..."

"I said he was as American as I am. I didn't say he was Owens."

"Ah, a question of semantics. Yes, I see. Still one could only conclude from your remarks."

"Charles, what the hell difference does it make now?"

"None I suppose.

The door opened and a nurse came in. She gave Charles a brief disapproving look and bent over the bed, fluffing the pillows, disconnecting the IV. "Are we feeling better after our little sleep?" She asked, busying herself about the bed. She turned a crank on the side and he was raised to a more upright position. "Not too long," she said to Charles as she went out.

"I only meant, Christopher, that you were quite right about Sokolov. Mikhail Sokolov was, as you are so fond of saying, born and bred in American."

"What?"

"That's right. He was an only child and his father returned to Russia when he was quite young. Obviously, he was never told. We don't know if Moscow even knew. We've been able to confirm it though."

Storm closed his eyes and smiled, wondering what lay in store for Miki Sokol now? A new name, a new identity, a new life once the CIA was through with him. Exactly what he wanted. Storm knew he would never see him again.

"Well, I won't disturb you any longer," Charles said, getting to his feet. "I've brought you something to read, the first volume for your graduate studies. I think you'll recognize it, but find it entertaining nevertheless."

Charles produced a book from beneath the folds of his coat and laid it on the bedside table.

"What went wrong, Charles? Was it all for nothing?"

Charles was nearly at the door. "Oh, I wouldn't say that, not at all. There's every chance that Owens will recover his memory. His work will prove invaluable I should think. Sokolov is a bonus." Storm knew that's all he would be told. "Anyway, there's someone waiting to see you. Do come and see me when you're well, Christopher. We have a great deal to talk about." When Storm opened his eyes again, Charles was gone.

He was suddenly tired again. He started to ring for the nurse when he remembered the book. It was the volume of quotations: a leather bound copy of the book he'd taken from the room at Langley.

He picked it up and opened it. On the flyleaf, Charles had written a short note.

> To Christopher, with fondest regards. I think you'll find the passage I've marked most interesting. It might even answer your question.
> ---Charles

Storm flipped quickly to the page. It was a poem by Robert Burns and Charles had underlined one of the last stanzas.

> "...The best laid schemes o'mice an' men
> Go oft awry."

Storm began to laugh before he finished reading. He was still laughing when Valerie came in the room with his son Danny.

ABOUT THE AUTHOR

Jazz drummer and author Bill Moody has toured and recorded with Maynard Ferguson, Jon Hendricks and Lou Rawls. He lives in northern California where he hosts a weekly jazz radio show and continues to perform around the Bay Area. The author of seven novels featuring jazz pianist-amateur sleuth Evan Horne, Bill has also published a dozen short stories in various collections.

http://www.billmoodyjazz.com/

OTHER TITLES FROM DOWN AND OUT BOOKS

By J. L. Abramo
Catching Water in a Net
Clutching at Straws
Counting to Infinity
Gravesend
Chasing Charlie Chan (*)

By Trey R. Barker
2,000 Miles to Open Road
Road Gig: A Novella
Exit Blood

By Richard Barre
The Innocents
Bearing Secrets
Christmas Stories
The Ghosts of Morning
Blackheart Highway
Burning Moon
Echo Bay (*)

By Milton T. Burton
Texas Noir

By Reed Farrel Coleman
The Brooklyn Rules

By Frank De Blase
Pine Box for a Pin-Up (*)

By Jack Getze
Big Numbers (*)
Big Money (*)
Big Mojo (*)

By Don Herron
Willeford (*)

By Terry Holland
An Ice Cold Paradise
Chicago Shiver
Warm Hands, Cold Heart (*)

By David Housewright & Renée Valois
The Devil and the Diva

By David Housewright
Finders Keepers

By Jon Jordan
Interrogations

By Jon Jordan & Ruth Jordan
Murder and Mayhem in Muskego (Editors)

By Bill Moody
Czechmate: The Spy Who Played Jazz
The Man in Red Square

By Gary Phillips
The Perpetrators
Scoundrels: Tales of Greed, Murder and Financial Crimes (Editor)

By Lono Waiwaiole
Wiley's Lament
Wiley's Shuffle
Wiley's Refrain
Dark Paradise

(*)—Coming Soon

17895891R00157

Made in the USA
San Bernardino, CA
20 December 2014